Bannon's Brides

by

Loretta C. Rogers

Bannon's Brides

Cover Art by Angela Anderson

The Wild Rose Press
PO Box 708
Adams Basin, NY 14410-0706
Visit us at www.thewildrosepress.com

Publishing History
First Cactus Rose Edition, 2010
Print ISBN 1-60154-808-7

Published in the United States of America

"Draw up your skirts, Miss Quinn. It won't do for you to get tangled up in them and dragged under the wheels only to be crushed or drowned."

Her cheeks flushed red as she reached down and drew the length of material between her legs and tucked the hem snuggly inside her waistband. Her elegantly arched eyebrows spoke volumes. "Thank you for your concern," Fiona said with more than a trace of sarcasm in her voice.

Bannon had already dissolved into silent laughter, his shaking shoulders the only outward sign he found humor in the situation. "I admire your youthful vivaciousness, Miss Quinn."

Her face was raised to the sun's warming glare, long, coppery lashes resting against cheeks brightened with a healthy glow and a sprig of freckles across the bridge of her nose. Her small tongue ran lightly over her lips in an unconsciously sensual motion, deepening their pale rose color.

She's nervous and trying to hide it. A muscle in his jaw ticked, but he could not force his gaze from the luminous green eyes that stared up at him. He followed the thin column of her creamy throat and rested for a tormenting moment on the small rise of two perfect breasts. He called himself every kind of fool, disgusted he should be attracted to a woman who could never be his. Sure, she was an alternate bride, and sure, the first leg of the trip had gone without error or accident, still he knew the dangers that lay ahead and went without saying that death waited to claim a victim. When that happened Fiona's name would go into the lottery.

Dedication

To my daughter, Jodi,
whose inner beauty surpasses her outer beauty.

To Greg Bannon.
May he see a little of himself in the hero.

To my editor, Eve Mallary.
It's always a pleasure working with you.

Acknowledgements

Peter Hanen for gifting me with research books about the Old West and Native Americans. Thank you for these wonderful treasures.

Chapter One

March, 1847

Fiona Quinn sat in her starkly furnished one-room shanty. She stared down at the dress in her lap and wondered how many more times she could mend the waistband before the frayed material fell completely apart.

Her spirits weighed heavy from burying her father and brother, yet a deeper emotion pricked at her—*fear*. She knew Shanty Town wasn't a safe place for any woman.

Swiping at the tears threatening to spill down her cheeks, she let out a heavy sigh. "Oh, stuff and bother, I won't cry. I won't.

A frigid gust sent shivers through her as the door opened and slammed against the wall. Her body went weak as she looked with repugnance at the weasel-faced man filling the doorway.

For several agonizing seconds, she struggled to find her voice. Biting her lip, Fiona drew in a deep breath to steady her nerves. "How dare you break into my home."

Mocking laughter trickled from Blackie Sledge's darkly cloaked figure. "You call this rat's nest a home?"

Forcing herself to match the brothel owner's stare, she said with surprising calm, "Get out, or I'll..."

His dark eyes raked over her and settled on her face. "Or what, you'll call the constable?" He raised a

1

mocking brow. "His men don't like to venture into this hellhole after dark."

Fiona inched her fingers beneath the dress bundled in her lap to grip the shears. The goose bumps that rose on her arms had nothing to do with the cold air blasting through the open door.

Even before she could scream or sound an alarm, he reached out. To avoid his hands, she reared back in the rocking chair. "Don't touch me." The fetid odor of alcohol on his breath filled her nostrils. The lust in his eyes was unmistakable.

Blackie Sledge sneered. "You got nobody to protect you now, Fiona. Your poor ol' pa done gave it up to the black lung disease and what with your brother dead in the mine cave-in—" He offered a lascivious grin. "Why, you're all alone, lass. My offer still stands."

"Not on my mother's grave," Fiona bit out the words. "I will never work in your den of iniquity."

"Ah, but you will, me darlin'. When the hindside of your belly starts gnawin' at your backbone, you'll come crawling on your hands and knees and beggin' for sure."

She sat unmoving, staring into a pair of serpentine eyes. He was right. She was alone. Her job at the restaurant paid little enough to keep a roof over her head, to buy wood for her stove and other necessities.

Sleek as a panther, the brothel house owner leaned forward, gripped her by the arms, and hauled her roughly against his chest. "I'll dress you in fine gowns, lass. You won't have to work like the other girls. You'll be for my pleasure only—*queen of The Philadelphia House.*"

Fiona struggled against his steel grip. "I know about you, Mr. Sledge. You're a dealer of flesh, and when those poor girls are all used up, you...you...toss them aside like useless trash." She jutted out her chin as she clenched her teeth against a shudder. She refused to cry. What was the use?

His eyes glittered like cold stones in the lantern light, a wicked smile played on his face. A terrifying fear gripped its icy fingers around Fiona's heart. The strength of his hands bit into her arms. "Me wild Irish darl'n. Don't fight me so, girl." He laughed aloud, a deep sinister sound in the small space.

He reached around and laced strands of her burnished-gold hair through his fingers. With a vicious tug, he forced her head back so the white of her throat showed above the collar of her dress. Buttons clattered to the floor as he ripped the threadbare material. His lips caressed her flesh. He whispered, "Don't resist, lass. Let me teach you the finer points of pleasurin' a man."

In a surge of desperation, Fiona pushed away from Blackie Sledge. Sinking her teeth in her lower lip, she drew back her arm and sunk the shears she'd kept hidden in the folds of her skirt, deep into his forearm. She yanked the bloodied blades free and held them high as a formidable weapon.

He yowled as he gripped his wounded limb. "You damned Irish bitch."

"Get out of my house, Mr. Sledge." Fiona's voice quavered as her chest heaved. "I told you once, and now I'll tell you for the last time, I'll become no doxie of yours."

The tang of blood struck her nostrils as he pointed a bloody finger at her. His voice rasped, "When you get hungry enough, you'll come beggin', and maybe I'll still make you my queen." His grin befitted the devil. "Or maybe I'll *just* break that uppity spirit of yours before I toss you to the wolves."

She knew well enough the *wolves* were randy miners with the morals of guttersnipes.

"Next time, *Mr. Sledge*, it won't be your arm I'll be aiming at. Next time, I'll sink my shears into your heart that's as black as your own name." She maintained a death-grip on the pair of scissors. Bile stung the back of her throat, and she willed herself not to swoon.

A long hard look passed between Fiona and her enemy. His sinister laughter echoed in her ears as he cradled his arm and stepped from the cabin. "I'll be back, Fiona. I'll be back."

Fiona slammed the door behind Blackie Sledge. She pressed her back against the wooden planks as if to keep him out. Her knees buckled, and she felt herself go weak with a heavy wave of revulsion.

Moisture pooled on her lashes, and her vision was blurred as she snatched the flyer from beneath her pillow and quickly scanned the bold letters— *Brides Wanted for the town of Glory in Oregon Territory.*

With trembling fingers, she plaited her long hair into a single braid. She slipped on her best dress—a gray woolen frock. She prayed she wouldn't throw-up as she draped the frayed cloak around her shoulders. She pulled the hood over her head and before stepping into the night, blew out the lantern's flame.

It seemed the March wind pushed her down the dirt street that led to the church. She stayed to the middle of the road for fear some of Blackie's henchmen lurked in the alleys ready to snatch her away to his den of iniquity. Her hand gripped the flyer. For days she had wavered between crossing the prairie to become a mail-order bride to a man she had never met or remaining in Philadelphia and continuing to ward off the unwanted advances of Blackie Sledge.

Shanty Town had been her home since crossing the ocean from Ireland at the age of ten. In many ways, her life had been little better than during the potato famine that drove her father to scrape together his life's earnings to bring his family to

America.

Now at the age of nineteen, she hadn't anticipated burying the two men she'd loved most within a month of each other. Without his knowing, Blackie Sledge had made the decision for her. *Surely crossing the prairie can't be as dangerous as remaining here.*

Contemplating her future, she didn't hear the clattering hooves until the horses were almost on top of her. One of the riders shouted as he veered his mount, missing her by inches. "What's the matter? You drunk or got a death wish?"

It was the other rider's words that chilled her to the bone. "Probably one of Blackie's whores. Once them poor women catch the pox they get a little tetched in the head. Best thing is to put 'em outta their misery, 'cause they're for certain gonna die a painful death when the grim reaper comes a callin'."

Wind kicked up, blowing frigid air against Fiona's face. She clenched her jaw and sped up her pace, entering the church with brisk steps. Two thoughts struck her as she stood inside the vestibule—the first how good the warmth inside the church felt, and the other was the number of chattering women who filled the pews. Panic rippled through her. *I'm too late. Oh please, God, don't let me be too late.*

She observed women of every size and shape and age. Some whispered to one another. Some sat with heads bowed, and still others sat ramrod straight—waiting. She glanced around the room to see if she recognized anyone. She didn't.

"You were almost too late," a voice said.

"Oh, Reverend Parrish. You startled me." She pushed the hood from her head. "Umm, what do you mean—too late?"

"Meeting starts at eight o'clock sharp." He pulled a watch from his fob pocket, held it toward the light and counted to three.

The town clock chimed.

He smiled as he stepped around her to pull the double doors shut. "Go inside Miss Quinn. The other ladies will make room for you on one of the pews."

"I'm the last one?" It was a question that didn't need answering. Once again, she peered over the crowd inside the sanctuary. "How many are there— ladies, that is?"

"I'd say about eighty." He folded his hands as if in prayer and looked heavenward. "It'd be glorious if the pews were this packed on the Sabbath."

"Reverend Parrish, are all these women going to Oregon Territory?"

The aging minister placed a finger to his lips to silence her and waved his hands motioning her to find a seat. He leaned close and whispered. "Lawyer St. John will explain all the details, my child, but it's my understanding that only a handful will be selected."

Disappointment registered, and Fiona's hopes plummeted.

She pursed her lips and closed her eyes briefly as she whispered a quick prayer.

She feared her chance of getting picked as one of the brides was slim to none if she sat near the rear of the church. Searching for a place to sit, she made her way toward the front.

Her nerves jumped as a hand reached out and tugged on her cloak.

A hefty woman with hair the color of a storm gray cloud and pulled back in a bun narrowed her eyes at the lady seated next to her, "Scoot yourself over so we can make room for one more." Then she smiled up at Fiona. "Name's Althea Smalley. Most folks call me Ma."

Fiona released a deep sigh.

She removed her cape and seated herself. As she

folded the cloak neatly across her lap, she offered Althea Smalley a warm smile and then tried to calm the excited pace of her breathing. "Good luck to both us."

Chapter Two

Fiona craned her neck for a better look at the man wearing buckskins. Even though he was seated, she could tell he was tall. Thick sandy hair curled at the neck of his collar, and when he turned his head her way as he scanned the crowd, she had an unrestricted view of his face. Magnificent tawny brows gave him a rugged sensuous look. His lean jaw was square and showed a quiet strength beneath the muscles that flexed in it. His nose was thin and straight, and the only imperfection she could see was that it slanted slightly to the left, indicating it may have once been broken. But even that added an unquestionable manliness to his appearance.

As if she'd willed it, eyes the color of blue before a summer storm stared into hers, and her heart leaped in her chest. She sat transfixed, unable to blink or draw a breath, much less pull her gaze away from him. He was recklessly handsome, but his scowl unnerved her as he nodded.

Her gaze dipped to his full parted lips, and she suddenly wondered what it would be like to have him kiss her. The thought startled her out of her trance. She snapped her mouth shut, stiffened her spine, and averted her eyes. A puzzled frown curled her brow, the mood of the moment ago shattered, when her gaze fell upon a different man.

The Reverend Parrish strode down the aisle and stepped up on the platform. A hush fell over the sanctuary as he extended his arms as if reaching out to the women. He cleared his throat. "Ladies, each of you have your own reasons for attending tonight's meeting. Some of you will be chosen, and some of you will not."

After a brief prayer granting the women courage and strength, the reverend said, "Trevor St. John, attorney-at-law, will explain everything you need to know about this journey." He motioned the well-dressed man to the podium and then took the vacated chair.

A sparse man with a balding pate stepped to the podium. "The hour is upon us, so I'll be as brief as possible. Some years ago, a colleague of mine decided he was tired of city living and left for the frontier. He settled in a town named Glory, in Oregon Territory. I recently received a letter from him explaining Glory is a young town, a growing town. However, the men outnumber the women. A group of thirty gentlemen commissioned my friend asking him to find them wives, and, thus, he contacted me."

St. John held up a large brown envelope. "The men have sent tintypes, along with letters telling about themselves, and one hundred dollars from each man that will go toward supplies and travel expenses."

A woman from the audience shouted, "If all the money ain't spent, what happens to the rest of it?"

The lawyer searched until he spotted the besmirched face of the speaker. "In that case, madam, I have instructions to give the remaining funds to the bride-to-be."

Another woman stood, but with a challenging glare, he motioned for her to sit. "Ladies, be patient and hold your questions until you hear all of the details."

Sober-faced, he continued, "With me tonight are Constable O'Leary and Dr. Samuels. Some of you are quite familiar with the constable. Every one of you deserves a better life, but not all of you are qualified to make this journey." He motioned the policeman forward.

The constable pulled his billy stick and pointed it from left to right toward the crowd. "I don't need to call your names, but you ladies with a *P* tattooed on your cheek should take your leave now. Dr. Samuels won't give a clean bill of health to any one infected with the pox."

A ripple of murmurs filtered through the church as five garishly dressed women who worked in the brothels stepped from the pews and departed.

Again, the policeman pointed his club. He called the women by name. "Trixie, Eustis, Charmaine, you've all spent time in my jail. There's no place for pickpockets, thieves and disturbers of the peace on this trip." Before taking his seat, he scanned the group as if checking to make certain he hadn't missed anyone who needed further weeding.

Lawyer St. John resumed his position. "If you are a single woman...never married, widowed or divorced then you qualify as a candidate. However, we regret that no women with children are eligible."

"That ain't fair. Why cain't I take my young'uns if I'm one of the chosen?" a woman chortled.

"Because, my dear lady, the chances of children surviving this arduous trip are very slim, and additionally, it was one of the stipulations made by the men seeking wives."

Six more women gathered their skirts and quietly wished those remaining Godspeed.

The lawyer spoke again. "The women who are selected will be examined by Dr. Samuels. Anyone with consumption, bad teeth, pregnant, or who is misshapen won't go either."

A woman with a crooked back and leaning heavily on a cane was followed by a woman who held a yellowed handkerchief to her mouth, and another who turned and offered a grin showing badly swollen gums and blackened teeth.

The silence filled with chatter again as the preacher stood at the front with a bag in his hand. The lawyer said, "There are numbers inside the bag Reverend Parrish is holding. He will start here with this lady." St. John pointed to a slender woman seated at the end of the front pew. "She will reach in and draw out a number, then pass the bag to the next person. Don't worry there are enough numbers for each of you." He drew a deep breath and continued. "Before this night is over, you will be given the opportunity to state your reasons why you want to make this journey. I caution you, it'd better be more than just for the money.

"After we hear from you, the reverend will draw numbers from a second bag. The first thirty ladies will be the official brides-to-be.

"As much as I regret having to mention this, we realize some of you won't survive the trip. As such, we will also draw ten additional numbers. Those ladies will go as alternate brides."

As the numbers were passed among the women, St. John motioned the sun-darkened man dressed in buckskins to the podium. "Ladies, Mr. Cordell Bannon has been commissioned to escort you across the frontier. He is a rancher, former Indian scout and also an experienced wagon master. He knows the lay of the land between Philadelphia and Oregon Territory."

Bannon was taller than any man Fiona had ever seen, sturdy as an oak, and the buckskins he wore accentuated his broad chest and taut thighs.

"Oh my." She hadn't meant to speak aloud, but she did. A flush heated her cheeks.

****

Cordell Bannon stood beside the podium with his legs spread apart, his arms across his chest. He wanted the women to see the scowl on his face, to

11

know that when he spoke he meant business. He didn't like the idea of playing nursemaid to a bunch of greenhorn females across a thousand miles of danger. Money was money. This trip would pay enough to improve the livestock on his ranch.

As he swept the room, he settled on a pair of emerald eyes. Her weary face was a pale, luminous oval overshadowed by wide, green eyes, and her burnished copper hair tumbled in a mass of tangled curls around her face. He thought her beautiful. She blushed, and he almost laughed.

He, a man who'd always maintained control over his baser instincts, was struck by a sudden impulse to lay a kiss upon her moistly parted, beckoning red lips. Never mind that he was probably a decade her senior. Never mind that she was probably alone in the world, and only a scoundrel would take advantage of an innocent young lady.

Expectancy reflected in her eyes as he studied her. He'd been paid handsomely to escort these women west. A confirmed bachelor with a ranch waiting for him back in Oregon Territory, there was no room in his life for a wife. He wasn't a settling-down man. In addition, he'd signed a contract to protect the brides-to-be at all cost, even if it meant laying down his own life. He'd also placed his hand on the Bible and sworn an oath not to shilly-shally around with any of the women. And he was a man of his word.

The contradiction raged within him, for her beautiful, innocent-looking face did not coincide with the contract he'd signed with G. W. Daggert, Esquire, Attorney-at-Law, Glory, Oregon Territory.

An unreasonable anger ran through him. He stared at her until she flinched and looked down at her lap. In some inexplicable way, he felt as if he'd won a victory.

He shifted his weight, and then placed his hands

on his hips. "Ladies, as master of the wagon train that will take forty of you west, let's get a few things straight—" he enunciated his words as he pointed to his chest, "I am the boss. My word is law. My rules will be obeyed. Those who break the rules are subject to my punishment." He waited a moment to let his words sink in.

"The only other man on this trip is my scout, Isaiah Thomas. Mr. Thomas is not at your beck and call. You will be expected to change broken wagon wheels, ride or walk in the scorching heat, or pounding rain. You'll drive your teams until you feel as if your arms are being pulled out of your shoulder sockets, you'll fight mosquitoes, and some of you will die from snake bite, the fever, or from the arrow of hostile Indians.

"There's no one to nursemaid you or wipe your sniveling noses when the going gets unbearable, and there will be no turning back. Once you sign your contract the only way to get out of it is by death."

He watched the redhead's face pale as she gripped the hand of the woman seated next to her. He glanced around the room and witnessed the impact of his words. "Any of you not hale enough to tough it out to the end, I heartedly encourage you to leave now."

Bannon silently cursed himself. He knew how hurtful and frightening his words were—especially to the young woman whose hair glinted like fire in the lantern light, and with eyes as green as the Pacific Ocean.

A white-haired woman stood. "Two men aren't enough to protect us from all the dangers you've pointed out, Mr. Bannon. And surely you don't expect a bunch of women to dirty their hands with men's work?"

"Your name, madam?"

"My name has nothing to do with the question,

sir."

Bannon snorted, curling his lip in repugnance. "The bride contracts specify celibacy until wedded that is why we have two men only. I'd hate to put a noose around a man's neck...or a woman's because they couldn't keep their urges in check."

"You'd dare hang a woman?"

"As wagon master, my word is law. Pity to those who challenge it."

A gasp filtered around the room. Bannon felt the weight of the emerald-eyed beauty's frightened stare when she placed her hands to her throat as if to protect it. He shifted his gaze back toward the woman who'd asked the question. "As for dirtying your hands, madam, if you expect maid service on this trip, there won't be any."

He watched the woman's lips tighten to a pinched whiteness. As if unable to bear his mocking grin a moment longer, she gathered her cape around her shoulders and beat a retreat down the aisle.

Setting his feet wide apart and resting his fists on his hips, he knew his words had won the women's undivided attention.

****

Fiona's fingers tightened on Althea Smalley's hand. Heat coursed through Fiona, but passion wasn't the cause. Her features were taut with fear. She didn't know what was worse, to stay in Philadelphia and continuously fight off Blackie Sledge's advances until she lost the battle, or to go on a wagon train with a man whose blood was as cold as the snow on the grounds outside the church.

She leaned close and whispered, "Maybe I won't get chosen. I-I almost hope my number isn't called."

Ma Smalley patted her hand. "Don't pay him no never mind. Sure he's wagon boss, and I'll lay odds he's tough as beef jerky, but honey, if my instincts are right, and they always are, Mr. Cordell Bannon would give up the ghost before he'd let anything happen to his cargo. And that's what we are—cargo."

"Oh, but still..."

Ma Smalley shushed her. "The lawyer's going to speak."

Trevor St. John pursed his lips and rocked back on his heels as he looked at his watch. "It is now nine o'clock, and there are sixty-three of you. Starting with this lady," and he pointed at the same dark-haired woman as before, "stand up, state your name, and in one or two sentences give a reason why you think you can make this trip and why you qualify as a bride."

The process began. Women of all ages, sizes, shapes and financial status stated their reasons.

In the pew in front of Fiona, a tall slender woman with hair the color of a raven's wing stood. "My name is Bird LeBlanc. My father was a Frenchman, my mother Iroquois. We come to this place because trapping no more good in the north. I speak the language of my dead parents. Not so different from Ind'ans where we go. I know herbs for healing, and which are poison. I ride and shoot the long rifle plenty good. I sew and cook. No can read, but make good wife."

Likewise, Louise Shultz, Gerda Olsson and Mercy Anders introduced themselves, until it was Althea Smalley's turn.

Silently, Fiona wished she had the confidence of the woman who was now speaking.

Older than most, the woman stood and crossed her arms under her ample breasts. "Name is Althea Smalley. I prefer folks to call me Ma. Now before any of you gents get your bowels in a dither, I know I'm a little longer in the tooth than most of these ladies. I've seen fifty winters, buried two husbands and three sons." She shifted her eyes toward the wagon master. "Mr. Bannon, you said there would be no one to wipe these women's sniveling noses. Well, sir, I beg to differ. My late last husband, God rest his soul, was a traveling preacher man. I can read the Bible and pray when the fear gnaws away at some of the ladies. I can set broken bones. I've survived typhoid. I'm strong as a bull. I can drive a team of oxen or horses, and even as old as I am, I still know how to pleasure a man. Through sickness and sorrow, I'm true and honest." She brushed her hands together. "There, I've said my piece."

As she sat down, she patted Fiona's shoulder. "Don't be nervous, child. Make your voice heard."

Fiona's legs felt as if they'd fold under when she tried to stand. She gripped the pew in front of her until her knuckles turned white. Her throat had gone dry. Her color grew high as she forced herself to speak. "My name is Fiona Quinn. I can read and write and do sums. According to my late father, I'm a good cook. I play the harpsichord and know how to draw. Most of all, I'm a survivor, and though I know nothing of being a wife, I am willing to learn."

She squared her shoulders and lifted her chin as she met the scowl on Cordell Bannon's ruggedly handsome face.

Chapter Three

Intrusive thoughts filled Fiona's head. She dreaded walking the long and dark distance to her shanty. What would she do if she wasn't chosen as one of the brides? And worst, would Blackie Sledge have her arrested for attempted murder?

She knew by the buzzing and shuffling of feet that the women grew restless. Anxiety filled Fiona when Lawyer St John stepped forward. "Patience ladies. We'll begin the lottery, by selecting the brides first, and afterward the ten alternates."

He instructed the remaining women to gravitate to the center row of seats. "When your number is called, seat yourself on the pews to my right." He indicated the direction with a flourish of his hand. "Reverend Parrish will write down your name, age, and next of kin, if you have any."

Silence descended over the church as the minister reached into the bag and called the first number.

Have faith...have faith. Tension knotted Fiona's stomach. Although she'd committed her number to memory, she couldn't help but glance at the slip of paper each time the lawyer reached into the bag, drew out a numeral and then read it aloud. Silently, she willed number *thirty-six* to be the next one called.

Her pulse thumped a little louder as whoops of joy went up each time a woman rose from the center section and moved to the pews on the right to join the newly chosen brides. Fiona's heart hung in her throat when he called—thirty, and it sank when he finished with—nine.

"Glory be. Number thirty-nine. That's me." Ma Smalley reached over and hugged Fiona. Before moving to the designated bride's area, she whispered, "Don't worry. You're one of the chosen ones. I feel it in here," and she pointed to her heart.

I want to believe you. Really, I do. Fiona offered a watery smile as she watched her newly found friend join the others. Her heart sank as she did a mental count and realized there was only one slot left and the bride quota would be filled.

She rubbed her sweaty palms across the cloak in her lap, and, though it was only seconds, it seemed to her a lifetime has passed before the lawyer called the last number.

It wasn't hers.

Disappointment and even a streak of panic rifled through her.

She watched the French and Iroquois woman, Bird LeBlanc, pad on silent feet to sit apart from the others.

Fiona felt a little sorry for Lawyer St. John, who once again cleared his throat as he shook the bag as if to redistribute the remaining slips of paper. "All right, ladies. It's time to choose the ten alternates. When your number is called, you will please move to the left side of the room. Remain seated until the Reverend Parrish comes and records your information—same as with the brides."

Fiona was more than a little conscious of the intensity of Cordell Bannon's gaze. Why was he always looking at her like that? His piercing stare seemed to bore through her, causing her to look away, another blush tinged her fair cheeks. She must look a sight, indeed, she thought worriedly, for him to gawk like that. *Fuss and bother.* The man was probably just as much of a menace as her nemesis, Blackie Sledge. The thought of being forced to become one of the brothel owner's whores sickened her.

So intent in her thoughts, she didn't hear the number until it was repeated. "Thirty-six...going once...going twice...number thirty-six...for the last time."

She gave a tiny shriek. "Me...Fiona Quinn...I'm number thirty-six."

"Congratulations, Miss Quinn. You are the final alternate." She thought the lawyer looked sorrowful when he said, "My regrets to you ladies not chosen. It's been a long and tedious night, and I thank you for your patience. We cannot make life easier for you, but before you leave, each of you will be paid one dollar for your time." He glanced over his shoulder. "Constable O'Leary will pay you on your way out."

Inhaling deeply, St. John said to the forty selected women, "Mr. Bannon has final instructions for you," and then to the pastor, he said, "Reverend Parrish, the hour is late. My supper is cold, and I am tired. In the morning, bring the list of brides' names to my office so that I might draw up the legal contracts." He bid the women goodnight and strode from the church.

****

Cordell Bannon assumed his earlier posture—shoulders wide, legs apart, his brows drawn together in a pensive frown. He spoke as if he were holding court. "The wagons and oxen are ready. Plan to leave before dawn day after tomorrow, and heed my word, you will take nothing more than you can pack in one valise."

"What about our furniture?"

"Yeah, I ain't got much, but I don't want to leave my mother's spinet behind."

"You have two days to either sell or give away

your personal belongings. If it can't be packed in *one* valise, then it isn't worth taking." Bannon sent a challenging stare at the women. "Your first priority is to go by the doctor's office tomorrow, then by the lawyer's office to give him the health certificate and sign your name to the bride's contract. Constable O'Leary wrote down the names of the women who just left. If Doc doesn't give you a clean bill of health, it won't take me long to round up one of the ladies off that list to replace you."

Fiona stood. Her voice was timid. "I don't understand, sir, why we are limited to one valise. Surely you don't expect us to pack enough clothes to last most of a year in one wee bag?"

As the group murmured their agreement, she squared her shoulders, and her voice grew bolder. "And what about blankets? 'Tis March, to be sure, and spring is on its way, but isn't it just as cold in other parts of the country as it is here in Philadelphia?"

He cursed himself for accepting this job. The thought of playing nursemaid to a bunch of mail-order brides hit him like a heavy fist to his gut. He found this young woman's quiet pride and dignity appealing and knew he'd have to keep a bridle on his emotions.

He blew out a long patient sigh. All it took was one rabble-rouser to create problems in a camp. His voice was curt. "Oxen are slow plodding animals. We need their strength to get us through the snow until we get to the Missouri River where we will trade them for mules. With four of you to a wagon, we can only make ten or fifteen miles a day. The lighter the load, the faster we travel. I won't watch good animals drop in their traces from exhaustion." He scrutinized the frail young woman and part of him hoped the doctor wouldn't certify her fit for the journey. "Each of you will be issued two clean blankets—free from vermin. Does that answer satisfy you, Miss..."

"Fiona Quinn." Her smile was wan.

After questioning the women to see which of them knew how to drive a yoke of oxen, Bannon explained the wagons would be divided into equal teams with a woman assigned as captain to each group. He'd already determined which of the women were able-bodied, strong-minded, and could handle most any situation that came along. He prided himself on knowing men and horses, and figured that except for being a little more temperamental, women weren't much different.

"Miz Smalley, you'll have an extra wagon in your team. You're in charge of wagons one through four."

Likewise, he assigned Louise Shultz to wagons five through seven, and Gerda Olsson was in charge of teams eight through ten. It'd been his experience that white women didn't generally cotton to squaws and decided to head off any trouble in advance.

"Bird LeBlanc," he singled out the half-Iroquois woman, "you and my scout, Mr. Thomas, will spell each other driving the supply wagon." He glanced around the room. "Any more questions?"

Ma Smalley stood. "Just what are our duties as captains of these here wagon teams?"

"Figured you'd be the one to ask." To answer her question he addressed the group as a whole. "Before we leave, I expect each captain to select the women for her group. How you go about it makes no difference to me. Just get it done."

He surveyed the expectant faces. "I don't have time for whining female grievances. Any woman who has a complaint, take it to your captain."

He crossed his arms over his chest. "Captains, I expect you to solve any complaints, wrong-headed notions, arguments, and female ague. As such, I expect you to meet on a regular basis then report to me every fortnight."

He sent up a challenge as he shifted his gaze, meeting expectant eyes. "Coming to me with a problem is the last resort. Any severe penalties that need doling out, I'll settle. As wagon master of this outfit, I am the judge and the jury, and rest assured you will not like my punishments. Understood?"

He left no room for further questions. "It's late. Go home, get some rest, put your belongings together, and meet me at dawn Saturday on Main Street."

Before anyone could react, Bannon disappeared through the side door.

****

Fiona laid her hand on Ma Smalley's arm as they stepped down from the church steps and onto the street. "I know we've only just met, and you don't know me from Adam's housecat, but I have a favor to ask." She hastened on. "Don't be feelin' bad if you're inclined to say no."

"Now...now," she patted Fiona's shoulder, "before you go putting words in my mouth, ask your favor. Let me decide how I'll answer."

Fiona shifted from one foot to the other. She hesitated. "Oh, stuff and bother. I'll say it right out. Tonight, before I came to the meeting, I stabbed Blackie Sledge."

Ma Smalley's voice was empathic, but her eyes opened wide. "He's a black-hearted snake, that one. From the gossip I hear, he's been the ruination of many an innocent young woman." She leaned close and dropped her voice to a whisper. "Bless my bones, did you kill 'im?"

Fiona almost choked at the thought of committing murder. "Nothing so drastic—stabbed him in the arm. Ever since the deaths of my sainted father and dear brother, Blackie's been after me to become his personal girl." She buried her face in her hands. "I need a place to stay until the wagon train leaves day after tomorrow. He'll come to get revenge, and I'm afraid when he does, he'll bring a few of his henchmen along."

Without hesitation Ma Smalley said, "I have a small room at the rear of the Denver House where I work in the kitchen. Only have the one cot—not big enough for both of us. If you're so inclined, I'll make a pallet on the floor."

Fiona readily agreed to the offer and hugged the woman. "I'm ever so grateful, Mrs. Smalley."

When Fiona stepped back, Ma Smalley dabbed her eyes at the unexpected rush of emotion. "If'n we're to be friends, call me Ma Smalley like most folks do." Mrs. Smalley continued, her throaty voice low and clear. "Can you get your belongings together tonight?"

Fiona shot her a questioning glance. "I suppose so. Why can't it wait 'til tomorrow?"

The older woman expelled an exaggerated snort. "Use your noggin, girl. Blackie Sledge'll nurse his wounded arm and that overstuffed ego of his tonight with as much rot-gut whiskey as he can slog down. Tomorrow, daylight or dark, he'll come with blood in his eye and revenge in his heart." She pointed to her chest. "I know these things."

"Then let's make haste. It won't take me long to stuff my few meager belongings into a valise." Fiona's chuckle was a hollow sound.

Walking as fast as possible she and Ma Smalley, in their black cloaks, were but mere shadows in the darkness. Before entering the one room shanty at the end of town, Ma Smalley cautioned, "Better listen at the door for sounds."

Fiona realized her mouth was dry and her heart pounded, not from exertion, but apprehension. She eased to the door and placed her ear against the wood. She looked over her shoulder and indicated with a nod she detected no movements or unusual sounds.

In spite of the cold, Fiona's palms were sweaty. She pulled the key from its place beneath the neck of her dress and inserted it into the lock. The click sounded deafening. Fiona held her breath—waited—eased the door open. Enough moonlight showed the room was empty save for the sparse furnishings.

She and Ma Smalley stepped inside. Fiona quickly barred the door. Groping her way to the table, she searched with her fingers until touching the match box. Striking a sulfur match, she lit a candle and then knelt down and reached under the bed. She pulled out a weather-beaten and scarred leather valise. Sitting it on the bed, she tugged at the rusted buckles and opened it wide. Walking to the one treasure her father had refused to sell to pay for doctor bills, she opened the chiffonier that he'd handcrafted as a gift for her.

"Mighty pretty piece of handiwork. Shame you cain't take it with you."

Fiona ran her hand lovingly over the ornate details on the chiffonier's door. "'Tis a replica of the one father built as a wedding gift for my mother." She expelled a long sigh. "Mother sold it to help buy passage to America."

Nearly the same size as her recently deceased brother, Fiona stuffed three pairs of woolen long-johns in the bag and a pair of his brogans along with woolen socks, three summer frocks, her only good petticoat, a sunbonnet, a nightgown, shawl, two sweaters, a hairbrush and the case that held her darning needles and spools of thread.

She scanned the small room. Her emotions reeled with anguish when she spotted her journal, drawing pencils, paintbrushes, and rectangular leather bound case that protected her drawing paper and sketches.

She picked up the folder and sighed. "It's too large."

Ma Smalley said, "Heard you say you could draw. Mind if I look?"

Fiona opened the portfolio and watched while the older woman stared in amazement at the charcoal drawings of birds, horses, scenes of the town and recognized many of the townspeople, including one of an evil-looking Blackie Sledge. "Shame to leave such talented work behind."

Fiona looked downcast when she said, "Isn't important. I'll draw smaller images in my journal." She lovingly tucked the medium-sized book inside the valise and buckled the straps. She lifted the case with both hands, blew out the candle and without a backward glance said, "I'm ready."

Chapter Four

Dawn was a scant hour old.

The morning air was cold and damp, the streets wet and puddled from an early spring snow. A hazy fog wafted near the ground, concealing the wheels of the covered wagons.

Fiona's first breath cleared her lungs with the sharp chill.

She felt more invigorated because of her past days huddled in Ma Smalley's room and her near disastrous encounter with Blackie Sledge.

Feeling both relief and regret, she sat silently beside Ma Smalley, her heavy woolen cloak wrapped around her, her hands clasped beneath the lap blanket that covered them both. Her pulse raced. She tried to calm the excited pace of her breathing as she listened to the eager oxen stamp their feet and waited for Cordell Bannon to give his order to roll the wagons.

Although each wagon was outfitted with two extra water barrels, the food and other supplies were in the one that brought up the rear of the train. Fiona now understood why Bannon had been so adamant about limiting personal belongings to one valise. With four women in each, the wagons' quarters were adequate, but cramped.

She leaned over the side and peered through the breaking haze at the waiting line of oxen. Bannon had explained the supply wagon would carry extra wheels, a bushel of beans which had been marked for each team leader's group, salt, tea and coffee, dried meat, salted fish, sides of cured bacon, and barrels of flour. It also included extra canvas, a keg of gunpowder, and two rifles along with fifty rounds of ammunition for each woman.

Ma Smalley questioned Bannon about the need for so many weapons. He merely shrugged and answered with a small smile, but there was no amusement in his eyes. "Once we enter Indian Territory, we'll need as much fire power as you ladies can muster."

In her usual manner, she drew her arms under her ample bosom. "My late husband, God rest his soul, anticipated going west to join missionaries to minister to the Indians. Surely they aren't all that hostile?"

What Bannon then said chilled Fiona to the core of her soul. He'd spoken quietly, matter-of-factly, and with no expression. "The Pawnee are a relatively peaceful lot, but they like to kidnap women and make them slaves. Being a slave is worse than dying. Now, some of the other tribes raid for the sake of stealing cattle, horses—women. And when they're done passing the woman around from brave to brave, and when she's all used up, they shoot arrows into her until God has mercy and she dies."

Mercy Anders pushed away from the group and stumbled behind a wagon. In a moment, Fiona heard the soft sounds of retching.

Not one woman spoke, and horror hung as thick as the fog. Bannon hadn't altered his scowl.

It was in this hush of silence that someone grabbed Fiona around the neck and dragged her a little away from the group. "Smart man, Bannon. Scaring these poor women into submission is a worthy tactic. Perhaps, I'll use the same on my sweet little Fiona."

She twisted around to meet the glittering

madness in Blackie Sledge's eyes. "Let me go. You're deranged if you think I'll stay here with you."

She tried to struggle from his grip. The hood from her cape had fallen from her head and he'd grasped her long braid, wrapping it around his hand, imprisoning her until she feared her neck would snap.

The crack of Isaiah Thomas' whip rent the stunned silence, jerking Blackie Sledge off his feet and into the mud. In his apparent surprise, the brothel owner released Fiona before his fall.

A hand reached out and touched her shoulder. "You all right?"

Not able to find her voice, she'd nodded her answer to Bannon who then handed her into the safety of Ma Smalley's arms.

He'd placed one foot on Blackie Sledge's heaving chest. "Miss Quinn your relative—a wife, maybe?" Bannon then leaned forward and placed the barrel of his .44 caliber Walker Colt between the bawdy house owner's eyes. "Careful you speak truthfully. This pistol of mine has a hair-trigger."

Sledge answered with a wide-eyed shake of his head. "N-no."

"Good. Because I have a signed contract saying she's spoken for as a bride-to-be."

"I'll buy her." Whether from the cold or from fear Blackie's hand shook as he made to reach inside his coat pocket.

"Wouldn't do that if I was you," Bannon warned. "Besides, she's not for sale—at any price." He glanced up at his scout. "Isaiah, escort this piece of trash over to the jail."

Almost as an afterthought, he said ominously, his eyes never wavering from Blackie Sledge's face. "Come after us, and I'll cut your heart out and feed it to the coyotes."

Fiona witnessed Bannon's jaw stiffen with

tension and then settle back into a bland expression.

His voice didn't just thunder, it rang, it pierced, it echoed. "To your wagons ladies. Ma Smalley...on my signal...move 'em out."

Chapter Five

Four weeks had passed, and harsh wind blew cold across the Cumberland Road as the women settled in for the night. Snowflakes splattered against the wagon's canvas. Fiona felt good, better than she'd felt since leaving Philadelphia. Grateful for the long underwear and woolen stockings beneath her frayed dress and the two sweaters she wore to ward off the chill, she sat crossed-legged on the rough-hewn top bunk. She recalled the cramped quarters on the ship that had brought her family to America from Ireland. Now her new home for the next four or five months was equally as small.

The lantern hanging from the center rung provided scant little warmth, yet the closeness of the wagon's interior felt like a safe cocoon that wrapped around her. Aside from herself, she shared the space with Ma Smalley, Mercy Anders, and Henrietta Hightower.

"I can't read much, but the pictures you draw sure are purty." Out of obvious curiosity, Mercy Anders stretched on her tiptoes to peer at the book cradled in Fiona's lap. "What is it you write in that little book of yours?"

Fiona smiled. "When Mr. Bannon said we couldn't bring any large personal items I decided to keep a journal to record my thoughts and to draw pictures of the things I see along the way. I hope I'm recording history, Mercy."

"Would you read something that you wrote?"

"Mercy," Ma Smalley scolded, "it's rude to ask

such liberties. Fiona's words are for herself.'"

The girl's face colored. "Beg pardon, Fiona. I didn't mean to pry."

Fiona let out a gentle laugh to show she took no offense at the girl's curiosity, though it actually mortified her, a little, to share such personal thoughts. "Well, if it shan't bore all of you to tears, I'll read today's entry."

"Hearing you read will be a nice way to end the evening." Ma Smalley snugged the heavy quilt up around her shoulders.

Feeling a bit shy about sharing her feelings, Fiona cleared her throat and began. "Mr. Bannon says our wagons are called Prairie Schooners. Sometimes the snow is too deep for the women to walk, so we ride in the wagons as often as possible. Oh, how I long for warm weather, blue skies, and wildflowers. Tonight, Mr. Bannon announced before we cross the great Missouri River he'll trade the oxen for horses and mules, so the going will be a little faster. He is a strict taskmaster and not the least friendly. I wonder if he will allow us a trip into the settlement we spotted earlier. We are one month on the trail. I think we all miss civilization."

She smiled, and as she closed the book, Mercy placed a hand on Fiona's arm. "Wait. Show them the picture." She turned with an expression of awe toward the captivated audience. "Fiona's drawn a likeness of Mr. Bannon."

Fiona passed the journal across the aisle to Ma Smalley who tilted the pencil rendering toward the lantern's light. "Fierce-looking as he is, you've captured the loneliness in his eyes, Fiona. I'd say under that heart of stone lays a man with a hurtin' soul." Ma Smalley leaned over and handed the book down to the next woman.

There was a long moment of silence before Mercy Anders stood on tiptoe again and blew out the flame in the lantern.

****

The first leg of their journey was so deceptively easy it was only natural for Fiona to doubt Bannon's warnings of the many dangers that lay ahead.

They had reached the river crossing late in the afternoon when Bannon rode to the lead wagon, held up his hand and signaled Fiona. She reluctantly pulled on the reins and brought her team to a halt. "Why are we stopping so early?" She brushed a wayward strand of hair from her face. "Are you taking us into the town?"

Bannon seemingly ignored her question. He waited for Isaiah Thomas to take up position at the fifth wagon before he raised his voice. From experience, Fiona knew it would only be heard as far back as the fourth wagon. "Ladies, we camp here for the night. Circle your wagons then meet me for a pow-wow in the center of the circle." He turned his eyes to Fiona and pointed. "Drive your team over to that copse of cottonwood trees."

Fiona watched him disappear behind a dip in the road. She flapped the reins over the broad backs of the oxen turning the beasts toward the trees.

****

An hour after the women had circled the wagons for the night, Bannon returned from his scouting trip as was his and Isaiah Thomas' daily routine.

By April's end, he was marveling at the way the women made good use of their time each evening, tending to their stock and setting up camp before seeing to their own needs.

In fact, he felt assured these women were faring better than most in wagon trains that traveled the same route year-after-year, searching for paradise.

It did concern him how the women would react to seeing the sun-bleached, dried bones of humans who'd died along the trail and whose bodies had been dug up by coyotes and wolves.

His gaze brushed past Ma Smalley and the other two wagon captains huddled together around a small fire to where Fiona, Bird LeBlanc, and Mercy Anders gathered edible roots and herbs a short distance outside the perimeter of the circle. Early on he'd warned the women not to stray too far and to never venture off alone.

He listened to the musical lilt of Fiona's laughter, followed by the other two women, and marveled at the Irish girl's capacity to welcome a half-breed woman as a friend.

He didn't consider that he was eavesdropping, just a phenomenon of nature how voices carried on the plains making conversations easily overheard.

Bird LeBlanc pointed out the difference between edible mushrooms and those which were poisonous. From where he stood, it appeared they'd also loaded their baskets with wild legumes and poke weed.

Dusk had fallen by the time Fiona and her friends returned to the circle of wagons, and Bannon was calling the routine camp meeting to order.

"All right ladies, settle down. Your wagon captains will speak for you, then I'll have my say."

Ma Smalley stepped forward. She drew the woolen cloak closer around her robust body as if trying to garner more warmth than the garment wanted to give. She matched Bannon's stare eye-for-eye. "Thankfully, there's no sign of sickness amongst any of us. We seem to be holding up well under the rigors of our travels. Now, nary a one of us is faulting you for the weather, but it's been more'n a month since we signed our bride contracts. The women have come to us three," she indicated Gerda Olsson and Lou Schultz, "with a few grievances." She pulled a piece of paper from beneath her cloak. "First, it's been a long time since leaving Philadelphia. We'd like a trip into the settlement.

It'd be nice to see some different faces other than our own for a change.

"Second, the women request a cow for fresh milk, and maybe a few chickens for eggs, and third, if the next leg of this journey is gonna get as hard as you keep predicting, then the women need a day or two's rest."

When she stopped to draw a breath, Bannon uttered a sarcastic chuckle. "A milk cow, chickens for eggs? Your ladies don't ask for much. Is there anything else?"

Ma Smalley didn't waver. "As a matter-of-fact, there is. We all figure that it's high-time we get a gander at the tintypes of the prospective bridegrooms, and we also desire to read the letters that lawyer feller said they wrote telling about themselves."

Bannon stood with his legs braced wide and not a semblance of a smile on his face. "Heed my words carefully, ladies." He sent a challenging glance that would cause the stoutest man to back down. "There will be no trips to the settlement—for any reason. The dangers along the trail are enough, but once a bunch of randy sonafabucks who haven't seen a white woman, hell, any woman, in a month of Sundays even gets the slightest hint this is a wagon train filled with women, none of you will be safe. They'll swarm down like a bunch of rabid wolves. Isaiah and I can't protect the whole lot of you if that happens. Trust me. These aren't the type men who go to church socials, and they won't care if they leave you dead or alive."

He stared at them in silence for so long that he didn't have to use his imagination to sense the women's tension. He shifted his gaze around the group. "Bird LeBlanc."

The Indian woman stepped through the crowd to stand in from of him. "I am here."

"You handle a team pretty well. I'll need you to haul back as many cages of chickens we can buy. We'll trade the oxen for mules, extra horses, and a milk cow."

A woman from Lou Schultz's group called, "Hey, that ain't fair. Why's she get to go?"

Lou whipped around. "Hush your mouth, Bertha Mae. Mr. Bannon don't owe anymore explanation than he's already given."

Bannon turned on his heel and then turned back. "Set up a table. I'll go get the tintypes of the men who've bought and paid for you."

He never looked over his shoulder as long strides moved him toward the supply wagon. He knew exactly where the oilskin packet of pictures and letters lay hidden beneath a false panel in the wagon's floorboards. He used his skinning knife to pry up the board. When he returned to the cluster of women, he unceremoniously dumped the packet onto the table. As the women rushed forward, he growled, "Back off. You remind me of a pack of hounds ready to fight over a handful of scraps." His glare caused the women to edge away from the table.

He directed his attention to the wagon captains. "Ma Smalley, I want you, Miz Shultz, and Miz Olsson to lay the tintypes out side-by-side. Each picture is numbered and has the man's name written on it. The letters the men have written are numbered same as their picture. Match 'em up." He continued in an acidic tone. "Any woman who fights over a picture will answer to me."

"And just what kind of punishment would you be handing out, Mr. Bannon?"

He directed his annoyed glint toward a stout woman with mousy brown hair. A pang of sympathy went through him for the man who wedded this shrew. "She'll feel the sting of my blacksnake across her back."

When she didn't back down from her challenging glare, he held out his hand. "Mr. Thomas."

The scout stepped forward and placed the whip in Bannon's outstretched palm. Bannon whirled the braided strip of leather over his head and flicked it so fast that it popped a button off the woman's dress. The astonished look on her face brought a sneer to his. "Anyone else dare to challenge my word?" He coiled the whip and handed it back to the man who stood at his side.

Glancing around, he searched for Fiona, who had shrunken back from the group. He saw the horror on her face and was aware his heart had begun to hammer dully within his chest. No woman had ever affected him like this diminutive, green-eyed beauty. He wasn't certain how she'd accomplished it, but she'd stolen his heart, and he knew with her being an alternate bride, the chances of him ever being able to give his heart to her didn't exist. He'd have to guard his emotions more than ever.

His voice was a deep rumble. "Just a reminder, those of you who are alternate brides will not choose. Brides-to-be, once you've made your choice, line up over by Miss Quinn. She will record your name and the name of the man whose tintype you've chosen." He placed his arms over his broad chest. "I caution you to choose well for there will be no swapping about once Miss Quinn writes down your name."

He stepped to where Fiona stood and handed her his log and a pencil nub. Even after a hard day of traveling, she smelled fresh and clean, like wildflowers. It distracted him. He noticed even though her lips were set into a thin line, they were enticingly red.

He shook himself from the distraction and turned to face the waiting women. "Any questions?"

Mercy Anders stepped forward. She kept her

eyes lowered as if concentrating on the toe of her dusty shoe. "I cain't read. How'm I gonna know what my letter says?"

Perhaps the most irritating thing of all was Bannon couldn't place his finger on the exact reason for his unaccountable anger. "Those who know how to read, help them that don't."

He glanced around until he spotted the Iroquois woman. "Bird LeBlanc, be quick about making your choice. After you've given Miss Quinn your information, join Isaiah and me. I intend to trade the oxen and get back to camp before nightfall."

****

Lantern light danced around the circled encampment. Fiona rested against the wheel of her wagon with a cup of hot tea in her hands. It'd been a long day, and her throat felt slightly parched from all the letters she'd read. She closed her eyes and thought about the curious look Bannon had given her earlier in the day—a look of irritation. She'd wanted to ask him why he was angry with her, but she didn't. Perhaps because she was afraid.

A sigh ensued as she lifted the cup of warm liquid and sipped. Many questions plagued her as she wrote in her journal. *What is my future? What if I make it all the way to Oregon Territory without having to marry? What then?*

She felt more than heard a silent presence. A startled little cry escaped her lips when she looked up into the dark eyes of Bird LeBlanc.

"I am sorry, Miss Quinn. I did not mean to frighten you."

"Please, not your fault. My head was someplace else, and I didn't hear you."

An awkward silence passed between them. "Won't you join me in a cup of tea, Miss LeBlanc?" Fiona rose to get another cup.

"I have come for that which you hold for me."

"Of course, forgive me. I'd forgotten." Fiona reached into her apron pocket, removed the tintype and letter and held it toward the Indian woman.

"You will read the letter to me?" Her voice sounded almost shy.

Fiona smiled. "It would be my pleasure."

"Then I will accept your offer for tea."

Bird LeBlanc held the picture toward the lantern's light. "He is not a big man, but sometimes it is the willow tree that is the strongest."

Fiona smiled as she adjusted the lantern so that its light cast over the page. She wetted her throat with a sip of tea. "It says...I am Jacques Medoro, and I await you. My mother was Ojibwa from the Yukon and my father French. My friends call me Jack. I am a trapper and a woodsman and work for the logging company." The letter went on to give his age and to say he owned his own cabin and would work hard to be a good husband.

Fiona folded the letter and handed it to the Iroquois woman. "Are you nervous, Miss LeBlanc, to wed with a man that you know only through a letter and a tintype?"

"Life does not hold much for mixed-blood women, Miss Quinn. We take what we get when the opportunity arises and hope in the end all will be right." Bird held the picture and letter to her heart. "Do you think the men were chosen as carefully as we women?"

Fiona tilted her head pondering the question. "Yes. I believe they must have been."

"Then I am not nervous. He is as I, a mixed-blood and will be a good man." Then as quietly as she had come, Bird LeBlanc disappeared into the shadows of the camp.

****

"He's not a particularly purty man, but then I'm no ravin' beauty myself." Mercy lamented from her bunk.

"Who're you referring to, Mercy?" Fiona leaned over her bed to peer down at the girl huddled in the blankets beneath her.

"Why, Mr. Henry Filmore, of course."

"There were lots of choices. Why did you select him?"

"Don't rightly know. Guess somehow I figured it just didn't much matter. One man's face seemed as good as the other." The girl sniffed.

"Are you crying, Mercy?" Fiona wanted to know.

"Maybe, a little." Mercy let her gaze glide up to Fiona. "At least I'll have a roof over my head, food to eat, and a man to look after me. Maybe even after a little bit, him and me will fall in love. Do you think that's possible?"

"You don't give yourself enough credit, Mercy. You're a lovely young woman with a lot to offer. I'd be willing to bet that Mr. Filmore will fall in love with you the moment the two of you meet." Fiona lay back on her pillow and placed her hands behind her head. "If he doesn't, then he's a foolish man."

There wasn't any need to say more. She'd seen the sparkle return to Mercy's eyes.

Fiona propped up on her elbow and smiled when Ma Smalley said, "Mrs. Otto Hackett." And then had clamped her hand over her mouth saying, "Reckon I was doing my thinking out loud."

Fiona and her bunkmates giggled. Fiona said, "You're already twittering like a bride, Ma Smalley."

"I've been wed to a farmer and a preacher. Buried them both. God rest their souls. Now it seems I'm to be a storekeeper's wife. I've been blessed." She adjusted her nightshift as she leaned forward and strained to see through the darkness. "Life will turn out all right for you, Fiona. Just you wait and see."

"How can you be so sure?"

"Instinct, mostly." Ma Smalley's voice was

emphatic.

"I suppose there are worse things than being alone."

"What can be worse than being alone, Fiona?" Henrietta Hightower expressed quizzical concern.

"Being forced to become one of Blackie Sledge's doxies." Fiona bit out the words.

A soft mewling caused Fiona to lean over the bunk. Her eyes swept downward to the frail girl who lay with knees curled to her chest. "Mercy, is something wrong?"

"Tain't nothing. G'night."

Before drifting off to sleep, Fiona wondered if the mention of Blackie Sledge had upset Mercy.

Chapter Six

Fiona sat wearily on the hard seat watching Cordell Bannon as he rode ahead of the wagon. True to his word, he'd returned from the settlement along the great Missouri River with one wire coop filled with two hens and a rooster for each wagon and one jersey milk cow.

Every time her wagon hit a rock it would set the cage of clucking chickens into a ruckus. "Oh, stuff and bother, biddies, if you don't stop squawking and lay some eggs you might find yourselves in the stew pot." She leaned around and grinned at the cage strapped to the side of the wagon.

She flapped the reins over the team's dusty backs and called the mules by name to increase their plodding speed. Several yards ahead, she observed Cordell Bannon's broad, powerful shoulders made even broader by the buckskin coat he wore. He was an extremely handsome man, and he piqued her interest more than she cared to admit.

After two months on the trail and after fifteen miles of hard traveling each day that began as soon as the mules could pick their way through the dim light of daybreak, one day grew into another. It had been that way all across Missouri, and she was tired. They were all tired.

She'd never seen anything like the plains. "Mr. Bannon?"

At the sound of her voice, Bannon swung his sorrel gelding around and sidled up next to her. "Yes ma'am?"

41

"I do wish you'd call me Fiona." His face was shadowed by a high-crowned, wide-brimmed hat, and she couldn't see his eyes.

"Yes ma'am." His voice was low and easy.

She expelled a resigned sigh. "I've never seen such beauty. It's like the plains stretch from the banks of the river to the horizon—like an ocean of undulating green, and stretching out in all directions as far as the eye can see."

Bannon smiled at her. "You'll grow mighty tired of that view when another few weeks of travelin's done."

She inhaled the sweet fragrance of prairie grass. "I don't think so, Mr. Bannon. It's a whole new world, and I can't imagine ever tiring of it."

"Yes ma'am." He doffed his hat and urged his gelding forward.

With powerful emotions roiling around inside her, Fiona watched him until he was but a speck in the distance. Had she not known better, she would have thought the land had simply swallowed him.

****

Fiona walked as much as possible, as did the other women. She wondered why it annoyed her Bannon had ridden past without the courtesy of a nod. *Why should he? Aren't I perhaps destined to be another man's bride?*

As was his routine, Bannon rejoined the wagon train when the sun began setting each night. She often wondered what he felt to have the freedom to come and go each day without ever having to answer to anyone.

His deep baritone voice interrupted her thought when he said, "Ma Smalley, up ahead about two miles is a small clearing." He shifted in the saddle and pointed the direction. "Pull your team in among the trees. We'll camp there for the night."

"You got it, Mr. Bannon."

"I'll pass the word." He flung the words over his shoulder as he urged his horse forward.

Hearing him barking orders brought memories of her departed father and brother, engulfing Fiona in sadness, as Bannon called out to each wagon, "Two miles. Follow the lead wagon. Circle up tight, ladies."

****

Fiona, like a bursting dam, let loose with a torrent of pent-up laughter at the wide-eyed expression on Ma Smalley's face. She'd completed her account of total mortification of accidentally letting a fart escape during a moment of silence at one of her late husband's prayer meetings.

Mercy Anders stamped her feet and all but fell over with laughter. Concerned about the girl's emaciated features, Fiona was glad Ma Smalley had entertained them with her outlandish story, bringing a little light to Mercy's eyes.

Fiona was still laughing when Louise Schultz and Gerda Olsson approached the low-burning campfire. Lou looked questioningly as Fiona lifted the hem of her skirt and wiped tears from her eyes. "You sound like a bunch of cackling hens. I could use a good laugh...mind sharing?"

Fiona opened her mouth only to bend double with another bout of hysterical giggles. Between gasps of breath she said, "Get Ma Smalley to tell you."

Managing to collect her wits, Fiona turned to leave. "I spotted a pool while I was gathering wood. While you ladies have your meeting, I'll have myself a wee bath."

"Don't know that it's a good idea for you to go wandering off by yourself. Never know what's hidin' behind the rocks." Gerda Olsson warned.

"Ah, she'll be okay, Gerda. You fret too much." Lou Schultz chided the woman seated across from her. A big rawboned woman, Louise Schultz didn't appear to be afraid of the devil himself. She lifted her arm and took a whiff. "I'd consider taking one myself if I knew how to swim."

Fiona laughed and strolled toward the wagon she shared with Ma Smalley and two other women, to fetch a bar of soap and a fresh pair of pantaloons.

Mercy Anders called, "Be careful, Fiona."

****

Fiona carefully picked her way to a small clearing to a near perfect circle among the trees. Silver moonlight illuminated a pool. The water was so still it seemed more a mirror reflecting the full moon and each sparkling dot in a sky filled with twinkling stars. The air was cool and fragrant with the perfume of wildflowers.

She glanced around to make sure the night didn't have prying eyes. "Silly goose, we're hundreds of miles from civilization. Who is there to spy on me?" The sound of her voice was reassuring. She stepped out of her clothes with sensual abandon.

When she tested the icy water with her big toe, goose bumps puckered her bare skin giving her second thoughts about fully submerging herself. "Oh, stuff and bother. I haven't had more than a spit bath in weeks and smell like a Billy goat."

She gasped and sputtered when she waded into the cold water.

A deep throaty laugh echoed around her. She swirled in the pool, her arms crossed to cover her bare breasts, while searching the shadows for the intruder. "Shoo. Go away, whoever you are."

"Shoo?" Bannon answered with a short laugh. "Can't imagine you scaring off a savage with, *shoo*."

Fiona caught the sarcasm in his voice. As her eyes adjusted to the darkness she spotted him standing in the center of the pool. "You're intruding on my bath. Go away, Mr. Bannon."

"Correct me if I'm wrong, Miss Quinn, but I do believe I was here first. In my estimation that makes you the intruder."

"Then for shame. You've given me such a fright." It occurred to her that Bannon had watched her undress. She dipped down until the water covered her shoulders. "Shame on you, Mr. Bannon. Have you no honor? A decent man would have made his presence known."

"Who said I was a decent man?"

She lifted her hand and slapped the water's surface. "You are a perplexing man, and I refuse to bandy words with you."

"Most women wouldn't jump into a darkened pool without checking to see if it was occupied. Guess you didn't hear my warning about venturing off alone?" He waded closer.

A strange stillness settled over the pool as the moon created a halo of light around Bannon. Fiona wanted to enjoy his closeness, to hear the soft laughter in his voice. The quiet was broken only by the rustle of breeze through the brush.

"Stuff and bother!" She wanted to hurl insults and degradations, and say how much she hated him. But she knew he'd only be amused at her theatrics. "I came for a little peace and privacy...and a bath."

"It seems we both had the same idea, Miss Quinn." He leaned slightly until moonlight revealed glittering droplets clinging to the hairs on his broad chest.

Her eyes drifted downward to where his hips narrowed. Embarrassed, she completely submerged herself.

She opened her eyes in the shimmering depth and found Bannon's legs, braced apart like two tree trunks. He bent and reached into the water, pulling her back above the surface. She came up gasping and pushing her mop of unruly hair from her face.

She placed her palms against his chest to steady herself.

His hands rose upward, from her sides, pressing against the side of her breasts, pushing the mounds together as he stared down at them. His mouth lowered to hers, his tongue teased, and without thought, she responded. His lips took hers, fiercely demanding. One of her arms encircled his broad shoulder, taking some of her weight from the muscular arm that supported her thighs. Her other hand caressed the side of his neck, feeling the corded tendons there. Her hand traveled down from his neck, across his shoulder and down the iron-hard bulge in his bicep and over his chest. She was lost in the kiss and in a sensual deliciousness that was new to her. She felt for the first time his large, probing shaft of manhood near her most intimate spot.

Her head fell back, and she arched to meet him as if they could not be close enough. She wondered what had come over her to be acting like one of Blackie Sledge's harlots.

Her nipples grew hard, and she moaned. She didn't expect to be released with a suddenness that sent her reeling across the pool. Her eyes flew open to see Cordell Bannon's tormented face. His hands ran through his sun-bleached golden hair, and his head shook in disbelief.

He said nothing more than her name. "Miss Quinn." But it was enough for her to sense his rage. "What the hell do you think you're doing?"

Modesty and innocence left her embarrassed. She spoke through chattering teeth. "I'm sorry. You must think that I'm...oh, you must believe me. I've never acted this way before." She opened her eyes to a face contorted in fury, and for a moment, she couldn't meet his gaze. "I'm so ashamed." Her voice was barely audible no matter how she struggled to make it strong.

His furious expression hardened into a mask of indifference that disturbed Fiona more than his anger. "I'm not a damned eunuch, Miss Quinn. Cover yourself before I spill your virgin blood!"

Fiona's breath caught in a shocked gasp, and she stumbled from the pool. She snatched her dress from a bush and with trembling fingers pulled the garment over her wet body.

"I'm bound by the same contract as you women. Now I have a man's need roiling in the pit of my belly." He turned sharply and swam to the other side of the pool.

Fiona felt her cheeks flame when he waded from the water. Before the night swallowed him, the moon's rays accentuated his body's hard, lean lines. Taking hold of her emotions, she shook herself. By heaven, she refused to allow him the last word. "You dare threaten me with rape?"

When he turned to face her she saw the fullness of his manhood.

"There's a word for women like you, Miss Quinn."

The words were flung at her in contempt—cold and hard dousing the desire he had aroused.

Chapter Seven

Thirty years older than his friend, Isaiah Thomas had ridden with Cordell Bannon for most of ten years.

Their horses plodded side-by-side. The silence gnawed at Isaiah. It wasn't as if he and Bannon made longwinded conversations. They'd often ride for hours, sometimes days exchanging no more than three or four words, but today was different. "I don't know what's eating at you, Cordell, but you been grumpy as a sore-tailed bear ever since morning coffee."

A muscle in Bannon's jaw flexed. His voice was gruff and his eyes straight ahead. "Women want a longer nooning. They want to reread the letters of the men who's bought and paid for them."

Isaiah sensed there was more to it than a gaggle of women yammering to take a gander at a bunch of tintypes, but he reined in his personal thoughts. "Well hell, that ain't nothing to go and get yourself all jowled up over. The solution's easy."

"How so?"

"Simple. Don't stop for the noon repast. Push on and make camp a coupla hours ahead of the usual time. You gotta admit, Cordell, this here is a tough lot of gals. Oh, shore, there's complainin', but we've heard worse from menfolk."

Fiona's voice drifted toward the men as she sang the words to an Irish ballad.

I laid me down upon a bank bewailing my sad fate,

That doomed me thus the slave of love and cruel Johnny's hate.

"She's got voice like an angel." The scout placed his hand over his heart and emitted an exaggerated sigh. "Don't she, Cordell?"

Bannon turned and scowled at his sidekick. The lines of hard living and toughness were etched like road maps on the face of Isaiah Thomas, and the dust of the plains lay caked under his fingernails.

"I could do without her caterwauling." Bannon wanted her to stop. He wanted everything to stop, the pictures inside his head, the ache inside his belly, the taste of her. Even after the last sweet notes of her voice died away, the song echoed in his head, buzzing around like an insect that you ducked to avoid...*and cruel Johnny's hate.*

He glowered over his shoulder at Fiona and when he spoke, his voice had the heavy-tooth snarl of a saw. "Ride down the line, Isaiah, and pass the word to the ladies that if they want to read the damned letters again, there'll be no time for napping on the trail."

"Where you off to, Cordell?"

"Going to scout out a stopping place for the night."

Isaiah reached out and grabbed the sorrel's cheek strap causing the animal to toss its head and sidle sideways. "I seen the way you look at her."

"Who?"

Isaiah winked. "Perhaps you should open your eyes a little wider, Cordell."

Bannon harrumphed. "All these women are bound by contract to wed once we get to Glory. Like you, I'm sworn by my word, and I've signed a contract that I'll deliver all those who survive the trip."

"What about the alternates? What if a particular Irish lassie with green eyes and hair like the setting sun were to make it all the way to Oregon Territory without having to marry up with one of them nob-headed, salivatin' yahoos?"

"There are no *what ifs*. Not for me. Not anymore."

Isaiah remained pensive for a second. "I was there, too, remember, Cordell? You cain't go beatin' up on yourself forever."

"Let go of the strap." The horse reared as Bannon gouged it with a spur, breaking the scout's grip on the bridle's cheek strap. "Go to hell, Isaiah." He set the horse off at a fast gallop.

Isaiah called after him. "I think the fates have made a wiser choice than you think, Cordell." Then he yelled, "You jug-headed mule. Dagnabit, you cain't stop fate."

****

Fiona followed the trail along the river, its banks swollen to the brim from thawing snow and spring storms. Like the other women, she helped make camp in a grove of elm trees while Bannon and Isaiah Thomas proved their worth by riding ahead to hunt. The men always returned each evening with a string of rabbit, quail, and sometimes venison, enough for the entire camp.

In the cool of the evening, Fiona went about her daily routine of gathering firewood while some replenished water barrels, others did laundry.

The Iroquois woman shyly approached Fiona. "I can show you how to set out fishing lines."

"Can I come, too?" Henrietta grinned with enthusiasm.

"Come. The more fish we catch, the more mouths we can feed." Bird LeBlanc shifted the fish trap she'd woven to a more comfortable position under her arm.

Fiona glanced to where Ma Smalley rested in the shade reading her Bible. "What about you, Ma

Smalley, want to come with us?"

The woman waved her away. "Nothing better than a mouthful of fresh fried trout. All the same, I think I'll just sit here and rest my weary bones."

****

Bannon waited until the evening meals were complete before he called the women to the circle. He raised his voice to make certain he was heard. "Tomorrow morning we ford the river. Earlier in the day, Isaiah and I scouted up ahead for places to cross. We don't know how muddy the bottom is, only that the water is belly deep on the horses. We figure this might be the best place to cross. Further down, the current is running swift, and we had to swim the horses. That's makes it too risky for wagons."

When he asked how many of the women had forded a river with a team pulling a wagon, it was as he expected—none. Concern gripped him. If the riverbed was nothing more than silt, it made crossing all the more dangerous.

"Tell us what to do, Mr. Bannon." Ma Smalley stepped from the circle. "We'll try our dangdest to do it or die trying."

Die trying. Truer words had never been spoken. Bannon had witnessed more drownings than he cared to remember—from greenhorns to experienced teamsters.

"That's all I ask." His smile was genuine. "Listen carefully, ladies. Decide among yourselves who'll drive the teams. Drivers, don't use the brake. Give the animals their head, let them do the work. Two of you will ride while the other two will walk on either side of a lead animal. Mules and horses are like people—some take to water—some don't. If you panic, they panic. Your job is to keep them calm and moving.

"The supply wagon is heavy, and the water is apt to rise over the wheels, if not higher. To keep it

51

from getting bogged down, we'll unload the food barrels and side meats and redistribute them amongst your wagons.

"Isaiah and Bird LeBlanc will lead out. The rest of you will watch for my signal to know when to bring your team into the water. Another thing..." instinct told him what he was about to say would bring about a horde of foolish twittering from the women. "...remove all your heavy petticoats. And one more thing, draw your skirts up between your legs and tuck the hems inside your waistbands."

Gasps filtered through the circle. Clovis Richmond huffed, "Ain't that a might indecent?"

"Wet clothing is heavy and will weigh you down like a stone, ma'am. If you have any notion of making it to the other side without drowning, you'll do as I say." He dismissed the group by directing them to begin dividing the supplies among their own wagons.

****

Fiona wasn't particularly interested in helping. Cordell Bannon had been cross-tempered throughout the journey, but more so since their chance encounter at the pool. She groaned, frustrated at the direction of her thoughts. If anyone found out that she'd acted like a wanton woman and had cavorted naked in a moonlit pool with a man she barely knew, her reputation would be ruined. A mixture of anger and longing bombarded her at the sight of him, and she remembered the way his mouth had felt on hers, his touch. Mortification flamed her cheeks. Hoping no one noticed, she ducked her head and wrapped her arms around her waist as she hastened her step toward the supply wagon to collect enough potatoes for the evening meal.

After a supper of char-cooked trout, roasted potatoes, and wild nettle, Ma Smalley dried the last plate. "You know, Fiona, I think now's a time to call a prayer meeting."

"'Twould be for certain. We're all little nervous about our first river crossing." Fiona smiled at Mercy who sat propped against the wagon wheel. "I think Mercy should ride in the wagon. I'll lead Rufus."

"And I'll get that stubborn Jonah across if I have to tote him on my back." Henrietta's statement brought a round of guffaws.

Fiona grabbed a tin pan and banged loudly on its bottom with a spoon. "Gather round ladies. Ma Smalley's going to hold a prayer meeting to bless our crossing tomorrow."

As soon as the women settled down, Ma Smalley lifted her voice, "Tomorrow after we cross the river, Mr. Bannon says we'll start the major leg of our journey. I figure that tonight, before we traverse to the other side, might be a good time to ask for the Lord's guidance and protection."

After she'd read a few scriptures, the meeting ended with the women singing. *Shall we gather at the river...*

****

Bannon wasn't much in the mood for praying. Hadn't been for a long time. Anger nestled in him like a contagious disease. It had become such a part of him that he couldn't remember when it hadn't been there. At first he'd thought he was angry because of his loss, because two of the most precious beings in his life had been so unjustly yanked away. But slowly he'd come to understand the anger was at himself for causing the deaths of his wife and baby, and that was a terrible truth to know about himself.

Chapter Eight

In the darkness, a snapping twig caused Bannon's senses to go on full alert. He whipped the revolver from his holster and crouched low as his eyes riveted toward the direction of the sound. "Whoever you are, show yourself."

A tall slender woman sashayed toward him. His eyes having grown accustomed to the darkness allowed him to see her unfasten the top buttons of her blouse. "My goodness, it certainly is warm this evening."

"Which one are you?" He didn't bother with courtesy as he holstered his weapon.

She fanned herself feigning warmth as she approached closer. "Why, Mr. Bannon, I'm Mavis Johns from Gerda Olsson's group."

The seductive richness of her voice beckoned him. A refined woman and a widow, Bannon knew a predator when he saw one. "Go back to your wagon, Mrs. Johns. It isn't safe for you or any of the women to be traipsin' around in the dark."

"I was thinking to cool myself down at the river." She slanted a glance at him. "Maybe you'd like to join me."

"Not tonight Mrs. Johns, nor any night. You know the rules." The corners of his mouth tucked into a frown as he turned to leave.

She stepped in front of him and cat-walked her fingers up the front of his buckskin shirt and gazed up at him. She licked her lips and sighed. "Don't you think I'm pretty?"

His voice was gruff. "We've got a long, hard day ahead of us tomorrow. I'm turning in for the night and so should you."

She reached up and toyed playfully with the strands of rawhide that laced across the shirt, sliding him a seductive smile. "It must be difficult for a virile man like you to hold his passion at bay; especially with so many women to choose from."

He deliberately took her hand and removed it from his shirt. "Maybe you'd like to feel the sting of my whip."

"It's not the sting of your whip I'm wanting to feel, Mr. Bannon." She sighed, lifting her eyes at him as she groped for his groin.

"Goodnight." His jaw clenched. Her touch seared him, and he stepped back, impatient to end this conversation. "Unless you've forgotten, let me remind you that you are betrothed, Mrs. Johns," and he walked away.

In a moment he heard the stamp of her foot. A disgusted snort escaped her lips as she turned and flounced back to her own camp.

Isaiah Thomas was already asleep by the time Bannon shook out his own bedroll a few feet from the fire. Bannon nudged the toe of the scout's boot. "You asleep or just pretending?"

Isaiah pushed back the hat covering his eyes. He chuckled. "Almost got yourself treed by a she-bear, didn't you?"

"I don't want to hear one word about that woman." Bannon eased down on his oilcloth and rested his head against his saddle. Damn. He didn't want to think about women—especially one with red hair and an Irish lilt to her voice. He yanked his hat down over his eyes as spasms of urgent desire burned in his throbbing manhood.

****

Morning sent the first gray light through the

clouds and with it brought cool breezes from the river. Bannon rode up and down the line of wagons barking last minute orders.

He stopped at the lead wagon. "You ladies set?"

Ma Smalley said, "Right as rain." She offered him a cheery grin. "Since I'm the strongest of the four, I'll drive. Mercy, here's been a little off her feed lately. She'll ride. Fiona and Henrietta will guide the leaders across."

He leaned over in his saddle taking a closer look at the timid girl who was a mere shadow next to the larger woman. "Anything I should be concerned about?"

Ma Smalley was quick to answer. "Just a touch of prairie weariness. I've seen it before. Nothing to concern yourself about." She lifted her eyes heavenward as if asking forgiveness.

He touched his fingers to the brim of his hat before he guided his horse around the wagon to where Fiona stood gently talking to the mule as if soothing a frightened child. "It's all right, Rufus. It's only a little water and nothing for you to fret about. Why, stuff and bother, all God's creatures need a good dousing every once in a while."

Bannon liked the musical lilt of her Irish accent more than he cared to admit. His glance shifted down to her feet, a scowl on his face. The morning rays filtered through her skirt outlining her long limbs. Certain she would slap him at the direction of his thoughts, he shifted in the saddle to ease his growing discomfort as he felt himself harden with desire. "Draw up your skirt, Miss Quinn. It won't do for you to get tangled up in them and dragged under the wheels only to be crushed or drown."

Her cheeks flushed red as she reached down and drew the length of material between her legs and tucked the hem snuggly inside her waistband. Her elegantly arched eyebrows spoke volumes. "Thank you for your concern," Fiona said, with more than a trace of sarcasm in her voice.

Bannon had already dissolved into silent laughter, his shaking shoulders the only outward sign he found humor in the situation. "I admire your youthful vivaciousness, Miss Quinn."

Her face was raised to the sun's warming glare, long, coppery lashes resting against cheeks brightened with a healthy glow and a sprig of freckles across the bridge of her nose. Her small tongue ran lightly over her lips in an unconsciously sensual motion, deepening their pale rose color.

She's nervous and trying to hide it. A muscle in his jaw ticked, but he could not force his gaze from the luminous green eyes that stared up at him. He followed the thin column of her creamy throat and rested for a tormenting moment on the small rise of two perfect breasts. He called himself every kind of fool, disgusted he should be attracted to a woman who could never be his. Sure, she was an alternate bride, and sure the first leg of the trip had gone without error or accident, still he knew the dangers that lay ahead and it went without saying that death waited to claim a victim. When that happened Fiona's name would go into the lottery. "If the mules balk, don't force 'em, sing out for me or Isaiah."

"Oh, stuff and bother. Rufus and me will do just fine."

Bannon had sworn a long time ago to never again be ruled by emotion for any woman. He would never again be vulnerable. He shifted his gaze away from Fiona and over the backs of the mules. "What about you, Miz Hightower?"

She offered him a bright smile. "Jonas is too ornery to let a little thing like crossing a river to upset him." She placed a loving pat on the mule's neck.

The moment he rode away, Fiona said, "The

river is beautiful isn't it, Henrietta?"

"I do like the cool breezes. Are you nervous, Fiona?"

"About crossing the river? No, I shan't think I am. Are you?"

"Not about the river...it's well, it's...somehow everything seems so big and distant, like I might never see civilization again."

"Why don't you put the face of Mr. Horace Winters in your mind, Henrietta? Might make it easier for you to know that with him waitin' in Oregon Territory to greet you there's truly a fairytale ending in your future."

"You've got a real insight for one so young, Miss Fiona Quinn."

Fiona laughed. "My dear papa used to quote an old Irish proverb, 'May you live as long as you want and want as long as you live.' In my heart, I feel you have a long life ahead of you."

On each side of the banks, Bannon and Isaiah Thomas had secured a rope to a tree. Holding on to the rope for guidance over the slippery, miry river bottom would act as a guide to help the women who couldn't swim stay to the shallowest part of the river.

Bannon yelled, "Unset your brakes, ladies. On my signal—" He rode back down the column to the near empty supply wagon at the front of the line, "Take it across, Isaiah, then get on your horse and come on back to lend a hand."

The scout gave a little salute as he flapped the reins and drove his wagon across with little trouble, though the mules had to struggle to pull the wheels out of the mire and onto the safety of the bank.

On Bannon's signal, Ma Smalley eased her team down the sloped embankment. In a matter of minutes, water rose over the wheels. The mules balked. "Hie up there, you lop-eared, jackasses."

"Sing to them, Fiona. Rufus and Jonas like your voice," Henrietta beckoned.

"*Oh father dear, I oft-times hear you speak of Erin's fields of green—*" Without hesitation, Fiona crooned as she tugged on the harness. The mules took a tentative step and then another, stepping forward until they'd pulled the wagon across the watery expanse and up the bank to the other side.

In less time than expected, one driver after another waited to bring their teams across.

"Last wagon and no casualties, Isaiah." Bannon lifted his arm and signaled the driver waiting patiently on the bank.

"Got me an itch 'tween my shoulders. You know what that means don't you?"

"Yeah, it means you need a bath." Bannon chuckled as Fiona pondered the scout's ominous sounding statement.

He lifted his arm and signaled. "Bring 'em across, Miz Johns."

The wagon didn't move.

"What the hell is she waitin' on, do you reckon, Cordell?"

"Damned if I know."

Bannon's voice exploded across the river. "Slap leather to those mules."

"Mr. Bannon, the mules are stubborn. They've decided to balk. We need your help."

Bannon grabbed the pinto's reins as Isaiah nudged the horse forward. "She's no better than the rest of the women. We'll sit right here until she brings her wagon across."

"I don't like it, Cordell. Got me a bad feelin'."

"Go on, Isaiah. I'll take care of this." Bannon squinted up at the sun. "Miz Johns, if you can't get the mules down the slope and into the water then get down off that wagon box and switch places with one of the ladies in the water."

An unexpected chill prickled the hairs on Fiona's arms. As she urged the mules toward a line of trees, she strained to hear Mavis Johns' answer.

"No-no. That's quite all right, Mr. Bannon."

By the time Mavis Johns brought her wagon into the water, the river bottom was trampled and rutted. The surefooted mules seemed to have trouble gaining a foothold, and midway across, the wagon's wheels stopped. Mavis' shout was frantic. "Mr. Bannon, help. We're stuck."

Bannon turned his horse back and rode across. He reached down and grabbed hold of one of the lead mule's cheek straps. He shouted at the animal as he spurred his sorrel and tugged on the harness. The mules strained. The wagon didn't budge. He climbed out of the saddle and onto the wagon's seat. He snatched the leads from Mavis' hands. He shouted and slapped the reins. He snapped the whip over the mules' backs. When that didn't work, he instructed all the women except Mavis Johns to wade on across the river. "Miz Johns, I'll need you to drive. Can you do that?"

A deep sensuous smile spread across the woman's lips. "With you next to me, I can do most anything, Mr. Bannon." The loud words carried over the noise of the river, and Fiona bristled.

Bannon emitted a sharp whistle, hoping to catch his sidekick's attention.

The mules' brays indicated their panic. They were having problems keeping their heads above water and clearly weren't inclined to pull the heavy wagon out of the mud.

"Mr. Thomas," Fiona called to the scout. "Bannon needs you."

From his position on the bank, Isaiah had watched the struggle. He untied his pinto from the supply wagon's tailgate and swung into the saddle. By the time he got to the middle of the river, he stepped off his horse and knee deep into mud as he slogged to the rear of the wagon. He didn't bother to restrain a string of oaths.

Bannon swore loudly as well as he reached down into the water to feel for the bottom of the wheel rim. "There's mud up to the axles."

"Miz Johns get on down from there and let me take the reins," the scout barked up at the woman.

"No, I can't swim. I'll drown."

This time Isaiah let go with an even worse string of oaths. "Hell fire woman. Get off that box."

"You don't understand, Mr. Thomas. I-I'm afraid." Mavis Johns gripped the edge of the seat until her knuckles turned white.

Bannon barely nodded a signal to his scout. He winked his acknowledgement as he lifted a water-sogged boot up on a wheel spoke and climbed up beside the terrified woman. Without giving her time to think, Isaiah wrapped his strong arms around her waist and tossed her into Bannon's waiting arms.

"Two of you women who ain't afraid of a little water come and get Mrs. Johns," Bannon yelled.

Without hesitation, Ma Smalley and Fiona waded in and sloshed toward the wagon. When they reached him, he had to pry the frightened woman's arms from around his shoulders. Between Ma Smalley and Fiona, the two of them got the woman to dry ground.

He watched Fiona hand the trembling Mrs. Johns over to Ma Smalley. Then, she walked to his sorrel and toed her foot into the stirrup. She dug her heels in the flanks of her mount and splashed into the water.

At the wagon, she climbed up on the box seat.

"What're you doing here?" Bannon yelled.

"I came to help. One man alone can't lift the wagon. I'll handle the mules while you put your shoulders to good use."

Bannon could hear the waiting women at the edge of the river calling their encouragement.

"Much obliged, young lady." Isaiah patted her on the shoulder as he handed over the reins and then stepped off into waist deep water.

Bannon said, "I'll put my shoulder to the back wheel and try to lift the wagon. You take the front on the opposite side, Isaiah."

He called to Fiona, "Get the mules moving, on my signal." He reached beneath the muddied water and grasped the lowest spoke with both hands and yelled, "Ready?"

Fiona responded, "Ready!"

Bannon put his weight into the wheels and heaved. He lifted and pushed until it felt as if his back were breaking, and he figured Isaiah was feeling the strain, too. Perspiration bathed his face. Air exploded from his lungs.

Fiona shouted at the team. The mules struggled in their traces, but nothing happened.

Bannon gulped air. "You okay, Isaiah?"

"Just found out I ain't as young as I use to be."

"What about you, Fiona?" It was the first time Bannon had spoken her given name. He paused, angry with himself for allowing the slip.

"Don't worry about me," she declared.

"If this doesn't work, we'll bring another team across. Maybe if we double team the mules, we can get this wagon to the other side before noon." He grated out the words unable to contain his disgruntlement.

Again, he and his scout leaned their weight against the wheels and shoved. At first Bannon thought their efforts were useless, and then, abruptly, the wheel moved. Not much, just an inch or two.

Fiona called encouragement as she slapped the long leather reins over the sweaty backs of the mules. The mules lunged again. The sudden lurch of forward motion was enough to throw Bannon off balance and send him down on one knee with a splash.

One of the mules reared in its traces, and just as suddenly as the wagon had moved forward, it rolled backward before Bannon could regain his balance. The roiled mud acted as quicksand and sucked at him. He tried to scramble out of the wheel's way. He felt a painful thump against his shoulder and then the weight, pulling him down. Not one to panic, he thought it would be all right. He tried to stand to no avail. He was trapped. He couldn't move. Before he realized it, water rushed over his head filling his mouth and his nose.

"Cordell, you're mighty quiet. You all right back there?" When Isaiah didn't get a response, he called again. "Cordell?"

Fiona leaned over as far as she could without falling off the seat. "Oh dear Lord. I don't see him, Mr. Thomas."

Isaiah bit out the order, "Hold them reins tight, girl. Don't let them mules move an inch until I tell you...you hear me girl?"

There was no mistaking the urgency in her answer. "I do."

Isaiah heaved through the water to where he'd last seen his friend and saw the space empty. He was all too familiar with death, and a stab of cold fear raced through him. "Cordell, answer me, boy."

He spotted the faint swirl of movement beneath the murky surface. "*Cordell*," his voice rasped as he saw his friend struggling to hold his breath. Isaiah shouted, "Fiona, Cordell is drowning."

He grabbed the wagon master by the shoulders and tugged. The few inches weren't enough to lift Bannon's face above the water.

Fiona's face drained of color as she splashed to

his side. "Let me try to get my hands under Cordell's shoulders while you pull."

Bannon's eyes bulged as he grasped hold of Fiona pulling her beneath the surface with his strength.

In an act of desperation, Isaiah squatted and used his hands to shovel away the mud, only to have it fill back into place.

"Hurry, please, Mr. Thomas. Do something." Fiona pleaded.

"I ain't a praying man, but right this minute I'm beggin'. Lord, this man don't deserve to die—least not this a way."

At that moment, Ma Smalley and Henrietta Hightower appeared at Fiona's side. "Merciful heaven," Ma Smalley whispered in horror. "Tell us what to do, Mr. Thomas."

"No offense ma'am, you reckon you can put your shoulder to the wheel?"

"None taken." Ma Smalley hunkered down and leaned her shoulder against the back wheel that pinned Bannon down.

"So be it. Miz Hightower, get up there on the seat," Isaiah shouted, "and get that team moving."

He cast an anxious glance at Fiona. "You grab hold his shoulders. Soon as you feel the wagon lift, try your dangdest to pull him free."

Isaiah watched Bannon's struggle to hold his breath as little bubbles of water rose to the surface. Some burst while others floated away. "Hellfire, instinct's gonna tell Cordell to gasp for air."

His urgency transferred to Fiona. She lowered her gaze to the muddied water. "No...don't." She ducked her head beneath the surface and pinched off Bannon's nose. She placed her lips over his and breathed into his mouth.

He clasped her arms. She lifted her head and refilled her lungs, and breathed more sustaining life into him.

Isaiah took up his position against the wheel and shouted, "Slap leather to them mules."

The wagon wheel shifted, sending a flood of fresh mud through the water. It seemed to take forever. The water dragged at Fiona's skirt, mud filled her boots and weighted her down. She heard Isaiah barking orders at Ma Smalley and at Henrietta and cursing the mules. She looked down and knew Bannon was dying.

Fiona heard splashing, and she saw Gerda Olsson and Bird LeBlanc had made their way to the scene. She heard the Iroquois woman say, "You get that mule, and I'll grab this one's head, Miz Olsson. Whatever happens, don't let the mules back up."

Fiona's voice betrayed her crumpling composure. "Quickly, he's drowning."

The world seemed to move in slow motion as she watched Bird breath into her hand then lift it to the wild-eyed mule's nostrils. "Do the same," she instructed the Swedish woman. "It will calm him."

On Isaiah's command Fiona heard the telltale snapping of reins as Henrietta whipped up the mules; Ma Smalley grunted as she strained and shoved against the wheel as the Swedish woman and the Iroquois woman tugged with all their might on the cheek straps of the two lead mules.

Silt drifted up like slimy ooze in the water, and Bannon's hand lost his grip on Fiona's. She tightened her lips against the scream that threatened to tear itself from her throat. She tried to lift his head and desperately tried to make her voice calm. "Hold on a little longer...please."

The mules gave a mighty lunge forward, and the wagon moved. The women continued to coax the lead mules. Slowly, the wagon yawned and lifted itself from the mud and rolled forward.

Fiona used the water's buoyancy to lift Bannon.

Her first instinct was to cradle him against her chest as one would do to comfort an injured child. She clung to him as the old scout splashed to her side and then climbed into the back of the wagon. "Can you hoist him up high enough for me to grab him under the arms?"

"To be sure, with Ma Smalley's help, we can," Fiona cried.

Isaiah grabbed hold and lifted his friend into the wagon. Fiona hoisted herself up next to Bannon. "He needs air."

Isaiah sang out, "Keep this wagon moving and don't stop 'til it's on dry land." Fiona watched as he rolled Bannon into a sitting position and used his fist to pound between the man's shoulder blades. From behind he placed Bannon in a bear hug and applied pressure to his chest, and repeated the action until Bannon was coughing and spewing filthy water from his lips, and gasping for air.

Fiona snatched a blanket off the bottom bunk and shoved it into the old man's hands. He wrapped it around Bannon's shivering body. "Shor'ly am glad today wasn't your day to die, boy."

Chapter Nine

Fiona climbed into the back of the wagon. "Mr. Thomas, the women will need your guidance now. I'll tend Mr. Bannon."

The scout frowned, "Don't reckon it's proper for a respectable young woman, such as yourself to be undressing a man down to his bare..." he stopped short.

Fiona offered him an understanding smile and spoke bolder than she felt. "Don't take on so, Mr. Thomas. I tended my poor papa 'til his dying day. There isn't much I haven't seen. Besides, I'm not bashful." Her cheeks flamed as she fleetingly remembered that night at the pool. She already knew what lay beneath the sodden buckskins clinging to the wagon master's lean body. "Would you be kind enough to relay to Miss LeBlanc that since I'll be staying in the supply wagon until Mr. Bannon regains his strength that she is to sleep in my bunk? Ma Smalley and the other two ladies will welcome her."

As Fiona reached out and slipped Bannon into her arms, Isaiah released him. Abruptly getting to his feet, he said, "If'n you need anything, send word. I'll see to it you get all you need."

He jumped down to the ground. Before taking his leave, he said gruffly, "Anything...anything at all...understand?"

"While I'm getting him warmed up, you might ask Miss LeBlanc to make a poultice to draw out any infection that might settle in his lungs, and one for

67

the injury to his shoulder. She knows all about herbs and healing, you know?" Fiona reassured the scout with an affirmative nod. "Get yourself into some dry clothes. And have Ma Smalley fix you a hot toddy. Won't do for you catch your death."

His craggy features softened into a smile. "Sure thing, Miss Fiona."

She brushed her hand over Bannon's forehead checking for fever. "Come on," her voice was shaky. "We need to get you into some dry clothes." When she raised his arm to lift the shirt over his head he winced and groaned. With firm but gentle touches she probed the injury. "Your shoulder doesn't feel broken, though I imagine 'tis badly bruised."

A spasm of coughing attacked him. When his eyes began to focus, and he looked at her, he rasped, "Thank you."

She lifted his shirt gently over his head. An angry purple bruise between his shoulder blades ran down his ribcage and disappeared beneath the waist of his buckskin leggings. She sucked in a breath and caught her bottom lip with her teeth.

Fiona talked about Bird LeBlanc's knowledge of herbs, and about Ma Smalley's funny stories. She knew she was rattling on to cover her nervousness as her fingers moved to unlace his leggings. It seemed the water had molded them tight to his muscular frame. His eyes were closed tightly, and his body felt cold and clammy to her touch. A chill set his teeth to chattering.

"I surely hope you have more than one pair of clean clothing. And I beg your forgiveness for ruining this pair." She whispered the words as she deftly removed the large skinning knife from the sheath strapped around his waist. Without hesitation, she slid the sharp blade beneath the waistband and sliced through the leather all the way down to Bannon's ankle, and then repeated the action on the other side. As the pants fell away, she tugged at them until they were free from his body.

Even with old scars that laced his back and chest, he was breathtakingly handsome. Softly, she felt him, her hands traveling the full expanse of his muscular body, exploring granite-hard ridges and the tangled blond hair at his chest. Light fingers followed that hair but stopped at the flat, firm stomach. A strange sensation fluttered inside her as she watched his manhood come to life and throb against his belly.

Once again she recalled their chance encounter at the pool, the feel of his fingers on her breast, the heat his touch had inspired, and Fiona wondered at her lusty musings and where they'd come from.

Curiosity caused her to extend her hand—desiring to explore further. A painful spasm of coughing broke the spell. Fiona moved quickly to cover him with a woolen blanket. She glanced around until spotting a flour sack and moved it to support his head. She opened a crate marked blankets and removed another blanket to tuck around Bannon's still shivering body.

A shy voice sounded in the waning light. "Fiona." The Iroquois woman spoke her name as if it were broken into three syllables.

"It's all right Miss LeBlanc, you may come in."

"I have brought the poultices."

Fiona accepted the medicinal pouch as the Indian woman climbed into the wagon. Fiona pulled back the blanket and leaned over Bannon to arrange one poultice under his shoulder and the other atop his chest.

"I had to cut his clothes off. He's...well...he's naked...all over." The words came out in a bashful refrain, and she was glad when the Indian woman didn't comment.

The Iroquois woman gathered the clothing. "I

mend his buckskins good as new."

"That's kind of you, Miss LeBlanc."

"Fiona, you will call me Bird? Miss LeBlanc is too fancy."

Fiona answered with a nod. She wrinkled her nose against the unpleasant odor. "What's in this, Bird?"

"Wild mustard and onion mixed with a little bacon fat and salt. It will draw down the swelling in his shoulder and will keep his lungs clear."

"How do you know about herbs and such?"

"Indian girls learn from their mothers and grandmothers at an early age. It is our way."

"These are good things to know. I was very young when my mother died. My father and brother worked in the mines, and there was no one to teach me such things. Will you?"

The Iroquois woman stared quietly for a moment. "You are not as the others. You do not look upon me as..." her voice quieted as if she'd said too much.

Fiona reached out and lifted a folded hand into her own. "Friends?"

"I would like that." Bird LeBlanc rose to her feet and gingerly stepped over the prone man and up on the wagon's bench seat. She gathered the reins in her strong brown hands. "The mules have rested. Mr. Thomas says I am to drive the wagon while you tend Mr. Bannon."

Fiona thought she'd seen tears glisten in Bird's ebony eyes before she'd ducked her head. The mules brayed as they lunged against the lines, and the wagon lurched forward and jostled across the rough ground until the scout commanded the women to circle the wagons for the night.

After seeing to his comfort, Fiona left her patient and strolled to the lead wagon.

"How is Mr. Bannon fairing?" Ma Smalley

handed her a plate of fried potatoes and a bowl of bean soup seasoned with fatback.

"Except for a groan or two when the wagon hits a rut, he's mostly slept." Fiona munched on a crisp potato wedge.

"Nothing better than a healing sleep." Ma Smalley settled back with a cup in her hand. Murmurs of agreement filtered around the group.

Finishing off the soup, Fiona poured two cups of steaming tea. "He's still clammy to the touch. I hope the tea will warm his insides and stop the shivers."

Henrietta Hightower strode to the pot over the fire. She ladled up bean broth into a mug. "He needs more'n tea. Got to have nourishment to keep him strong."

"Yep, and a toddy won't do any harm either." Ma Smalley hurried off to the wagon only to return with a bottle of spirits.

Fiona called her goodnights to the ladies. With two cups in each hand, she was careful not to slosh hot liquid as she made her way through the darkness.

She sat the mugs on the wagon's tailgate, climbed in, and struck a sulfur match to light the overhead lantern. "Mr. Bannon, are you awake? I've brought tea and a good, strong soup."

He opened his eyes and blinked up at her. "Where are my clothes?" he rasped.

"I couldn't get them off...the water must have shrunk them. Don't worry. Bird LeBlanc will mend them good as new."

"What did you do to them?" He eyed her with skepticism.

"Oh, stuff and bother, don't fuss." She tried to sound cheery. "It was a clean slice I made with your knife to get them off your body. What was I to do, let you shiver your insides out? Answer me that."

He propped up against the flour sack bringing

the blanket to his chin, and with a bare arm accepted the meager meal with a sheepish grin. Fiona sat the whiskey laced tea within easy reach and silently observed him.

"I remember everything, Miss Quinn. I'm indebted to you for saving my life."

She looked at him over the rim of her cup, her voice quiet, almost shy, "You called me Fiona just before you..." she shuddered remembering the panic in his eyes as water covered his face, and he'd struggled to hold his breath. "Miss Quinn sounds old and stuffy."

He drew a ragged breath as if it pained him to breathe. He stared into his cup. After a moment, he said, "Nothing would pleasure me more, Fiona, but I signed a contract and swore an oath not to get personal with any of the women. You are as bound as I am."

She watched the seriousness of his expression. "What happens if we get to Oregon Territory without my being chosen?"

"I'm not usually a betting man, but the odds of that happening are very slim."

She faced him with an earnest gaze. "I don't understand."

"The prairie is a dangerous place, and much as I'd rather it didn't happen, death is inevitable. I'm helpless to stop it and so are you."

He exhaled impatiently. "From here on to Oregon Territory, it's strictly business between the two of us. I will treat you no different from the other women." He tore his gaze away from her, and she knew the moment of magic was broken.

She stepped down from the wagon and drew water from the barrel attached to the sideboard and rinsed the empty cups clean. Back inside, she blew out the lantern and lay on the pallet she'd made on top of Bird LeBlanc's bunk. "May God hold you in the hollow of His hand, Mr. Bannon." She rolled to her side and closed her eyes.

Sometime during the night, Fiona awakened to harsh raspy coughs. She moved quickly to lift Bannon into her arms. She felt the fever against her cool skin, felt the jerking tremors that seized him, and without hesitation slipped under the blankets. She fitted against him spoon-fashion and wrapped her arms and legs around him so he could garner the heat from her body.

Clad only in her waist shirt, she crooned a lullaby and listened as he coughed again. There was still a slight rattle to his breathing even after the coughing passed. For the first time, Fiona realized death could strike at any moment and claim anyone of them, or all of them, and she might never see the town of Glory.

****

Ma Smalley returned to the perimeter of the camp from taking care of her evening necessities. She settled on an upturned bucket next to Isaiah. In the setting sun, she could see the supply wagon's canvas with clarity as Fiona bent over Bannon and put her hands on his unclothed chest and how she sat close to him, their heads almost touching.

She nudged Isaiah and nodded toward the banker's widow. "Had a rooster once who strutted around the hen yard like he was a king. Miz Johns' sorta reminds me of that ole cockadoodle."

"Yep. She does lean toward highfalutin."

She rotated her hands. "I wrung that rooster's scrawny neck."

"You wouldn't be suggestin'—"

Ma Smalley's lips winged into a dour grin. "My intuition says she's up to no good."

She watched Mavis hustle over to a group of women preparing beans and biscuits. "She's a brazen hussy. Why she has no business tending a sick man all by herself." Mavis' voice was spiteful.

Placing her hands on slim hips, Mavis paced around the area as if in an agitated state. "Why, I even offered to make Mr. Bannon a rich broth thinned down and seasoned with spices. And that high and mighty little Irish hussy refused."

One of the women who shared Mavis' wagon, Luana Skittle, straightened from her position over the fire and rubbed the small of her back. "Admit it, Mavis, you're jealous. We've all seen the way you look at him."

Then, Hilda Detz said, "Better not let Ma Smalley hear you badmouthing one of her ladies."

Mavis strutted around the fire. She kicked a little clod of dirt with the toe of her shoe. "I'm not afraid of Mrs. Smalley." In a louder voice, she said, "Fiona Quinn is a brazen hussy."

Ma tapped her sharply on the shoulder. Startled, Mavis turned. She drew herself up and smoothed down her skirt. "Why if it isn't Mrs. Smalley and her crew of misfits. And to what do I owe this visit?"

"Sound carries at night, Mrs. Johns." Ma Smalley stood erect, shoulders squared.

"I don't care if it does. The truth is the truth."

Ma Smalley stepped closer and shoved a stout finger against Mavis' thin chest. "Mr. Bannon almost died because you were too arrogant to let one of the other women drive the mules across—didn't want to get your dainty feet wet. And it was Fiona who breathed her own breath into his lungs to keep him alive until we could get that wagon off'n him. It's her right to nurse him back to health. She don't need my permission and certainly don't need you to act as chaperone. I'd suggest you take back that vile name you called her."

Mavis' cheeks deepened to a mottled red. She scoffed. "I've already said it, and I'll say it again,

Fiona Quinn is a trollop and is a disgrace to the rest of the ladies on this train." She swept her arms wide to indicate the gathering crowd.

Ma Smalley's hand made contact with Mavis Johns' cheek. The slap stung Ma's hand and was fierce enough to rock Mavis Johns back on her heels.

"Kinda like the pot callin' the kettle black, ain't it? I always was a little partial to listening to tidbits of gossip when I worked at the Denver House. I heard what Mrs. Reinhardt and the other society ladies had to say about you. Seems your secret trysts weren't as secret as you thought. Why there was even speculation about the circumstances of poor Mr. Johns' death." Ma Smalley winged her brows up. She took a step closer. Her face was hot and had to be dark red with rage. "I'll have no more blasphemous talk from the likes of you, Mavis Johns. Be warned to keep your foul mouth shut, or I'll hold a council meetin' with Lou and Gerda to determine a suitable punishment for you."

Lou Shultz and Gerda Olsson had pushed through the group and stood on either side. Gerda Olsson said, "As captain of your group, Mrs. Johns, let me warn you that whatever punishment we decide upon will not be pleasant." She pointed at Mavis. "I suggest you retire for the night and think on your own past sins before casting judgment on Fiona Quinn or any other woman in this outfit."

Mavis reached up and rubbed what had to be a painful sting on her already reddening cheek. Tears glistened in her eyes as she crossed her arms and strode off into the twilight. Ma smiled at the other two wagon captains.

"'Scuse me, ladies. Time to patrol the camp before turning in." Isaiah's eyes held no warmth as he called a warning to Mavis Johns. "Wouldn't wonder off too far, ma'am. Never know what's lurking in the dark."

****

A while later Isaiah sidestepped to keep Mavis from bumping into him. Beneath his beard, he couldn't keep a sneer from twisting his lips.

She gasped, "You've scared a year off my life—skulking around like an Indian."

The night was still. Not the slightest breeze stirred the air. A full moon rising above the hills gave the world a silvery hue dotted with black shadows. Only the stamping of the mules' hooves broke the silence.

When he moved away, Mavis reached out and grabbed his arm. "Mr. Thomas," she said sweetly, "I'd truly like to take Mr. Bannon a bowl of my special broth, but Miss Quinn seems to have taken it upon herself to keep me from saying how much I regret today's incident."

He made a sound and to his ears it was akin to that of a grizzly before it attacked. "Incident," he growled. "You call what happened today a danged incident?" He shook a finger gnarled with rheumatism under her nose. "Woman, if I t'weren't a gentleman, I'd knock you four ways to Sunday." He pointed to his ear. "I ain't deaf, neither. Heard what you called Miss Fiona."

He stepped around her. "Best stay away from the supply wagon, or it won't be the wagon captains you'll answer to."

****

The only excuse Bannon could give himself for having been awakened from the dream was simply he'd realized he wasn't alone on his pallet. His mind refused to shut out the events of this day, and the vision of Fiona's frightened eyes as she'd placed her lips over his and breathed sustaining life into his lungs repeatedly flashed before his eyes. As events began to uncurl in his mind, he felt as if this had been one of the longest and most tiring days of his life.

Every muscle in his body ached. The poultice had eased the soreness from his shoulder, and the herbed tea had quieted the rattle in his chest.

He had become uncomfortable and felt the need to shift positions without awakening the girl who lay curled against his back with her arm draped over his bare chest. He wished he had someone with whom to share his quiet times. He thought of Fiona, but no smile graced his lips. A frown drew his tawny brows together. The conditions of the contract were very clear, and he'd made the conditions equally clear to her.

A cloud shifted, casting moonbeams that illuminated the wagon's canvas bonnet. He rolled from his side and propped on his elbow. His pulse quickened the instant the rays enshrouded her. Ivory skin, sensuous pink lips, and the tip of a slim nose peeked beneath the auburn curls that spilled across her shoulder.

It seemed the soft glow of moonlight suddenly filled the dark corners of the wagon, and Bannon found himself preferring the shadowy darkness right now.

His eyes raked over her as he studied the sleeping figure, and he thought of the things he'd learned about her. She was well read, her pencil sketches were better than any dime novel's artist, and her beauty far surpassed the comeliness of any women he'd encountered. And he admired her stubborn, Irish spirit.

With a finger he eased the hair from her shoulder to reveal the swells of two rounded breasts above her waist shirt. The rise and fall of them with each breath mesmerized him. His desire stirred as if she held a mystical power over him.

His body turned against the contract he'd signed, the oath of celibacy he'd sworn, as need raged uncontrollably within him. The smell of her, her silken skin, the feel of her slender frame molded against his, were too much for him to pretend they didn't affect him. He wanted her as he'd wanted no other woman. Without the will to bring an end to his desires, Bannon leaned over until his lips met Fiona's. He would claim her as his and worry about the outcome later.

He felt Fiona's slight shiver as his fingers lifted her petticoat and inched the garment above her hips. The heavy brush of silken lashes lay on cheeks rosy and fair as her soft sighing breath slipped through temptingly parted lips. She moaned and then whispered, "Cordell..."

"Hush," he murmured against her lips. "I won't hurt you." His pledge seemed to ease her, yet he knew he must be gentle with her, for he doubted a few stolen kisses could have readied her for what was to come.

Cupping her face in his large hands, he brushed his lips against hers while he fought the urgent cravings of his body. His lean tanned fingers worked loose the laces of her camisole and freed the ivory breasts from their restraints. He trailed a hot path to a rose-colored peak, his tongue teasing, his teeth nibbling softly. She snuggled against him as if her passion were mounting. His wide hands drew her close to his nakedness and held her as he sampled the second treasure he had found, claiming it with his open mouth to suck greedily while her fingers reached to entwine themselves in the thick mane of wind-bleached hair as if to guide him and hold him close.

Impatient now to have her, Bannon raised up over her delicate form. His mouth covered hers in a savage kiss. His breathing quickened, and his passion ran high.

He hungrily feasted on the beauty of her ripe

breasts, the perfect curves of her hips and waist, the long length of her willowy legs, and the lust burning in her eyes. Towering over her, he parted her trembling thighs with his knee and slowly lowered himself down, his hands braced on either side of her head, her lips parted expectant of the kiss.

Fiona's mind reeled with confusion. The moonlight danced alluringly over Bannon's handsome face, enhancing his bronze complexion and vividly accentuating the corded muscles of his shoulders, chest and arms. The masculine scent of him, his rugged good looks, and the dark lustful gleam in his blue eyes turned her blood to fire. Her body thrilled at the expectation of him pressed against her, of his manhood, hot and hard thrusting against her belly.

Innocent of the pleasures to be had, she was eager to learn. Her womanly instincts took over, and while she studied his face, his parted lips, the passion burning in his eyes, she ran her hands over the sinewy breadth of his shoulders and chest, and down lean hips to the taut flesh of his buttocks as she pulled him down to her.

A clash of lightning coursed across the sky, bringing with it a rumble of thunder so violent that it vibrated the wagon to the core of shaking it apart.

Before the fiery pain of his manhood entered her, another bright flash of red light instantly brought Fiona to her senses. She grabbed the blanket and covered herself as she scooted as far away from Bannon as she could in the small confines of the wagon. The pleasing warmth that had enveloped her only moments ago disappeared and brought with it a chilling realization of what she'd almost allowed to happen. She stared at him and with trembling fingers quickly donned her chemise, and tied the laces in record time. She reached for her petticoat while using the wool blanket as a shield to hide behind, slipped the garment over her legs.

She breathed, the horror of her actions clearly etched in her mind. "You have made it abundantly clear, Mr. Bannon, you speak out of both sides of your mouth."

When his lips parted, she held up her hand to silence him. "You so piously talk about the precious contract you're bound to, but out of the other side, you play on my innocence to satisfy your beastly urges. Did you think to service me the way a stallion does a mare, then cast me aside like an old worn out shoe once we get to Oregon Territory?"

Her chin sagged to her chest, tears spilled down her cheeks. A sob choked her as she lifted her eyes to look at him.

She raised her hand and groped the top of a black powder barrel until her fingers wrapped around the clean set of buckskins. A smack sounded as the soft leather hit his chest. "Do me the courtesy of leaving this wagon for the remainder of the night. And spare me any lame excuses, and most of all spare me any further unwanted attentions. My virginity belongs to me, and I plan to arrive in Glory a chaste woman."

Fiona knew she'd have to remain in the supply wagon until predawn life stirred in the camp. She needed time to compose herself and had no need for questions she wasn't inclined to answer.

"You...you lecher!" She hissed through gritted teeth. "You uncouth, vile barbarian...get out."

Gathering his wits about him, Bannon watched the spirit go out of her. *Good God. What have I done?*

"Damn," he growled as he tugged the leather leggings up to his waist. He grabbed the soft doeskin shirt, the blanket and jumped barefoot to the ground. "Toss me another blanket. A man could catch his death on a cold ground."

He grunted when a wad of wool hit him square

in the face. He crawled beneath the supply wagon and tried to find a comfortable position as he lay on the hard ground. Suddenly drained of energy, he rolled to his back. He stared idly up at the bottom of the wagon that separated him and Fiona, the lingering fragrance of her scent invading his senses. He felt an intense aversion to another man claiming her.

How had he allowed the pert little Irish woman to capture his heart?

Chapter Ten

The traveling gradually grew more difficult with each passing day. The fiery June sun, a red-gold ball in the cloudless azure sky, blazed directly overhead. The wild land and hard traveling seemed to go on forever. Every muscle, every bone in Fiona's body was sore, her head throbbed, and her legs and buttocks were raw where perspiration had caused chafing from walking so far the day before.

Sitting on the wagon's hard bench seat did little to ease her discomfort. The constant sawing motion of the reins had raised a new crop of blisters on her hands. When the sun was halfway down the western sky, she judged it was about three o'clock, and her aching body couldn't stand much more torture.

Sometimes the stretches of the Mormon Trail were so rough that she could fill the churn with fresh cream in the morning, and the wagon would bounce around enough to churn a small lump of butter for the evening meal.

The simple leaf springs under the driver's seat made the perch tenable, but not particularly comfortable.

A pure panic poured into her veins, and a strong fear shook her the moment the wagon rounded the bend into a line of gruesomely painted faces of Indians. For an endless moment, she couldn't breathe. It whipped up her pulse and scrambled her brain, bombarded it with one question after another. *What did the Indians want? Were they friendly or hostile? Would all the women be carried off, murdered or worse? And where were Bannon and Isaiah Thomas?*

"Fiona?" the frightened voice of Mercy Anders called to her.

"I see them Mercy. Hurry, get in the back of the wagon before they spot you." Fiona tugged on the reins to slow the mules enough for the girl to hop on the tailgate and scramble inside. In spite of the searing heat, nervous tremors sent chills to slither like snakes through her veins. Vivid images of the things Bannon had said Indians did to captive women sprang behind her eyes.

"I'm in, Fiona. Where are Mr. Bannon and Mr. Thomas?"

"I wish I knew. Listen carefully, Mercy. Make sure the rifles are loaded, and if one of those painted heathens tries to get at you, blow him to smithereens."

"I'm scared, Fiona."

"So am I."

The consuming fear tried to rise again, but Fiona fought it down. Known for her level head, she'd never been one to panic.

One of the braves galloped his pony up along side her wagon. He hugged the body of his pinto with his bare legs and reached up to grab her.

She snatched the whip from its holder and lashed at him like a she-panther bent on revenge. "Get your filthy hands off me."

When he lost his balance, she swiveled around and kicked out her foot hitting him square in the chest and knocking him from his pony.

"God save us," Ma Smalley shouted. "Drivers, circle your wagons, and if'n one of them heathens gets in your way don't stop, run him over." She cupped her hands to her mouth and yelled. "Ladies, take up the rifles and get ready to blast these redskins to kingdom come."

From habit, Fiona sawed the reins to the left knowing the other drivers would follow. Bannon had taught them early on how to circle the wagons, and it had become their nightly routine. She kept moving until her team nosed up to the tailgate of the supply wagon closing the circle.

She locked the brake in place and climbed over the seat into the back to help Mercy hand down the rifles to Ma Smalley and Henrietta. She watched women scramble for cover under the wagons, inside wagons, and heard their high-pitched screams of fear and panic.

"Mercy, you stay inside," Ma Smalley instructed. "Grab your rifles girls. Let's get under the wagon. Maybe we can pop the noggin's off a few of them red devils."

Fiona skittered on her belly between Henrietta and the older woman. She watched the legs of horses galloping by, kicking dust into her eyes and up her nostrils to choke her.

Piercing cries echoed throughout the circled wagons. Someone yelled, "They're stealing the mules."

Fiona scooted around to face the interior of the circle in time to see warriors grabbing the harnesses of mules, to create an opening between the wagons.

The band of Indians was like a battalion of giant locusts swarming to choke the life out of the women. *Where is Bannon?*

Raucous whoops mingled with frightened screams until Fiona wanted to cover her ears to shut out the sounds.

"Oh God...oh God. One of them heathens has Eloise Gosselin. He's dragging her off." Fiona watched, horrified, as the brave leaned down, grabbed the woman and hauled her belly down across his pony.

Trying desperately to recall all the instructions

Bannon and Isaiah Thomas had given the women on the few occasions to teach them how to load and shoot, Fiona drew the rifle to her shoulder. Her throat was parched; she tried to swallow. She didn't know if the pounding in her ears was from her heart or the thunder of hoof beats. *In the event of an attack, Bannon had said, choose your target, take aim, ease back on the hammer, and squeeze. Don't jerk the trigger.*

All this filtered through her mind as she recalled each step. She didn't remember closing her eyes when she pulled the trigger. The rifle's recoil hit her with such force that it felt as if her shoulder were broken. The loud explosion still echoing in her ears, the pungent scent of gun powder stinging her nostrils, her eyes widened and bile rose thick and acrid when blood spewed from a gaping hole between the warrior's shoulder blades.

His limp body yawed sideways. The pinto pony reared, sending the dead Indian to the ground and landing heavily on top of Eloise Gosselin. Fiona watched the frightened woman fling the body away and then scurry on hands and knees to safety beneath the nearest wagon.

Henrietta screamed. Fiona twisted around in time to see a hideously painted face reach under the wagon and grab the rifle's barrel.

"Pull the trigger, Henrietta," Fiona implored.

By this time he had a handful of Henrietta's thick brown hair and was tearing at her clothes as he tried to wrestle her to the ground.

Fiona heard the ominous click as Ma Smalley pulled the trigger. Nothing happened, no explosion, no acrid smoke, no dead Indian. The rifle had misfired. Fiona felt as if her body was rooted to the ground.

While Fiona collected her wits over committing murder, Ma Smalley lunged forward and wrapped her arms around Henrietta's legs. "Help...Fiona."

The desperate plea restored Fiona's senses. There was no time to reload the rifle with shot and powder. Instead, she rushed from her place of security dragging the rifle with her. Wrapping her hands around the barrel, she used it as a bat and swung with a force she didn't realize existed. The wooden stock shattered as it connected with the brave's forehead.

She tamped down the hysterical giggle that threatened to escape as she watched the comical way his eyes crossed and the surprised expression on his face, before he wilted to the ground.

"You killed him deader'n a doorknob." Ma Smalley clapped Fiona on the back.

"I'm beholding to you, Fiona." Henrietta's voice trembled as she spoke.

"God forgive me." Fiona's hand groped for the crucifix that hung between her heaving breasts.

****

Days of riding long hours in the hot sun had gradually cleared the congestion from Bannon's lungs. Sometimes he awoke at night reliving the nightmare of being trapped under water. He wasn't the kind of man who understood fear, but he now thought he knew what the women felt every grueling mile of this journey.

He worried about the mood of the women. They'd stopped laughing and had grown withdrawn. This attitude caused carelessness, and carelessness caused accidents. He mentally calculated the number of months left before reaching Oregon Territory.

He searched the skies for signs of rain. As was their routine, he and his scout had ridden ahead looking for water, game to hunt, and a suitable place to camp for the night.

Bannon stood in the stirrups. He squinted at the

rapidly approaching cloud of dust. Until he spotted Isaiah's pinto running hard and fast, he hadn't realized the tension that rolled between his shoulders. He settled in the saddle and waited for the scout to draw up the horse with a skidding halt. "What's your hurry, ole timer?"

"I tell you, Cordell, I got me an itch 'tween my shoulders."

"Like I always say, Isaiah, a bar of soap and a little water will cure that itch." It was an old joke between them, but he knew from experience when Isaiah got one of his twinges, something bad usually happened.

It seemed the air had changed, become electrified. It was for this reason that Bannon's own senses shifted, acutely attuned to any signs of danger. He stood in the stirrups and pointed in the direction of the wagons.

"Mighty big cloud of dust for 'leven wagons. Don't you think, Cordell?"

"Could be rawhiders. Maybe Indians." Bannon focused his eyes on the horizon, listening hard.

"Don't matter. One's bad as t'other. We gotta hightail it back." The edge to the scout's voice was unmistakable.

The two men spurred their horses and rode high over sweating withers pushing for more speed. Two hundred yards from the wagons, a knot of fear gnawed at Bannon's gut as rifle shots split the air.

Sweat trickled into his eyes and oozed from his armpits and down his sides.

The ground echoed with the thunder of hooves as Indians whooped and swarmed in and around the wagons.

"Oh hell, Shawnee. We'd better pray none of the women are good shots. C'mon." Bannon motioned for the scout to follow him. They rode straight for a bronzed figure astride a long-legged black and white horse, sitting off in the distance.

"Looks like ole Lame Bull's band." The scout reached into his beard and scratched his chin. "Be hell to pay if'n one of the women accidently got off a killin' shot."

"Yeah, but the women don't know the Shawnee are out for a little sport and to count coup."

"We'd better make tracks, Cordell. Don't make no never mind to Injuns how hard they whap a body on the head with their war clubs, long as they can count it as a victory blow."

Digging his spurs into the gelding's sides, Bannon blinked away the vision of Fiona lying bloodied and broken.

****

From her place under the wagon, Fiona watched Bannon ride toward the lone Indian seated regally on a black and white horse and holding a staff decorated with red feathers. Bannon came to a halt in front of the bare-chested man, lifted his hands and moved them in a fashion that looked as if he were creating drawings in the air. She glanced over at Ma Smalley. "What's Bannon doing?"

"Maybe it's some kind of sign-language."

Fiona's heart was beating so fast she could hardly breathe. Her hands were slippery on the stock of the rifle. "You don't think he's surrendering do you?"

"Cordell Bannon? Not likely." Ma Smalley pointed. "I think they're havin' some kind of palavering."

Shortly, the Indian sounded a series of loud whoops. He raised the lance above his head and yelled something guttural. When he didn't get a response, Fiona watched him knee his pony and set off at a gallop toward the wagons.

He rode into the melee of circling braves, reared his horse and threw the lance with such force it stuck into the ground. Red feathers fluttered in the wind. He yelled again. Fiona thought it sounded as if he were yodeling.

"Look," Fiona pointed, "they're leaving."

"Oh, merciful heavens, I don't know what that big galoot said, but I surely feel like plantin' a big slobbery kiss on that handsome face of his right about now."

The next sight caused Fiona to scoot on her hands and knees from beneath the wagon, dragging the rifle with her. She stood, braced her feet apart, the way Bannon had taught her and the other women. She lifted the rifle to her shoulder and peered down the barrel, taking aim. Just as she fired a hand gripped the barrel and jerked it upward yanking the weapon from her hands.

Stunned, her green eyes flared wide. She screamed at Bannon, "They're stealing Bossy."

"Calm down, Fiona." He grabbed her arm to keep her from racing after the warriors. "Be glad it's only the milk cow they're taking."

She slapped at his hands, struggled to free herself from his iron grip. She caught her breath with this shocking piece of news. Her fury quieted. "Why?"

"We're on their land. Call it payment—like paying a toll."

"What will they do with her?"

When he didn't answer, tears welled in her eyes. She felt like a foolish child as realization dawned. "Well, I suppose they don't drink milk, do they?" Her fear dwindled to be replaced by anger. She wanted to lash out at Bannon, the Indians, the endless sea of prairie, and had clenched her hands into fists when a woman's scream, loud, terror-stricken shrieks filled the camp.

All eyes turned to Mercy Anders. Her face was a gray sheen and a glossy glare covered her terror-widened eyes. Fiona willed her feet to move and sprinted alongside Bannon to where Mercy knelt. She reached and lifted the girl to her feet. Mercy buried her head against Fiona's shoulder and sobbed. "She's d-dead."

"Faith and Begorrah." Fiona fought down the gorge that rose in her throat as she looked down at the mangled body of Mavis Johns crumpled like a limp rag doll. "Hush now, Mercy."

"Get her out of here." In the next breath, Bannon shouted, "Isaiah."

Fiona handed the distraught girl into the arms of Ma Smalley. "What happened to her, Mr. Bannon?"

He stared down at the mangled body, his brows furrowing into a deep frown. "'Pears like she fell, and was trampled to death."

Fiona screamed, "I hate them...I hate all of them. Murdering savages. We paid them a toll, and for what...for this? Why didn't they just ask for the damned cow? They didn't have to kill for it. Did they?"

The scout called out, "Got another one over here, Cordell."

"Go back, Fiona. You don't need to see this." Bannon's voice was loud and commanding.

She didn't understand the reason but felt compelled to follow. The strong pungent sweet odor of fresh blood assaulted her nostrils. She stared at the gaping hole in the back of the head of the woman who lay face down. Blood, brain matter, and dirt now matted hair that had once reminded Fiona of corn silk.

Bannon gently rolled the body over. "Did you know her?"

Her voice was so soft it was barely audible. "Trudy Adler. She was in wagon number four," Fiona sobbed. "Poor Trudy, she didn't deserve this. She was bright and funny and optimistic about her future."

"Was she one of the brides?"

"An alternate...like me." She didn't understand Bannon's cold detachment.

Her knees buckled. She didn't feel Bannon's arms lift her to rest against his chest. She was unaware that he carried her back to her wagon, and gently handed her up to Henrietta Hightower or that he'd lifted her into her bunk and pulled a coverlet over her.

"She's in shock. Go to the supply wagon and bring a cup of brandy."

Images of blood and broken bodies flashed through her mind. Through her whimpers she heard Bannon calling her name. She wanted to answer. Her mind wouldn't allow it. Bannon called her name over and over again, shaking her shoulders as if in an effort to reach her.

Reality dawned as the sound of her name being called came through to her. Her hands pressed firmly against her mouth, her eyes cleared of their glazed stare. But the terror of the Shawnee's attack, the Indians she'd killed, and the gruesome deaths of the two women replayed in her mind.

Bannon accepted the cup from Henrietta. "It's all right Miz Hightower. You're needed outside. I'll tend to Fiona."

Henrietta nodded her understanding and stepped down from the tailgate. Before she took her leave, she said, "Fiona was brave today. Killing is never easy. She did what she had to do." A tear rolled down her cheek. "You should've told us about the Shawnee, Mr. Bannon."

Her words roiled him with guilt. He should have warned the women. The Shawnee were basically harmless, and they usually counted coup by rapping the enemy on the head or shoulder with the tip of a lance or a war cudgel. Still with him and Isaiah away, a group of women without the protection of men was an open invitation to pillage and rape.

"Bannon." Fiona whispered.

He swung easily to the top bunk, pulling her into his embrace, holding her tightly against his body, his arms wrapped around her. "Sh, sh, Fiona. It's all right. You're safe," he murmured, his tone deep and comforting, drawing her senses back to sanity. He lifted the cup to her lips, watched her grimace as she gulped the fiery liquid.

Her small body shook with tremors, and dry sea-green eyes tried hard to focus on her surroundings. Her cheek pressed into the warmth of his chest. "Will they come back and take revenge?"

"Isaiah took over a side of bacon as a peace offering. We've seen the last of them."

"I committed murder...tonight. I snuffed out two lives...like it was nothing." She tried to snap her fingers and failed.

It took a long while before she calmed down. In all that time, Bannon remained, holding her, smoothing the coppery tangles of her hair, whispering soothing words of comfort.

"I'm sorry. I'm so sorry," she repeated over and over. "It isn't like me to be a ninny."

"Death is never easy. Especially when it's violent."

She drew a ragged breath. "How much longer until we reach Glory?"

"September."

"Almost three months."

She lay back and flung an arm over her eyes. "If you don't mind, I need to be alone."

"You rest. Isaiah rode back into camp awhile ago. We've work to do." His frame too tall to stand his full height in the wagon, his wide expanse of shoulders curled forward to keep from scraping his head on the bonnet canvas.

"Mr. Bannon?"

He turned and looked up at where she leaned over the bunk. Sanity had returned to her eyes. "Thank you."

He smiled warmly at her.

Bannon had held her so tightly against him that he feared his own strength might hurt Fiona. Her quiet courage was a rare quality he admired. He respected how she'd strove to conquer her hysteria. He'd witnessed first hand hardened buffalo hunters, even soldiers, break down, go into shock under extreme duress. Sometimes it happened that way. He found no fault in Fiona's reaction and felt a surge of protective feelings.

Tomorrow would be the first of how many more funerals? Tomorrow, the first lottery to select an alternate bride to take Mavis Johns place would be held with nine candidates remaining.

Bannon sighed heavily. A new worry plagued him.

Chapter Eleven

The early June morning was hot—hot enough to suck the air out of Fiona's lungs. Perspiration soaked through her clothes. Still shaken from the Shawnee attack on the wagons and the grisly deaths, she joined hands with Mercy Anders as the women formed a circle around the two mounds of dirt.

While some of the women had prepared the bodies for burial, she and Bird LeBlanc had picked armloads of sunflowers which now adorned the graves.

Not having fully recovered her composure from the day before, Fiona's eyes shifted around at the haggard faces of the women—Flora Newcomb cradled a broken arm in a sling, one entire side of Astrid Lute's face was swollen black and blue. Others suffered from scrapes and bruises, too.

Dreams had plagued her last night, horrible dreams, dreams she must learn to deal with alone. Her thoughts shifted to the things Bannon had said about death and killing never coming easy.

He was probably right, she thought, but his words didn't help the emotions warring inside of her. When she had begun this trip, she had felt nothing—not fear, eagerness, or excitement.

She held her hands, fingers laced together. In those few brief moments when the Shawnee had attacked, and death had closed its icy hand around her throat, she had felt everything more intensely than she'd ever had in her life, and she vowed fear would no longer hold any power over her.

Her vision blurred, and involuntary tears stung her cheeks.

She didn't hear the scriptures Ma Smalley read, didn't realize she'd finished until Ma Smalley reached down and grabbed a handful of dirt and sprinkled dust over the forlorn graves.

"Ashes to ashes, dust to dust, and so shall Mavis Johns and Trudy Adler return." Ma Smalley lifted her eyes heavenward. "We ask Thee ole Lord to accept these fine women into Your loving arms."

Fiona whispered, "Amen."

An unexpected wind kicked up, blowing Fiona's hair across her face. Dark clouds blotted out the sun, bringing an unexpected cool breeze.

"Rain. Glory be, rain." Ma Smalley laughed.

Like the other women, Fiona lifted her face to drink in the fat drops that splattered them. They pushed back their sunbonnets to let the water wash through their hair and soak their sweat-stained dresses.

"We can freshen the water barrels," Henrietta Hightower exclaimed.

"And take a bath." Mercy's eyes twinkled up at Fiona.

A sudden gust of wind caught Fiona's skirts and like long fingers propelled her forward. She slapped down her garment.

The wind snatched at Bannon's voice as he shouted, "Get to your wagons, ladies. Make haste. And don't forget what I said earlier—drive your wagons straight over the graves."

Fiona followed the line of his arm as he pointed toward a slanting sheet of silvery rain moving east and west toward them as far as the eye could see. A bank of dark clouds curtained the expanse making it difficult to distinguish where the horizon stopped and the sky began. Jagged lightning streaked like spiny glowing fingers, followed by a crack of thunder so loud Fiona's teeth ground together.

She linked arms with her wagon mates, and the women lowered their heads against the stinging sand that lashed their faces and pushed against the wind toward the safety of their wagon.

She darted a glance at Bannon as he sprinted to his sorrel, swinging into the saddle without using the stirrups. His horse reared and bucked. He fought to bring the frightened animal under control. "Move 'em out ladies. Storm's coming out of the east. Let's make tracks and see if we can outrun the worst of it." The brim of his hat flattened against his forehead as he spurred his horse up and down the line bellowing to make his voice heard.

Fiona climbed on the seat beside Ma Smalley who slapped the reins across the backs of the mules. The mules brayed and reared against their traces. "They're afraid," Fiona cupped her hands around her mouth and shouted.

Ma Smalley nodded and started to climb down off the wagon box. "Gotta get 'em...moving."

"Nooo." Fiona yelled above the wind. "I'll do it." Slashing needles of rain hit her as she reached the mules' heads. She stood between the traces and tugged on the harness. "Come on Rufus, Jonah, move your feet, please. Now's not the time to stubborn up." The frightened mules stiffened their legs and refused to budge.

"Get back in the wagon, Miss Quinn." Bannon's hat flew from his head. It reminded Fiona of a ballerina as the wind danced it across the prairie.

Ducking her head and fighting the tangle of her skirts, she used the mules to steady her way back to the wagon. She climbed on the wagon box and huddled under the canvas tarp Ma Smalley lifted.

Bannon whirled the whip over his head and with a snap of his wrist lashed the tip between the ears of Rufus, and then Jonah's. The sting put the mules in motion which such force it nearly dragged Ma Smalley off the wagon box, had it not been for Fiona grabbing the woman around the waist, it would have. Apparently, theirs wasn't the only teams refusing to budge. She listened to the repetition of sharp cracks as Bannon whipped the teams into action.

Lightning popped and snapped at rapid intervals leaving seconds between splinters. The rain was coming in torrents and slammed against the canvas bonnets.

Fiona struggled to catch the sound of Bannon's voice as he rode from one wagon to the next, shouting orders no one could hear, mostly trying to keep the mules moving.

For a long as she remembered, she'd always hated thunderstorms. The bright flashes of light and ear-piercing cracks of thunder shook the wagons. Another flash and the ensuing crack of thunder made her jump, and she hugged her arms tighter around her waist. Even so, she refused to leave Ma Smalley's side for the dry interior of the wagon. Both of them huddled under the canvas draped around them as Ma Smalley manned the reins and shouted encouragement to the mules.

Fiona's fist went to her mouth as the scout's horse went down. She screamed Isaiah's name. Wide-eyed with fear she watched him struggle to his feet, grasping for the reins as Bannon brought the pinto around. Sobs of relief and fright shuddered in her throat.

Seconds later an explosion of blue and white fire stabbed the earth, and the wagon rocked perilously back and forth. Fear dug inside Fiona's skull, crawling between her breast and her knees down to her shoes.

She whirled around, thinking she'd heard a

woman's scream. Not one wagon was visible in the gray that blotted out the sun. She turned back to see Ma Smalley trembling with exertion. Her sodden bonnet was plastered to her head. Fiona put her mouth close to the older woman's ear and shouted above the wind's roar. "Let me take the reins while you go get out of those wet clothes. You need to rest."

Alarm and exhaustion in Ma Smalley's eyes was evident. She handed over the reins and scrambled over the seat to the damp interior of the wagon.

The wind drove knife points of rain into Fiona's back. She scrubbed the palm of her hand across her face, straining to see the backs of the mules. She could see nothing, nothing at all except sheeting gray water and flashes of blue and silver streaks that stabbed the earth.

Trust the mules...trust the mules...keep them moving. She talked inside her head as she punished the backs of the animals with the reins. Her fingers wound so tight around the leather leads her hands were numb. She clung to the reins with the same ferocity that she clung to life as the wagon creaked and swayed across the muddied ground.

She wanted to pray, to ask deliverance from her sins, and wondered if God was punishing her. She thought of Bannon and worried if he was safe. She was afraid he and Isaiah Thomas had been washed away, or worse struck by lightning.

Her mind screamed, *no more...no more...please.*

It took several seconds for her to realize the thunderous downpour had slowed to a drizzle. Exhaustion weighed her down as a hand reached out and touched her shoulder. Ma Smalley said, "It's over. Glory be. The worst of it is over."

Already billowy white clouds and azure skies replaced the gray darkness. Drops of rain, clinging to tenacious spider webs on stems of purple flowers, glistened like diamonds against the sun's bright rays.

Bannon's still damp hair curled darkly, giving a boyish look to his haggard face, and his wet clothes clung to his body when he rode up beside Fiona's wagon. She sensed by the determined set of his eyes and firm mouth that tragedy had struck again. She steeled herself not wanting to hear the news.

"You and the other ladies all right, Fiona?"

Except for the suction of mud against wagon wheels, the air was crisp and silent. "Aye, we are," she managed weakly. "Is it over?"

"All but the burying."

She strangled on a sob. "Who?"

"That last bolt of lightning, the one just before the storm ended..." his voice struggled as if he couldn't get the words out, and then said quietly, "Circle up, Fiona. I'll pass the word to the others."

****

Fiona stepped down to the ground and braced herself against the wagon. Her legs were shaky, and her arms ached as her muscles slowly unclenched.

Ma Smalley stood beside her. "Never in my born days have I witnessed a storm with such ferocity."

"Mr. Bannon said we're to have another burying." Fiona's voice was low and filled with emotion.

"Sweet mother in heaven. Do you know who?"

Fiona chewed her bottom lip. She shrugged her shoulders. "Guess we'll find out soon enough, here he comes."

Bannon was covered with grass and mud, his wet hat slapping against his thigh. "We'll camp here for a few days. We can all do with a rest."

Ma Smalley touched his arm. "Fiona said we'd have another burying. We'd like to know who."

His words sounded almost apologetic, as if he were somehow responsible. "That last bolt of lightning. It jumped over the supply wagon, spared wagon number nine and struck dead center in wagon number eight like a big ball of fire. Not much left of it."

To numb to even think much less reply, Fiona stood with her chin sagging, her breathing shallow and tears spilling down her cheeks.

"Merciful heaven." Ma Smalley wrapped her arms around Fiona. "All of four of 'em?"

He nodded. "There's plenty of brandy if any of the women need a libation to calm their nerves." His warm blue eyes sought Fiona's. "I'm sorry."

She thought he smelled of rain and mud, perspiration and exhaustion. Swallowing the knot in her throat, she lifted her hand to his cheek. "It's not your fault."

He sighed heavily. "Isaiah and I will see to the graves."

Though barely visible in the fading light, she thought his shoulders drooped a little when he turned on his heel and strode away.

****

That night Fiona sat on her top bunk recording the day's events in her diary.

There was no time to say proper good-byes to Mavis Johns and Trudy Adler before the storm struck. It seemed sacrilegious that we should drive the wagons over their unmarked graves even with Mr. Bannon's explanation that it was necessary to leave no traces because sometimes Indians dug up the graves to take scalps or steal what they could from the bodies; and too keep animals from feeding off the carrion.

Six lost souls in one day with the addition of Irma Lewis, Hilda Detz, Octavia Herman, and Iris Molpe. Morale is low.

Beneath the entry, she sketched six graves with crosses, and in the finest print wrote the names of the deceased.

A distant rumble of thunder caused her to jump, and she hugged the quilt tighter around her waiting for the lightning to strike.

Her heart pounded in her chest. There was no reason for her to be afraid of the storm. It was only a lot of noise and rain, something her father had always tried to tell her.

"It's too far off in the distance," Althea Smalley spoke. "We won't see any more storms for a while."

"I've always hated storms." Fiona closed her diary and tucked it beneath her pillow.

"I've seen a lot of bad ones before," Henrietta Hightower said, "but nothing like what we experienced today."

Mercy Anders swung her legs over the side of her cot and sat up. "Why do you hate storms, Fiona?"

"Mercy," Ma Smalley scolded. "Leave Fiona be with your infernal curiosity."

"I'm sorry, Fiona. Ma Smalley's right to scold me. 'Tain't none of my business why you're afraid of storms."

A blinding flash of light filled the wagon and vanished, hurting Fiona's eyes. She was surprised at how chilly it had gotten.

Closing her eyes a moment, Fiona collected her wits. "'Tis all right, Mercy. Perhaps I've kept it within me long enough." She began, "When my father booked passage for us to leave Ireland, my mother was with child, but she didn't tell my father for fear he'd change his mind about coming to America.

"Times were hard in Ireland. Between high taxes and little work, Father found it difficult to keep kit and kin alive. So, he sold every stick of furniture in the cottage, what few sheep he owned. He sold his good plow horse, and my mother sacrificed her few heirlooms to help buy ship's passage for she refused to be left behind.

"By the time her condition was obvious, it was too late, for we had sailed hundreds of miles from our homeland. Between the morning sickness and the seasickness, we none thought she or the *báibín* within her would live.

"The ship's captain had so gladly accepted the peoples' fares, then crowded all of us down in the hold of the ship, like criminals. There was precious little room for the three hundred of us...barely enough room for any of us to lay toe-to-toe in the wooden bunks, never mind milling about. Privacy didn't exist when we needed to bathe or to use the slops.

"The hatches had to be kept closed in foul weather, and since there was no other ventilation for that low deck, the damp, stale air held the odors from the bilge, the breath of many people close together, and the reek of the necessaries, which were of the most primitive kind.

"All too often water from crashing waves dripped through from the upper decks, and in the winter the water froze on us while we slept.

"And then one night a violent storm hit. Over the steady roar of the ocean, I could hear the pummeling rain. The gale kept us below deck for days, and none of us could remember the last time we'd even nibbled a scrap of hard tack or slaked our thirst with anything other than foul-tasting briny water. Worst of all were the sanitary conditions.

"The night mother went into labor..." Fiona struggled to keep her composure. "Even a wee child such as myself, I knew it was too early for the babe to arrive. The storm's violence increased so that it tossed the ship about as if it were a mere toy in a gigantic pool of swirling water. Thunder and lightning, and the wind's howling sounded like banshees wailing over the moors, and salt water sloshing through the grated hatch soaked us to our skins. Nary a dry spot was there in that stinkin' hold.

"Mother developed a fever—burning up one minute, then teeth-chattering chills the next. She swore she'd go mad if the storm didn't stop. Then one night a horrific blue-white streak seared across the deck and up the main spar setting the sails on fire. That's when my mother's labor started. Her screams blended with the thunder as the babe ripped from her body." Soft sobs mingled with her own as Fiona finished the tale. "The next morning, amid the rain and thunder and lightning, Father gave my dear gentle mother and the wee *báibín* over to the sea." Anger laced her voice. "Father wasn't even allowed to sew their bodies inside sailcloth."

Lantern light glimmered across Fiona's tortured features. Althea Smalley tsked, "Terrible, just terrible for a child to experience such a thing. How old were you?"

Fiona blinked, swallowed hard, and sucked in a deep, trembling breath. "I had just seen my ninth birthday, and my brother was eleven."

"I don't know about the rest of you, but I say this calls for a drop or two of brandy." Althea Smalley uncorked the bottle that Cordell Bannon had brought earlier. "Medicinal purposes, of course." She filled four tin cups and handed one to each woman, then offered a toast, "To better days ahead and a bright future for all us."

In spite of the encouraging words, an ominous dread filled Fiona.

Chapter Twelve

A cloudless blue sky, warm sunshine, and soft breezes marked the day. "Oooee." Isaiah Thomas slapped his knee. "If you don't stop that infernal pacing, Cordell, you're gonna dig yourself clear down to China."

Bannon hadn't slept well that previous night. While every inch of his body begged for rest, his mind refused to shut out yesterday's storm and the vision of Fiona, the way the color had drained from her face when he'd carried the sad news of the women who'd died in the wagon.

The anger crimping his brow deepened as he continued to pace. It was time to hold the first lottery, and with the death of Trudy Adler at the hands of the Shawnee, only nine alternate bride's names remained to assume the bridal contracts of the buried women.

"You ain't answered me, boy. What's eatin' you?"

Bannon spun around. His tall frame stiffened. "I swear, Isaiah, you're worse than a nagging woman."

The old scout chuckled and scratched under his beard. "You gonna tell me, or am I gonna have to whup it out of you?"

Bannon's sour gaze drifted over the camp and watched the activity as the women went about their morning chores in quiet solemnness. He frowned as he watched Fiona study the horizon. Her long auburn braid shimmered down her back. She closed her eyes, drew in a deep breath of air, and tilted her head back turning her face to the sun.

"She has all the attributes of a fine wife, Cordell. She's honest, innocent, and brave."

For a moment Bannon had been caught up in his thoughts and had forgotten about his scout. "She's not mine to claim."

"Blasted contract. When you gonna hold the lottery?"

Bannon fingered the slips of paper holding the names of the alternate brides. He laughed half-heartedly. "Now."

"Could be her name won't get drawn." A mischievousness glint appeared in Isaiah's eyes. "You could take it out, you know."

The expression on Bannon's face caused the deviltry on the old man's face to disappear. Isaiah kicked a clot of dirt and said, "That's what I've always admired about you—honest to the bone."

Bannon didn't miss the sarcasm in his friend's voice. He squared his shoulders and watched Fiona a moment, noticing how the wind teased a stray tendril of her hair and molded her dress against her slender body. Since the death of his wife, he'd freely taken all that women would give him without a moment's thought, never desiring to share a permanent life with them. And now the one woman he wanted could never be his.

As if she sensed she was the object of conversation, Fiona lifted her emerald eyes to look at him, and his heart lurched in his chest when she smiled.

He growled. "Might as well get this over with." He placed the slips of paper inside his journal, slapped it shut and strode toward the camp's inner circle.

The figure of authority, he stood with his legs splayed, hands on hips. Impatient to get the drawing over and done, he said, "Gather round, ladies. Isaiah, lend me your hat."

He opened the journal and placed the nine strips of paper in the leather hat, then he removed his own hat and placed the names of the deceased women inside. He addressed the waiting group. "I never expected we'd lose so many fine women in such a short time and all at once. Even so, you know what that means?"

A low buzz of voices filtered around the group. He handed the journal to Fiona. "You ladies know the terms of the contracts you signed. Upon the death of one of the brides, a lottery will be held to select an alternate who will fulfill the obligation." He shifted irritably from one foot to the other.

"Bird LeBlanc will assist me. She will draw a name from each hat then hand them to me to read out. Miss Quinn will record the new information in my journal. You can ask her the name of the man you're betrothed to—it's in the book."

Fiona's green eyes fairly crackled with fire as they shot to Bannon's. He wished he knew what she was thinking. He only knew she looked more appealing than ever with rosy cheeks against sun-browned skin and mussed hair. The brown wool dress she wore fit her snugly, the bodice clearly revealing the hardened peaks of her breasts.

She bit her lower lip, then released it from her small, even teeth, leaving it lush and red as blood. Bannon tried not to stare at her mouth, which was bow-shaped and eminently kissable. And God help him, what was he going to do without her?

****

Fiona blinked as she looked down at the journal that lay open in her lap. *Oh, stuff and bother.* She refused to cry. She was also more than a little conscious of the intensity of Bannon's gaze. He must know she could never be more to him than a friend. Especially if her name was drawn from the lottery. She shifted uncomfortably on the barrel. Damn him anyway. Why did he have to almost make love to her? Why had he awakened a desire in her so deeply that it hurt?

She swallowed involuntarily, her auburn eyelashes lowered, afraid to look into his enchanting blue eyes—eyes that were harsh one minute and kind the next. As she held the pencil nub poised above the page, she tamped down the nervous flutter in her stomach. She'd wanted so much to escape Philadelphia to avoid a condemned life as one of Blackie Sledge's doxies that she'd prayed extra hard to be one of the chosen brides. She'd been relieved to become an alternate. Her heart thrummed in her ears, now she desired what she'd never have— Cordell Bannon.

An awareness of silence caused her to look up. Bird LeBlanc reached into one hat and then the other. She handed the slips of paper to the wagon master. Fiona's breath hung in her throat as he read the two names, "Marnie Brown—Constance West."

Relief washed over her as she penned the names of the alternate brides on the journal page.

And for ten minutes this was the way it went until time to select alternate bride number six. Again, the Iroquois woman pulled out two slips of paper and handed them to Bannon.

Fiona was unnerved at the way he frowned at her. His muscular arms crossed over his chest. She almost fainted when he announced, "Doreen Blair, you will assume the contract of the recently deceased, Mavis Johns."

Fiona's heart clenched. She worked to gain control of her emotions, drawing from an inner strength and dignity. And within her sparked a dim ray of hope.

Chapter Thirteen

The traveling grew harder over the next few days. The trees, and streams, and creek beds grew fewer and farther between. Fire wood became more and more scarce resulting in the daily harvesting of buffalo chips.

The sun was hot and dry, and insects crackled in the air. Fiona sat with her legs apart and her elbows resting on her knees to ease the strain on her back; the brown pioneer bonnet was pulled forward to shade her face, but the wind had already unwound her braid into a tangled mass of wayward curls across her neck and shoulders. Her face was bronzed by the sun and dust, the sleeves of her dress rolled up above her elbows.

Bannon rode up beside the wagon. He grinned. "You could almost pass for a muleskinner."

She scowled. "You don't exactly look like one of those dandified fellows in a dime novel."

Her scowl deepened. Even now with his bronzed skin and blue eyes that crinkled against the sun's glare, she wanted to run her fingers through hair the color of honey and wheat.

She turned her attention back to the mules and tried not the think about getting to Glory. Their little group had dwindled to thirty-four. She worried about it a lot. She prayed no more tragedies would happen.

"Leave me alone, Mr. Bannon. Go scout for water, or a place to camp for the night, but leave me be."

"Fiona—"

"No. Bannon." Her voice was sharper than she intended. "There are few remaining alternate brides, and I'm one of them." She gave him a long, hard look. "You said it yourself. We're bound by contract—both you and I, and I fully intend to honor mine."

A long time passed with nothing but the creak of leather and the jangle of traces and the rattle of the wheels for company. He trailed alongside in silence then set spurs to his gelding and galloped away.

****

The sound of thunder worried Fiona. Her eyes automatically searched the sky. She'd learned afternoon storms were not unusual. She leaned over to look down at Ma Smalley who trudged beside the wagon. "The sky looks to blue and clear for a storm."

"Slow this contraption down so I can climb up."

Fiona nodded. She tugged back on the reins, slowing the mules' pace.

With practiced ease, the older woman hiked her foot up onto the single tree and seated herself next to Fiona. "Something's bothering the mules. Listen to 'em blowing, and see how they keep twisting their ears."

Although the floppy-brimmed hat shaded her face, Fiona didn't miss the worry in her friend's eyes. "What do you think it is?"

Althea Smalley swatted at a bug buzzing around her face. "Wish I knew. Doesn't sound like regular thunder."

Then they spotted Bannon racing toward them from the west, and Isaiah Thomas pushing his pinto straight toward them. The men weren't just riding—they were racing, bent low and using their hats to beat their horses, kicking up a cloud of dust in their wake. Bannon was shouting before he reached them, but Fiona and Ma Smalley couldn't hear him.

"Haul up on the reins, Fiona. I can't make out what he's yelling."

She obeyed, bringing the wagon to a halt. Bannon and the scout's lathered horses skidded up to the wagon choking the women with dust. Bannon shouted, "Oglala, headed this way."

Fiona shuddered, the incident with the Shawnee still fresh in her mind. She fought the rising panic as she craned her neck searching the horizon. The sight paralyzed her. The distant figures grew close enough to identify as men...and not just men, but brown-skinned gruesomely painted men with lances who were known to steal horses and women, then ransom the women off as slaves, or worse.

Her throat went dry and fear settled cold in her stomach. "Indians? Can't we just pay a toll like we did before?"

Bannon shouted, "The Oglala Sioux don't settle for tolls."

Fiona's fingers clutched the reins, and she felt she might split apart at the seams. "Can't we outrun them?"

"'Fraid not. They're the finest horsemen on the prairie."

"What should we do?" There was a tight edge to her voice. She shifted a worried glance from Bannon to Isaiah Thomas.

Bannon cut a sharp look toward his scout. "You were flailing your pinto mighty hard, Isaiah. Not more Indians, I hope?"

"No, sir. Buff'lo." The old scout dragged an arm across his sweaty brow. "Small herd, bout five hunnerd or so." He twisted in his saddle and pointed.

Bannon said, "If we can cut across in front of them, the herd will wipe out any traces of wagon wheels. That should buy us enough time to get away."

Fiona listened to the men rough out a harried plan. She shifted both reins to her left hand while she gripped Althea Smalley's with the right. "Oh, Ma Smalley, I'm only nineteen. I never expected to look death in the face more than once."

"Know what you mean, girl. Suddenly fifty don't seem so old anymore." Althea Smalley said, squeezing Fiona's hand.

Fiona's heart quickened at the scout's reply. "Can't do it, Cordell. Them buff'l'er are meandering, placid like, in the same direction as us."

She watched a troubled frown pinch Bannon's face. His voice carried strongly above the creak of wagon wheels. "Placid like, huh? Here's what we'll do, we'll mix right in amongst the herd, easy like and trail along with them until we're in the clear. Clouds of thick dust will hide any trace of us, and two thousand hoof prints will wipe out our wagon tracks."

"Better hope them Injuns ain't looking to kill a few of them ugly critters for supper."

It took a moment for Fiona to realize what the scout meant. Along the way, they'd passed small knots of the huge, foul-smelling, hairy beasts. Isaiah Thomas had warned them about the damage even one of the brutes could do if it took a notion to charge one of the wagons. He'd said buffalo were cantankerous animals and a gnat's fart could trigger a stampede.

"Fiona, Miz Smalley, keep the mules moving. Don't allow them to balk or to run. Look for a gap in the herd and push in amongst them. Sing to the mules, talk to 'em, anything to keep these lop-eared jackasses from braying." Bannon looked up at Fiona. There was something in his eyes she'd not seen before. She saw his chiseled features had twisted into the picture of contriteness.

He smiled up at her, his voice low and intense.

"You really don't look like a muleskinner, Fiona." He saluted her with two fingers. "Isaiah and I will ride up and down the line explaining to the other wagons."

"See you on the other side, Mr. Bannon." *If we make it through alive.* She offered him a tenuous smile.

"Merciful heaven, get a move on, Fiona. Do what he says." Althea Smalley twisted on the seat and called to the back of the wagon. "Mercy...Henrietta, stay quiet as church mice, you hear?"

Fiona heard the intensity in Bannon's voice as he rode away. "Your pinto looks done in, Isaiah. Meet me at the remuda. We both need fresh mounts."

"Yep, don't relish gettin' trampled to death if'n my pony stumbles."

By the time Bannon and his scout rode up on fresh mounts, Fiona's stomach was in knots.

"Follow me." He raised his arm and waved them forward.

Fiona's heart pounded in her ears as she flapped the mules into action. Sweat trickled down her nose and dripped off her chin.

The ground vibrated beneath the wagon from the thunder of hooves. Then she looked up and the full impact of what she saw hit her with a powerful force.

The horizon was black with swarms of buffalo spread out over the prairie like armies of ants. Not just a few, but as far as her eye could see.

Her mind couldn't comprehend what her eyes were seeing. *Lord protect us.* She looked over her shoulder and saw the stricken faces of her friends. Bannon shouted something to her, but his words were lost amongst the rumbling herd.

The wagon rocked a little as Henrietta moved forward to peek over Fiona's shoulder. Fiona snapped, "Be still."

"God save us," Henrietta's voice squeaked with fear.

"And don't talk," Fiona commanded breathlessly. Her heart slammed against her ribs. "If you see an opening, Ma Smalley, point it out." Fiona forced herself to loosen her grip on the reins to give the mules their head.

The woman seated next to her, tied a bandana around Fiona's face, and then one for her own. "Maybe this'll keep us from choking to death."

Above the rim of the bandana, Fiona's eyes scanned back and forth, seeking an opening large enough to drive the wagon through. The last thing she wanted was to be trampled.

Althea Smalley touched Fiona's arm and pointed. Fiona nodded her understanding and turned the mules, expertly guiding them. Her palms sweated. Inside her head she screamed with terror as she maneuvered the wagon amongst an ocean of monstrous hairy beasts. The roar of tramping hooves echoed in her ears; the heat and dust and stench were equally oppressive. She couldn't breath. She wondered if this was what it felt like to die—alone and defenseless.

She worried about Bannon and Isaiah. She worried about the other wagons. She didn't dare think about splinters beneath a rampage of thundering hooves, or the broken bodies of women trampled beyond recognition. Sweat streamed down her face and caked her eyes. Every breath was a struggle. A shred of relief filtered through her at the sight of another wagon. The dust-coated driver was barely recognizable as a woman.

She caught sight of Bannon marbling through the maze. A sea of buffalo surged around him. She watched his horse dance and turn in a circle as it found itself in the thick of the herd. She feared the frightened animal would whinny and create a stampede or worse rear up and dump Bannon into a tangled death trap.

She imagined the soothing words he spoke to the nervous horse as he leaned forward and patted the buckskin's neck. Yet, Bannon held his place in the saddle as huge shoulders jostled against his legs.

Sweat crawled between her breasts and down to soak the waistband of her skirt. Her heart was beating so hard she found it difficult to draw a breath. She wondered if the other women were as frightened as she was at this moment.

Beside her, Althea Smalley's face was contorted with terror. Her chin braced on top of clasped hands, Fiona knew her friend was praying for their safety.

Fiona wanted to sob, but her throat was too dry. She wanted to cover her head and hide under the covers like a frightened child. A mule's panicked bray tightened her stomach muscles. Her eyes darted like nervous birds for signs of agitation in the herd.

One jittery behemoth creature bellowed, lowered its massive head and rammed the wagon, tipping it precariously until it finally settled on all four wheels. Her heart hung in her throat for one breath-robbing second. *Don't scream, Mercy. Please don't scream.* Fiona silently implored the nervous young woman huddled on the cot with Henrietta Hightower.

Fiona knew the slightest anything always brought a panicked squeal from the young girl.

She managed to muster enough saliva to moisten her throat and in a quiet soothing voice crooned an Irish lullaby to the sea of animals surrounding the wagon.

Numb with fear and the terrible resignation of dying, she guided the mules for what seemed like a lifetime until she spotted Bannon and Isaiah

Thomas with lifted arms signaling. She gently clucked the mules in their direction and moved along with a plodding pace until she'd cleared the buffalo herd and halted the mules on a grassy knoll above the swarm of animals. As far as her eyes could see the grass was churned up into chunks like a freshly plowed field.

As the other women drove through the herd, it wasn't until she'd counted the last wagon that the full force of realizing what they had all survived hit Fiona. Only now did she allow herself to think how incredible it was they had all lived to see another day.

Behind her she heard a dry sob. Mercy Anders buried her face in dust caked hands and wept. Fiona turned on the wagon seat and looked at the girl's shuddering shoulders. "We're safe, Mercy. We're safe."

Fiona and Althea Smalley climbed down from the wagon. They hugged each other. "Praise be. We made it," Ma Smalley choked on a sob.

Fiona's heart clenched when Bannon rode toward her. His shoulders were slumped, and it seemed he moved toward them with excruciating slowness. She loosened the bandana and swiped at the gray dust caked in the corner of her eyes.

She was afraid to ask if there were any losses. She swallowed hard. "Did all the wagons make it?"

Bannon slid off his sweat-caked horse and let it stand. "Except for a torn canvas on Miz Ward's wagon and a broken wheel on Miz Thigpen's everyone's all safe and accounted for." She heard the relief in his voice.

"What about the Indians?" she asked hoarsely.

His eyes moved around at the dirty, disheveled women climbing down off their wagon seats. "We out foxed them, this time. But we need to push on." He extended his arm and pointed. "About five miles from here is Devil's Gate. There's plenty of sweet water for drinkin' and freshin' up. Look for an outcropping of boulders and make camp there. Isaiah and I will catch up to you later."

He smiled and traced his finger down her cheek. "Stay out of the canyon. If it rains, you could all drown."

Her eyes stung with unshed tears as she stared up at him. She wanted to wrap her arms around his dirt-smeared leather shirt and hug him. She wanted him to hold her. Instead, she allowed him to help her up on the wagon's box seat.

She lamely nodded her head. "We'll get a fire going. Coffee will be hot by the time you and Isaiah ride into camp."

She resisted temptation to look back as Althea Smalley guided the team of mules over the grassy knoll. Fiona forced her eyes on the trail ahead and listened to the echoing of rattling wagon wheels closing in behind them.

Chapter Fourteen

The sun blazed high in a cloudless blue sky by the time the wagon train circled to make camp for the night. Weariness from her harrowing experience tugged at Fiona as she helped Althea Smalley and the other women in her group tend to the livestock.

"Except for one other time, I've never been as scared as I was going through that herd of buffalo, today." Mercy Anders sniffed back tears. "How much longer 'til we get to Oregon Territory?"

Fiona grabbed the rope handles of two wooden buckets. "We were all frightened." The girl did look a little worse for wear, her eyes rimmed with bluish-black circles. "I looked at my map, and if my calculations are correct, we'll cross out of Wyoming and into Idaho territory tomorrow."

"Mind if I walk with you down to the waterhole?"

Fiona handed the waifish girl a bucket. "Sure, c'mon." She looked out over the grassland and pointed toward an unusual outcropping of rocks. "That's where Mr. Bannon said we'd find a pool of water." She shuddered. Her eyes searched for an unseen enemy.

"What is it, Fiona? What do you see?"

She tried to make her voice sound calm and cheery. "Nothing, Mercy. Just jumping at shadows, I guess." She lifted her hand to brush a wisp of hair from her face. "Grab another bucket."

The two young women trudged along in silence until the light touch on her arm interrupted Fiona's solitude. "Fiona?"

"Mmm-hmmm?"

"I've got a secret. Part of me is busting out all over to tell it, and the other part of me is purely afraid of what will happen if I do tell."

Fiona watched heat wash up the girl's neck and flood freckled cheeks. Mercy muttered something that sounded very much like a curse as she picked up a rock and let it fly.

When Fiona didn't respond, Mercy said, "Can you keep a secret, Fiona?"

Fiona was tired and hungry and not in any mood for playing childish games. "I'm no jabbering magpie if that's what you mean."

She glanced over at the girl scuffing her feet, kicking up small clouds of yellow dust and buzzing insects as they walked. Fiona scowled. "Well?"

Two blonde braids flapped against the girl's frail shoulders. "Never mind, Fiona. It ain't important."

Her gaze ran over Mercy, noting she seemed thinner than when they'd first begun the journey. She dismissed it as nothing to fret about. Even the stoutest of women had lost weight from long miles of daily walking.

Approaching the rocks, Fiona's hand shot out with lightning quickness as she grabbed the rope handle of her companion's swinging bucket. "Pick up a few rocks and chunk them toward the water, Mercy."

A puzzled gaze met Fiona as if she'd lost her mind. "Whatever for?"

"I don't know. To shoo away snakes, maybe."

With an audible gasp, Mercy drew back. "Snakes." She paled and fainted, falling to the ground in a crumpled heap.

Fiona shouted the girl's name over and over again, shaking her shoulders in an effort to reach her.

Mercy's eyes fluttered open, but terror remained reflected in her gaunt features. Her hands pressed firmly against her mouth to muffle the whimpering.

"Sh, sh, Mercy. It's all right." Fiona murmured, her tone comforting. "I'm sorry. I didn't mean to frighten you. Really."

Mercy's small body shook with the tremors of fear, and dry brown eyes tried hard to focus on her surroundings. "I-I'm mortally afraid of snakes. T-that's why I mostly ride in the wagon."

Mercy's eyes grew round and wide as she placed her hands against her face and sobbed. A gray sheen and a glassy glare covered her widened eyes.

Fiona clanged the two wooden buckets together. She picked up a handful of rocks and tossed them toward the pool of gurgling water. She wasn't overly fond of the slithering reptiles either. She placed her hands around Mercy's waist and helped the girl to stand.

"C'mon. After we fill our buckets, we'll cool ourselves off." Fiona's eyes riveted to sound of pebbles splashing against water. Her eyes scanned the top of the ridge above the gorge.

"You're making me nervous, Fiona. Do you think the Indians followed us?"

Fiona drew a deep breath. Her heart pounded in trepidation. Her smile was forced, but she attempted to calm the girl by teasing her. "Oh, stuff and bother. Just my imagination playing tricks on me. 'Tis nothing."

With buckets swinging from each hand, she ran the last short distance toward the gurgling pool. "C'mon with your worrying self. A good cold soak is just what we need."

After filling all four buckets, the girls sat on rocks warmed by the sun and removed their shoes and stockings. As they dangled their feet in the water, Fiona noticed the tears sliding down her friend's cheeks. "'Tisn't Indians or the buffalo that's upsetting you, is it?"

Mercy drew her feet from the water and wrapped her arms around her knees, hugging them tight. When she didn't answer, Fiona said, "'Tis the secret, that's eatin' way at you?"

The girl nodded. Her sobs grew louder. Fiona untied her apron, pulled the sash from around her waist and dipped the faded material into the water. Wringing out the excess moisture, she wiped Mercy's face with the cool cloth. "If it's burdening you all that much, you can tell me. I promise to keep your secret." Fiona crossed her heart. "Honest."

Mercy shook her head, took a deep breath, and dissolved into fresh tears.

"Do you wish to be alone, Mercy?"

"Not really."

"Are you homesick, then? Do you long to return to Philadelphia?"

Mercy let out a long shuddering sigh. "You promise, Fiona? You really promise not to tell?"

Fiona crossed her heart and said, "Aye. May the *cailleach* swoop down on her *scuab chailli* and steal me away if I do." The puzzled frown on the girl's face brought a smile to Fiona's. "Sorry. 'Tis the witch on her witch's broom I be meaning."

Mercy brushed away the last of her tears. Her eyes were luminous under dark lashes. "I'm pregnant." A shudder wracked her frail body. "There, I've said it. That's my secret."

Fiona fixed an astonished gaze on the girl. She tried to speak but had trouble forming the words. "How...I mean, I know how babes are made...oh, stuff and bother, Mercy...d-did you know before...I mean, the doctor examined you, didn't he?"

Fiona watched the internal struggle on Mercy's face until a breath burst from the girl's lungs as if something had knocked the wind out of her. "When it happened, I didn't think about gettin' with child. I didn't know. 'Til I missed my woman's-time a few months ago, I tried to pretend it didn't happen. You've got to believe that I'd never lie about such a thing."

The girl stared at Fiona blankly for a moment, then, with a strangled sob, she buried her face in the damp apron she held as tears flowed and violent tremors shook her body.

Fiona focused her attention on the sobbing girl, allowing her time to collect her thoughts.

"I was afraid." Mercy spoke through chattering teeth. "So very afraid."

Fiona wrapped her arms around the girl's shoulders and held her close, rocking her as if she were a child. A sense of dread filled her. "Tell me, Mercy."

The words came in snatches as Mercy spoke. "It only happened the one time." She grabbed Fiona's arm, her eyes pleading. "Honest, you must believe me."

"I do, Mercy, I do. Who is the father? Surely, you'd want him to know?"

"Never...never. He's the devil himself."

Seconds ticked by. A premonition shivered through Fiona. "Unburden yourself, lass. I'll pass no judgment over you."

The girl's fingers were wound together until her knuckles turned white. "For months he'd been after me, and I'd managed to keep out of his clutches. I'd never been with a man and haven't since that...that awful night," she whispered brokenly. "I'd heard the preacher tell about how men from Glory were paying for mail-order brides and knew it was my chance to get away. T-then the week before the meeting at the church, it happened. I'd finished washing up all the supper dishes at Dempsey's."

Fiona knew Dempsey's Café was located in the

seedier section of Philadelphia. She remained quiet waiting for the girl to continue.

"I was in the alley walking to the shanty I shared with two other girls who work for Mr. Dempsey. Anyhow, someone threw a gunnysack over my head. I struggled. When I screamed, my lights were punched out. It wasn't until after I'd come to my senses that I knew...that I knew..."

"It's okay, Mercy, you don't have to say another word." Fiona's eyes brimmed with tears.

"No. I need to...to tell all of it, please."

Fiona nodded.

"My mouth was swollen and tasted of blood. I could already feel a bruise forming on the side of my face. The front of my dress was ripped, and there were teeth marks on my b-breasts, and my petticoat was torn and splotched with blood. And I hurt, terribly, you know, down there." Mercy's chalk-white face and her eyes were filled with horror.

Fiona felt herself go weak with a heavy wave of nausea and revulsion. It was clear what had happened to the girl.

After a moment, Mercy gathered herself and continued. "He said that he'd tried to ask me nicely on several occasions to be his queen, and this was my punishment for resisting him. He said that all women were bitches and deserved to be treated like whores." She spoke through broken sobs. "And then he laughed, saying that him and his men had taken turns ridin' me while I was knocked out, and that I wasn't good 'nuf. He said sows did it better than me, and that I was only fit for the *hog* farm."

Having heard the term from some of the diners where she worked, Fiona choked a gasp. "Do you know what the hog farm is?"

Mercy nodded. Her breath came in ragged heaves. "It's where all the used up or diseased girls are sent because they can't get more'n a dime from the *rooters.*"

Knowing what she'd escaped, Fiona shook off her morbid thoughts. "You said he wanted you to be his queen?"

"Life is hard enough when you don't have a family or a man to protect you, Fiona." Mercy's eyes, dark and soul-catching, pleaded for understanding. "You've got to honestly believe me. I never wanted to be his queen. I'd rather starve to death before I worked in such a place."

"Who is he, Mercy? Say his name."

The slender blonde with eyes the color of chocolate looked at Fiona with uncertainty. "I can't."

"If you won't, then I will—Blackie Sledge." She spat the brothel owner's name as if were as venomous as the rattlesnakes they both feared.

The girl's eyes widened, she placed her hands against her mouth. "How did you know?"

"Because he came to me the same night the meeting was held at the church. He promised to make me his *queen*, too."

"Oh, not you...he didn't...hurt you, too?"

"No, he didn't hurt me."

"What did you do? How did you get away?"

"I stabbed him with my sewing shears...only in the arm. Now, I wish I'd aimed for his wicked heart."

Mercy twisted her hands together. "I don't know what to do, Fiona. By the time we reach Glory, my secret will be showin', and Mr. Henry Filmore won't be obligated to accept me as his bride." She balled up her fist. "I don't want this baby. How can I possibly love the spawn of a devil like Blackie Sledge?"

"I'll hear no such blasphemy. Why would you say such a thing?"

Mercy sobbed hysterically. She splayed her fingers across her still flat belly. "I don't mean to sound blasphemous against an innocent child." She hiccupped. "All I ever wanted was a chance at a new life and with a husband who'll give me his children. I don't know what to do. Tell me what to do, Fiona."

She smoothed the girl's limp blonde hair. "Worrying takes a toll on your mind and body. Stop your frettin', you hear me?"

Mercy nodded. "What about Mr. Filmore? He won't want me now that I'm...ruined."

"We none ever suspected. Me poor mother had the morning sickness all the time, but you...you eat like a horse." Fiona giggled. "Sorry, I didn't mean—"

"Nothing you could say would ever insult me, Fiona. You're the best friend I've ever had."

Fiona patted the girl's arm reassuringly. "I'm going to think on this."

Mercy snuffled. "There's lots of hazards along the way. Maybe..."

"You hush up that kind of thinking, right this minute. The worse that could happen to you has already happened."

"I wish I'd had the courage to cut out Blackie Sledge's gizzard and fed it to vultures."

Fiona managed to say, "No sense crying over spilt milk, now is it?" She quickly added, "We'd better get back to the wagons." She reached down to grab two water filled buckets. "Don't worry, Mercy. As tiny as you are, it'll be weeks more before your condition is obvious. Until we can figure a way around this, your secret is safe with me."

"Even though it wasn't my fault, I know people will judge me as a loose woman."

"The devil with what others think, Mercy. And don't fret yourself, I'll help you and your babe all I can."

Mercy wrapped her arms around Fiona and hugged her tight. Without saying a word, the two girls walked back to camp.

Chapter Fifteen

The month of July roared in like a blazing furnace leaving the days and nights intolerably hot. Unable to sleep, Fiona dangled her legs over the rough hewn rail, her toes seeking the bunk frame below. A soft moan from the girl in the bottom bed momentarily stilled Fiona. Assured the girl slept, she stretched until her bare feet touched the floor. On tiptoes, she reached up and lifted her pair of brogans from the end posts of her bunk. She clasped the shoes in one hand while she used the other to steady herself as she hiked up her cotton shift to lift her legs over the wagon's closed end gate.

Knowing it wasn't safe to traipse around in the dark in bare feet, she quickly slipped on the shoes and laced them.

She stretched, tilted her head back, and gazed up at the millions of stars littering the inky sky.

She lifted the heavy mass of hair off her neck as she sucked in the fragrant air and felt the soft summer breeze mold the cotton fabric of her nightgown to her damp body. Crickets chirped from somewhere off in the distance, and she could hear the occasional grunt of a buffalo.

It was peaceful here. She didn't miss the noise of the city, the daily hustle and bustle of trying to meet the demands of her waitress job. She wondered if any of the customers missed her. It wasn't long before her thoughts betrayed her, and her mind wandered off to the plight of Mercy Anders' pregnancy. How could a man, even one as despicable as Blackie Sledge, violate an innocent young woman? And why hadn't Mercy reported the rape to the constable? Fiona knew the answer to that question and retracted the thought. Almost everyone in Philadelphia knew that Blackie Sledge secretly paid to keep the law on his side. Not many dared to come against him and most certainly not a frail young woman without a spare penny to her name.

The brothel owner's evil grin floated in front of Fiona's face as she recalled the night he'd come to her home, making his offer. She shuddered knowing the terrible fate she had escaped, and a part of her mourned all the unemployed young women forced to work in his fleshpot as a way to keep a roof over their heads and food in their bellies. She wondered what was worse—dying of starvation, freezing to death in the winter for lack of money to buy coal, or suffering a slow and agonizing death from the pox.

Survival! She harrumphed at the word.

Walking to the water barrel, she lifted the lid and drew out a ladle of water. After quenching her thirst, she used a small amount to cool her cheeks.

A distant campfire drew her thoughts to Cordell Bannon. She liked watching him while he rode horse back, the way sweat made the soft leather shirt cling to his well-muscled back. Her breath would catch in her throat whenever he'd glance her way, offering a smile. She enjoyed the rare occasions of his laughter and the deep resonance of his voice when he spoke. She liked the way he walked, the way he smelled, the way he cursed. He was firm with the women, yet he was kind, and caring, and determined to deliver the remaining brides safely to their waiting husbands.

Bannon's Brides. She smiled at the nickname the women had given themselves. He was the sort of man any woman would be proud to claim as a husband. *But not me—not as long as the possibility remains that another woman could die along the trail.* Fiona offered up a silent prayer they would rapidly close the gap on the miles between Idaho and Oregon territory without her name being chosen from the lottery.

There was no point dwelling on what she could not change. She felt deeply and hopelessly alone. A chill darted through her when a distant memory shook her. What had Bannon meant, on that night so long ago, when she heard him confess that he was responsible for his wife's death?

She sighed knowing she was powerless to change the past or the future.

She looked out over the grassland, thinking it would be virtually impossible for anyone to sneak up on the camp. Her body went on instant alert the moment a calloused, soot-blackened hand covered over her mouth, preventing her from screaming at the top of her lungs. Her arms and legs were seized, and although she fought with all her might, she was no match for the assailant who wrapped his massive hand around her throat and squeezed until she slipped into unconsciousness.

****

The only excuse Bannon could give himself for having been awakened was simply he hadn't been that soundly asleep in the first place. He didn't understand why he hadn't fallen into a deep slumber the second he crawled into his bedroll, since he'd put in one of the longest, most stressful days of his life.

Every muscle in his body ached. He longed for a hot soak in a tub, and a shot of good bourbon. With his arms behind his head, he used his hands as a cushion. Looking up at the sky, he picked out the constellations and mentally named each one.

He turned his head to stare out across the prairie. His broad, bare chest was wet with perspiration, and he tossed aside the horse blanket.

Restless, he rummaged around inside his saddlebag and pulled out a cheroot, then rising to his knees he leaned close to the dying campfire embers and lifted a burnt twig to light the end of the cigar while drawing the tobacco's earthy flavor into the back of his throat.

A strange gnawing played upon his conscience as he thought about a certain red-haired beauty. He silently damned himself for his mistreatment of her. Only a coward preyed on the innocence of young women.

He inhaled another puff of smoke, feeling the effects of the long day, first with rampaging Oglala and then the harrowing experience of guiding a wagon train of inexperienced women drivers through a herd of buffalo. He rolled his head from left to right and back again to stretch the tensed muscles in his neck.

A soft breeze wafted through the night. He listened to his sidekick's puttering snores and wondered how the old man slept so soundly on the rough ground, yet knowing that at the first sound of danger, Isaiah Thomas would be fully alert and ready for a fight.

Bannon drew in a deep breath, his nostrils filling with myriad scents—dry earth, sage, the stink of his own unwashed body. In his frustration he recalled the fragrant scent of Fiona.

He chided himself again for his treatment of her—first by leading her to the pinnacle of willingly giving away her virginity, then rejecting what she offered. He rolled to his side and stared for a long, contemplative moment into the campfire's dying embers.

You poor female deprived man. It's a shame you've allowed grief to shrivel you up and ruin your manhood. He smiled lamely. At the time the old scout had spouted them off, Bannon had misinterpreted the meaning behind the words.

Sometimes just glancing at Fiona would catch him unawares with a pain in his chest, plunging him briefly into the past.

A dark frown settled over his brow as he thought about Fiona. Since the death of his wife, there had been a few women in his life, some whose memory lasted longer than others, some whose names he couldn't remember.

Fiona is young and innocent in the ways of men and certainly not mine for the simple pleasure of slaking the lustful fire burning in my belly.

The mere thought of her caused his manhood to stiffen bringing about a frustrated growl. "Dammit to hell."

"Gawl dang it, Cordell, cain't believe yer still awake."

Bannon tossed the spent stogie into the campfire's cooling embers. "Thought you were asleep."

"Was, but your thinking interrupted my dreams." The old scout grunted.

"Guess we can add mind reading to your many talents." Bannon chuckled derisively.

Isaiah Thomas sat up, yawned, and scratched himself all over. "Ain't ever knowed you to let a woman get under yer skin, not since—" his voice trailed off. "Get some sleep, Cordell. It'll make the night go faster."

"Go ahead and say it—since Annie." Bannon spoke his wife's name with reverence.

Isaiah softened his gravely voice. "You gotta stop blaming yerself. 'Tweren't your fault."

"My head knows you're right, but my heart hasn't wrapped around it yet."

As he laid back down on his bedroll, Isaiah said, "Only got six hunnerd miles left. That's 'bout a month, more or less. Mebbe she'll make it all the way to Oregon Territory without her name gettin' drawn."

"Who?"

Isaiah slapped his thigh. "Dagnabit, Cordell. Sometimes I think you've got mush for brains. *Fiona.* Ain't another women in the whole of this bunch whose twisted yer insides in knots."

Bannon's lifted his shoulders in a careless shrug. He settled on his bedroll, shifting to find a comfortable position. "Go to sleep, Isaiah. And I wish you'd stop walking around in my mind."

Uttering a disgusted grunt, the scout pulled the leather slouch hat over his eyes.

Angry and frustrated, Bannon closed his eyes and willed away the image of Fiona's dimpled smile. He tried to look toward the future and saw only emptiness.

****

Dawn was hours away when Bannon felt a foot roughly nudging his shoulder. He eased his hand down and grabbed the hilt of his knife, ready to whip it from the leather sheath tied around his waist.

"Wake up, Cordell."

"What's eatin' you ole-timer?" Bannon groaned, but didn't miss the urgency in his friend's voice.

"Got me an itch 'tween my shoulders."

Bannon yawned. "You disturbed my sleep just to share that bit of information. Like I keep saying, Isaiah, nothing a bar of soap and a bath wouldn't cure." An uneasy feeling swept over Bannon bringing him instantly awake. He threw back his blanket, but the sense of unease remained.

He stood, his eyes seeking out the wagons a few hundred yards away. Bird LeBlanc was awake, and he saw her stirring life into cold embers. Aida Bills came out of her wagon, looking worriedly up at the yellowish sky.

The hairs on the back of his neck prickled when

Althea Smalley came racing toward him with Henrietta Hightower and petite Mercy Anders hot on Ma Smalley's heels.

Bannon grabbed up his rifle which he always kept next to him while he slept, he spoke sharply. "You and your damned itches, Isaiah."

He and the scout jogged toward the women. Questions in Bannon's head joined the shouts of Althea Smalley's words, like broken syllables, all mixed up and meaning nothing.

There was an uneasiness in him, like a thundercloud gathering in the back of his mind. Althea Smalley's words caused the cloud in his mind to grow darker. He cradled the rifle in one arm while he grabbed her shoulder. "What's happened, Miz Smalley?"

The plump woman wrung the apron around her hands. "It's Fiona. She ain't in the camp."

Bannon shifted his gaze away. "Maybe she's off taking care of her morning necessaries."

"No...no, she ain't." Althea tried to calm the excited pace of her voice.

"That was our first thought," chimed in Henrietta Hightower.

"That's right, Mr. Bannon. I ran fast as I could to the pool." Mercy Anders turned to point to the water. "And she weren't there. Nary a sign that she'd been there, either."

Bannon scanned the horizon, searching the ridge-line along Devil's Gate. "Could be she took that sketch book of hers to draw pictures of flowers. I wouldn't worry. She'll turn up before breakfast."

Althea Smalley gripped his arm. "Fiona's not in the habit of walking around in her night-shift. And her bunk ain't made."

Like an echo, Henrietta said, "She's a creature of habit. Makes her bed, neat as a pin, first thing."

"How do you know she's in her nightgown?"

131

Bannon spoke quietly, addressing no one in particular.

"Her dress," Althea put in sharply, "is still hanging on its hook, but her shoes are gone."

"Yes, that's right." Henrietta responded firmly. "I figure she got up during the night to take care of" she fidgeted, "personal callings. Well, of course, she'd put on her shoes—rattlers, don't ya know?" She ran her hands up and down her arms as if warding off a chill.

Bannon was silent for a long time. When he spoke it was almost like saying nothing at all. "Isaiah and I will take a look around the camp—see if anything looks out of the ordinary."

"Injuns, Cordell?" Isaiah Thomas' eyes were hard and his lips tight.

"Don't go jumping to conclusions, Isaiah."

With extra long strides, Bannon approached the camp with the scout matching each step; the women jogged to keep pace. Bannon lowered his eyes. He pointed to a set of foot prints. "Whoever was here wore moccasins."

Isaiah squatted and feathered his finger over the slight imprint. "Cold. She was took mebbe three—four hours ago."

The words made Bannon feel ashamed for doubting Althea's concerns.

"Indians, Mr. Bannon?" A worried frown pinched Althea's face.

He didn't answer. Instead he walked toward the Iroquois woman who stood tending her cook fire. "Good morning, Bird LeBlanc."

She straightened, smiled and returned his greeting. "*Shé:kan*, Bannon."

"Miss Quinn is missing. We spotted moccasin footprints inside the camp's interior circle," Bannon said. "Did you hear anything out of the ordinary last night?"

A line of puzzlement creased the woman's forehead. "I had a dream of many buffalo, and then I heard a horse whinny. I thought it was part of my dream."

Bannon drew back his shoulders and tightened his fist around the stock of the Sharps Buffalo rifle. He spoke almost to himself. "Anyone else missing?"

Althea said, "Don't think so, or we'd known by now."

"Ladies, get your morning possibles taken care of, then harness the mules, get your wagons lined up and ready to roll by the time Isaiah and I return." His voice was short and clipped.

"How long will that be, Mr. Bannon?" Henrietta wrung her hands together.

"Half an hour, maybe longer." There was a sharp edge to his voice. "No time to saddle up, Isaiah. We'll ride bareback."

"I'm with you all the way, Cordell." The old man muttered under his breath, but loud enough that all who stood close heard his words. "Harm one hair on that little gal's head and I'll split him from asshole to brisket so the vultures can peck at his innards whilst he's beggin' the Almighty to take mercy on his black soul."

"And I'll sharpen the knife," Bannon agreed soberly.

Chapter Sixteen

A change in weather caused Bannon to examine the sky. Clouds multiplied like breeding rabbits.

"Rain's comin'," he said, as he and the scout slid from the backs of their horses. Dropping the reins, the men left the animals ground-tied.

"You check the cave, Isaiah. I'll climb up there to see what I can spot. Meet back here in ten minutes."

As the older man turned to go, Bannon said, "If you find them, don't do anything foolish."

The scout simply nodded his understanding. The two men split up, heading in different directions. A gust of warm, humid air forecast a stormy morning. Bannon swore under his breath. The last thing he needed was for rain to wash away any evidence of who'd kidnapped Fiona. His best hope was for Isaiah to surprise the scoundrels napping inside the cave's cool interior.

Meanwhile he worried about the camp being unprotected. Anything could happen to a bunch of frightened women.

At the top of the butte, Bannon lifted his hand to shade his eyes against the glaring sun, the heavy Sharps rifle held loosely at his side. He scanned the horizon, looking for a cloud of dust that might indicate riders. He turned in a circle and noticed the activity at the wagon train located no more than a mile away. He swallowed hard. "No sign. None."

Frustrated, he skittered down the slope, careful not to let his feet go faster than his body. No sense risking a busted leg, or worse, a broken neck.

He jogged to where his sorrel and Isaiah's pinto stood munching on dried buffalo grass. As his friend approached, the old man answered Bannon's unspoken question.

"Ain't nothing but four-legged varmints been in the cave." He cast a sorrowful glance at Bannon. "Did find horse tracks leading through the chasm." He pointed toward the crack that separated the two massive rock structures.

"How many?"

"Two. And by the looks of it, one of 'em's packin' heavy."

"Shod?"

"Nope, but Cordell, you know that don't mean nothing out here in the territories. It ain't only Injuns who ride unshod ponies."

"You're thinking white men—buffalo hunters?"

"Yup. Not worth the powder to blow 'em to hell and back."

"Makes me sick to my stomach to think what they'll do to Fiona." Bannon swallowed hard. His dark brows gathered in an angry frown.

"Dirty low-down, stinkin' heathens," Isaiah said, flatly. "You got a plan?"

Bannon grabbed a hank of mane and with the agility of a cat, swung up on the sorrel's back. "Tell you back at the camp."

The old man did likewise, spurring his pinto into action.

****

Shaking his head to the women's unspoken questions, Bannon slid off the back of his horse. He and Isaiah accepted the plates of food and cups of steaming coffee shoved into their hands.

Knowing it might be days before he ate another full meal, he knew the importance of keeping up his strength and forced himself to be patient long enough to consume the food on the plate. "Fine vittles," he said to no one in particular. He drained his cup and held it out for a refill.

While he waited for the liquid to cool, he said, "Isaiah, you'll stay with the women. I'll go it alone."

The scout scrunched his face into a mass of angry wrinkles. "Now listen just a gawl dang minute, Cordell. You need me to watch your back. These ain't no Sunday go-to-meetin' youngsters you're fixin' to tangle with."

"The wagons need to keep moving if we expect to make Glory by September. Somebody has to lead the women. That's you." Bannon spoke with infinite patience, authority steeling his voice.

Bird LeBlanc stepped forward. "You should listen, Mr. Bannon. What good are you to Fiona if you get yourself killed?"

"Mr. Bannon, please," Althea Smalley pleaded. "We ladies have adapted well to the hardships along the trail. We can load our rifles and shoot straight. I think we've proven that. Tell us the direction we're to go, and we'll stay the course, but I beg of you to take Isaiah with you."

Bannon spoke quietly, matter-of-factly, and with no expression. "So be it, then."

He turned to the scout. "Sling a saddle on the horses. Grab two extra boxes of cartridges—one for our side-arms and one for the carbines."

"Don't have to tell me twice." Isaiah Thomas swung up on his pinto. He reached for the sorrel's reins and rode off to their night camp to saddle the horses.

Bannon surveyed the group of trail weary women. They'd fought gnats and droves of mosquitoes, defended each other against an Indian attack, and did the impossible by driving their wagons through a herd of buffalo. They'd buried their dead, had worked hard, and silently suffered.

He clamped down firm on the direction of his

thoughts as he addressed the women. "Ladies, this is the truest test of your courage. I expect you to listen to your wagon captains—trust them to make the right decisions."

"How long you plan to be gone, Mr. Bannon?" Gerda Olsson wanted to know.

"As long as it takes, Miz Olsson." He waited to see if others had questions. His expression didn't change as he met their eyes. He could sense their apprehension. There was a brief hesitation when he called, "Bird LeBlanc?"

"I am here." The Iroquois woman stepped forward.

"In my absence, you will act as scout. Choose one of the ladies to ride with you. Safety in pairs. In the event of danger, don't play the hero. Put the spurs to your ponies and high-tail it back to the wagons."

The Iroquois woman looked up at him, her dark eyes filled with pride. "I choose, Henrietta Hightower to ride with me. She good horsewoman. Shoot plenty good, too."

Henrietta stepped forward to stand shoulder-to-shoulder with Bird LeBlanc. "We won't let you down, Mr. Bannon."

His face grave with concern, he turned and pointed. "Keep moving due west. Try to make fifteen miles each day. If you reach the desert before Isaiah and I return, don't be foolhardy and try to cross it." Again, he pointed, his voice deadly serious, "Veer to the north and follow the base of the mountains, north by northwest. The way is longer, but there's water, shelter, and it's safer."

"I will do as you say, Mr. Bannon."

"Me, too," said Henrietta.

"Use the saddle horses in the remuda. You'll need to scout ahead to find a place to set-up camp each night." As an afterthought, he added, "Ladies, drive your wagons up to the spring and fill the barrels with fresh water before leaving this place. This time of year, what few watering holes are left between here and Oregon Territory might be dried up. If you come across one with scum floating on the surface, don't let the animals drink. They'll want to balk, but take the whip to 'em."

"What'd be wrong with the water, Mr. Bannon?" said Louise Schultz.

"Contaminated. Any living creature partaking of the smallest amount will die. And that includes humans." He glared at the women, waiting for a challenge. His voice softened, "With a lot of luck, Isaiah and I will find Fiona and return before the week is out."

Althea Smalley and Mercy Anders pushed through the group to hand him two rawhide pouches. "Vittles."

Bannon's eyebrows lifted in question as Althea handed him a neatly folded green garment. Her throat was thick as she said, "As worn and faded as this dress is, Fiona'll need something else to wear besides her nightshift. And tucked inside is a fresh pair of drawers."

When Isaiah rode up, he tossed Bannon the sorrel's reins. "Ready to ride, Cordell?"

Bannon touched the brim of his hat. "Ladies, good luck to you."

Althea blinked back the tears rimming her eyes. "Bring our Fiona back to us safe and sound."

With a reassuring nod to the women, he accepted the rawhide parfleches filled with food and two canteens of water. He walked over to Isaiah's horse and stuffed one sack of food inside the saddlebag, then a sack for himself. "We're burnin' daylight, Isaiah."

"Speak fer yourself, Cordell."

The men spurred their horses and rode off in the

direction of Devil's Gate.

****

The day was gray and misty and muddy. It wasn't the cold, damp ground that caused Fiona to clamp her teeth together to still her quivering chin. The bottom of her nightgown had been ripped off and stuffed in her mouth. Pain seeped through her shock, and agony crawled along her scalp and limbs, while her bruised cheek and jaw set up a torturous throbbing.

Her wrists were tied, and her ankles bound tightly together with strips of leather. She flexed her fingers against the numbness from lack of circulation, and her wrists hurt from the rawhide burns. Tears blurred her vision of the men, but in her mind she saw them very clearly.

Buffalo hunters and rawhiders were more treacherous than renegade Indians. Living for months on the prairie, killing and skinning buffalo, Bannon had said these men showed up at the yearly prairie jamborees to trade the hides for whiskey and supplies. A scrofulous bunch, they were usually considered less than human. Isaiah Thomas had further explained that these men often suffered from Prairie Fever. He'd pointed to his head, making a circular motion with his finger. *Leaves 'em crazy as rabid coyotes and twice as dangerous. Respected by none and feared by most.*

Men's voices instantly brought Fiona to full awareness. Her mind raced in every direction as she realized her fate. She pulled her knees up to her chest, wanting to curl up in Bannon's arms and tell him how scared she was. A lump of terror formed in her throat. *Bannon, where are you?*

A wild cackle drifted across the camp fire. She opened her eyes to mere slits. The men were unshaven. Matted hair hung beneath their hats. She crinkled her nose at their stench.

Grease dribbling down his chin, one man squatted across the fire tore at the piece of charred meat held in his beefy hands. A rabbit or a bird, she guessed. Responding to the aroma, her stomach made little squeezing noises.

He wiped his hand across the back of his mouth. "Why'd you have to go and hit 'er so hard, Rufus?"

"Hellfire, I only tapped her on the chin. What'd you 'spect after she bit a plug outta me." His laughter sounded phlegmy. "Ain't had me a white woman, in so long, I can't rightly disremember."

"Yeah, white women's got spunk." The buffalo skinner watched Fiona for a minute, grinning. He pushed from the ground and walked toward her, a leering grin on his face.

The lanky man stuck out his foot and sent his partner sprawling face down in the dirt. The grizzled buffalo skinner whined, "Now why'd you go and do that for, Rufus?"

"Who was it that spied out that wagon train, Otis?"

"You."

"Dang right. And whose idea was it to get us one of them women?"

"Your'n."

The taller of the two men pointed a sooty finger at his partner. "You ain't a dumb as you look, Otis."

Fiona thought that if the thickset man behind the grease-caked beard was capable of pouting, he was doing it right now, with his head hung low and muttering obscenities under his breath.

Rufus tapped his temple. "I'm the brains of this here outfit. You'd best remember that."

Otis shoved to his knees and shimmied to his side of the fire. He uncorked the bottle next to his bedroll. After chugging down a generous gulp, he winced as if the liquid burned his throat. He turned mean, rheumy eyes toward Rufus. "Yeah, and I'm yer brother. Mama allowed how we was to share 'n share alike, and don't you go forgittin' that."

Rufus surrendered a wry grin. "Reckon it's time to wake the little gal up. What say you, brother?" "We gonna do 'er now?" The skinner slapped his hands together and cackled. "I got me an ache bigger'n buff'lo balls." He massaged his crotch and groaned.

"Hold yer taters, Otis. You always were too impatient. 'Sides, I'm the oldest, so I get the first go at 'er."

Fiona clamped her eyes shut feigning sleep. The one called Rufus squatted next to her. He pulled the skinning knife from its leather sheath, using the tip of the razor sharp blade to lift a strand of hair draped across her shoulder.

The man's overpowering stench caused Fiona to draw in a deep breath. She tried not to breathe.

"Ooowee. Same color as a blood moon." With a swift movement, he sliced off the auburn curl and lifted it to his nose inhaling its fragrance before opening his scalp sack that hung around his waist, placing the curl inside. He sheathed the knife. Lifting another strand of hair, he rubbed it between his thumb and forefinger. "Feels like silk."

"How'd you know, Rufus? When'd you ever feel of silk?"

Fiona heard the slap and then the responding grunt. She visualized the wallop the man called Rufus had laid on his brother.

In a reverent tone that suggested some far away memory, Rufus said, "Had me a hurdy-gurdy whore onct. She wore a red silk dress. Feel 'er hair Otis, softer than ermine."

Finding the stench of two sweat-caked, unwashed bodies overpowering, Fiona gasped out the breath she was holding. Her eyes flew open. She jerked back.

Otis jabbed an elbow at his brother. "Hot damn. Green eyes."

"What's your name, girl?"

She squinted up at him. "Go to hell."

The lanky man slapped his thigh as he let out a belly-busting laugh. "Ooowee, that's a good'un. *Go to hell.*" He grinned over at his brother.

Otis said, "It's plain as the nose on your face that this here is a re-fined woman. You gotta introduce yourself then ask polite-like."

"Prob'ly right, Otis. Me and you got to get to a town more often so's to practice up our manners."

He fixed his dark gaze on her, silently mocking her. "My name's Rufus, and this here's my baby brother, Otis."

She looked at the squat-legged, squint-eyed man with a tobacco stained beard and two missing front teeth. "My mule is named Rufus. And you're as butt-ugly as him."

The blood instantly drained from her face when he jerked her up. After hours of having her ankles tightly bound, pain shot up her legs, causing her to sag against the man for support.

"I-I'll tell you my name if you'll untie my hands and feet." A rush of emotions filled her, and tears burned behind her eyelids.

"Don't matter what you're called, girlie. The outcome's gonna be the same. 'Sides you might try to run off." His fingers bit into her arms.

"Ah, come on, Rufus. Cut 'er loose. How far can an itty-bitty, green-eyed witch get without water?"

Her wrist ached from being bound, her back was sore from lying on the hard ground. She held out her hands. "Untie me."

Tears of self-pity welled in her eyes, and she blinked them back. She wouldn't cry. She wouldn't give Rufus and his brother the satisfaction of knowing how afraid she was.

She struggled for something to say. Her eyes roamed to the charred meat dripping over the fire on a make-shift spit.

"I'm hungry." She shoved her hands toward him.

Rufus pulled out the knife and with expert precision, the rawhide straps fell to the ground. She rubbed her wrist while he bent and sliced through the leather binding her ankles and knew he wouldn't hesitate to slit her throat with the same accuracy.

"Please take me back to the wagon train, or point me in the right direction and I'll walk. I won't say anything about you, honest. I'll just say I went out to take care of my necessities and got lost in the dark."

Rufus grasped her chin in his hand so hard that she bit down on her lip to keep from crying out. "Don't think you understand, girlie. You're me and brother's play pretty. You ain't going no where 'til we've wrung all the fun outta you."

Arms akimbo, she yanked loose of his grip. Her breath drawn, she hurled every vile, contemptible name she could lay on him. The words caught in her throat when he whipped out the knife, the tip biting into the soft under-flesh of her chin.

Otis grabbed his brother's arm. "You can carve on her later." He pointed, and Fiona followed the direction of his arm. "Look yonder."

Rufus' eyes narrowed as he squinted into the sun. "Riders, moving fast."

"How many, you reckon?"

"By the size of the dust they're kickin' up, I'd say two, mebbe, three."

"Bannon," Fiona whispered. Hope surged through her.

"Git 'er on a horse, pronto." Rufus grabbed up his saddle.

"What 'bout our stuff?"

"Leave it."

Otis took a step toward her, arms extended, and recoiled with a jerk when she punched hard with her fist. Blood dripped from the man's blob of a nose.

She retreated backward, shocked at what she'd done, while he roared and dabbed at his nose with his greasy sleeve.

Her feet took flight. He tripped her, then reached down and grabbed a fistful of hair, hauling Fiona upright. Her temper raged. She lashed out with her foot, landing a blow to his shin with her brogan. He howled and hopped on one foot.

He made a grab for her and quickly backed away when she doubled up her fist again and growled at him.

She swallowed the knot in her throat and sucked in a deep breath, trying to quell her fear and forced herself to think logically.

Her mistake was thinking she could outrun her kidnappers. She clutched the skirt of her nightgown in both hands and bolted, running as hard and fast as she could.

"Rufus, the girl," Otis shouted.

She glanced over her shoulder to see Otis put the spurs to his gelding. She had a good head start on her captors. Even so, the horse's speed cut the distance in half.

She didn't know if it was the sound of the hooves or the thumping of her heart that thundered in her ears. She chanced a glance over her shoulder. Desperation filled her at the sight of the buffalo hunter's maniacal grin.

The horse's hot breath bore down on her, its left shoulder ramming into her, throwing her to the ground.

She felt as if the very life had been knocked out of her. She sprang to her feet oblivious to the scrapes on her knees and the palms of her hands and the pain in her shoulder.

When Rufus wheeled the horse around, her face drained of color and a terror widened her eyes. A cry of anguish escaped her lips as she fell to her knees and clamped her hands together.

Chapter Seventeen

Fiona struggled for air. She clawed at the hands around her neck. If God willed it, she would live to see her captors dead before she allowed either to violate her.

Otis pulled his horse to a skidding halt. Leaping from the saddle, he grabbed his brother from behind, wrapping him in a bear hug. "Rufus...Rufus. Let go. You cain't be killin' no white woman."

Fiona toppled to her side, sucking air into her starving lungs. The glaze over her eyes cleared as she watched Rufus whip out his knife. The brothers crouched, circling like two grizzly bears spoiling for a fight.

The knife Rufus held glinted bright in the sunlight. Fiona lifted a hand to shade her eyes against the momentary blinding glare. She didn't know how long the men circled each other. A second, a minute, an hour—time had lost all meaning. Otis sidestepped as his brother swathed the knife through the air.

Otis stumbled backward over Fiona and sprawled flat of his back. She had no idea he could move that fast when he shoved her out of the way, reached down, grabbed a handful of dirt and tossed it in his brother's face.

Dropping the knife, Rufus' hands flew protectively toward his eyes. He yowled, "I'm blind. You'll pay for this, Otis."

With the agility of an acrobat, Otis sprang to his feet, bunched his fist, hurled a mighty swing and

146

knocked Rufus to the ground. Heaving deep breaths, Otis said, "Yer plumb tetched in the noggin, brother. Ain't you heerd what I said...you cain't kill a white woman. It's agin the law."

A frown contorted Rufus' face as he used the back of his hands to wipe his eyes. "Well, c'mon then." He squinted at the horizon. "That cloud of dust yonder is gettin' closer."

Fiona silently damned the pair and watched Rufus gather the reins and prepare to mount. "Prob'ly Injuns. Either way, the girl's our'n and we ain't sharin'."

Otis reached down and roughly yanked Fiona to her feet and tossed her wriggling form up to his brother. Rufus cautioned, as he straddled her across the saddle in front of him. "Don't you try to jump off this here horse, girlie. 'Cause next time I'll trample you in the dirt, 'stead of knocking you down."

A combination of fear and anger crimped Fiona's brow. "You and your mangy brother will rue the day you laid your filthy hands on me."

Rufus used the heel of his hand to club her on the back of the head. "Shet your hole, girlie. I'll deal with you later." He wrapped his arm around her, trapping her against his chest. He spurred the gelding. "We're 'bout two hours from the Big Hill. We'll hide out there."

"Stop yer jabbering and get a move on. I ain't fer dodging bullets," Otis shouted.

****

The sun shimmered off the ground in waves of scorching heat, making travel brutal.

Fiona squeezed her eyes shut and prayed wordlessly. The hoof beats behind them were growing further away. A sob burst inside her. She clamped her lips together refusing to let it out.

She wanted to go home, except she had no home. Even if she escaped, where would she go? She had no idea where she was. She longed for the comfort of the bumpy covered wagon she shared with her friends, and as ugly and cantankerous as they were, she missed the mules. She closed her eyes against the sun that burned them and thought of Ireland, her father's fiddle playing, and her brother's playful teasing. They were dead, and soon she would be, too.

She wanted to cry, but had no tears. And after two hours of riding, the insides of her bare thighs were chafed raw from scrubbing against the saddle and the constant forward motion of the galloping horse.

Where are you, Bannon? Please save me.

She placed a hand across her closed eyes hoping to shield them from the coppery rays of the sun. Her head lolled against her chest. Exhaustion took over.

She gave a little cry that came out as a croak. How long had she slept? She scrambled to her hands and knees, her eyes searching through the darkness, and her heart wildly pounding. She was in a cool, quiet place. Stars twinkled overhead.

Fire flickered, and she made out the hidden form of Rufus within the shadows of the tall aspen trees. He stood guard, rifle in hand while Otis squatted at a fire roasting meat on a stick. She knew that her very life depended on how clearheaded she remained.

Panic knotted her stomach. She struggled with her restraints, wincing at the pain she inflicted upon herself when the rawhide dug into her flesh. If only they hadn't bound her ankles, she could push herself up on her feet and charge Otis, knocking him into the fire, maybe even kick him in the head and make a run for it. Scanning the area, she spotted the horses, saddled, but hobbled.

The buffalo hunters hadn't given her even the smallest advantage. She forced herself to concentrate on the leather strips binding her wrists.

Otis walked over and squatted next to Fiona. He jabbed a stick against her shoulder. "Supper."

"What is it?"

"Rattlesnake."

Fiona shook her head, her stomach rebelling at the thought of eating anything that slithered on its belly.

Otis gingerly slid a piece of hot meat off the stick. He blew to cool the morsel before popping it in his mouth. "Taste like prairie chicken." He smacked his lips as he chewed. "Better eat up, girlie. You gonna need your strength for what we got in mind." He laughed, excitedly, a sound that reminded Fiona of a braying mule.

She jerked her head aside and kept her face impassive, but everything from her toes up was tightening into hard, cold knots.

Vicious laughter filled her ears as she glared hatefully back at the man squatting in front of her. He reached forward and lifted a strand of hair, rubbing it between his greasy fingers. "Get yerself ready, girlie. Soon's me and Rufus fill our bellies, we gonna have us some de-ssert."

His fingers played down her throatlatch to the buttons lining her nightgown. Leisurely, he patted and teased. She tried to forget all feeling by staring at the indifferent moon. She frantically struggled with the restraints around her wrists. These were no ordinary men. Both Otis and his brother were insane, and once finished with their ravaging, they would kill her. This she knew for certain.

"Ain't never in my whole life seen skin like cream...all over..." He shoved her nightgown up to her waist, his fingers probing between the fine coppery hairs of her mound.

She became wild, almost senseless. "No...please no..." Her mind working frantically, she said, "Rufus will kill you. He said so...remember?"

Otis sat back on his haunches. The moonlight flashed on his bared teeth. At length, he unbuttoned his breeches and relieved himself, making gurgling noises of enjoyment.

Fiona tried not to look at him and turned her head as far as she could and stared out in the darkness.

Rufus called for his brother. "Otis, git your fat ass on back here." He growled, "I'll split your guts if'n you're trying to bust that girl. I'm the oldest, and I've already told you I get first rights."

Otis' mouth sought hers in a passionate frenzy, and it seemed an eternity passed before he broke away with a sigh, leaving her gagging and spent.

"Gotta spell Rufus while he eats." Otis ambled off into the shadows.

Fiona desperately worked the straps binding her wrists, twisting and turning her hands in an effort to stretch the leather enough to free one hand. Her arms and shoulders ached, the delicate bones in her wrists bruised, the flesh bleeding.

She brought her hands to her mouth and used her teeth to chew at the knot. The leather didn't give.

A twig snapped, drawing her attention away from her task. It was the way he walked, the leer on his face that brought her defenses up. She had thought it was impossible to feel terror again. She thought her poor brain was too dulled even to register the emotion, her body too exhausted and drained to fight.

Rufus squatted, he slid his knife from the leather sheath at his waist, and one-by-one, snipped the buttons from her nightgown. He used the blade to part the fabric. He stared at her breasts. He straightened her legs out in front of her and then sliced through the rawhide, freeing her ankles. He raised the blade high, then brought it down forcefully, stabbing the dirt next to her head.

Fiona's blood flowed icy cold, then feverishly, with dizzying rapidity. She could smell the layers of perspiration and buffalo grease clinging to his skin.

"No," she whispered, crossed her legs and drew her knees up under her.

Rufus grabbed her hair, grunting. "Just a little kiss, girlie." With the other hand, he fumbled with the strap holding up his leather breeches. He flung away the scalp sack and the empty scabbard that hung around his waist.

As he reached for her, Fiona lashed out with her feet, hitting him square in the chest. She rolled to her knees, but before she could stand and flee, Rufus grabbed hold and flung her down. He forced her legs apart with his knee, while he held her arms above her head.

"Got us a real wildcat, brother. Ooowee, I'm gonna squirt afore I can get me a poke. Git over here and spread-eagle her."

She heard Otis' gleeful shout as he supported the Sharps rifle against the tree he'd been leaning on. He clapped his hands together and danced a jig, giggling.

"Don't you worry none, girlie. After the first poke or two, you won't feel nothing." Otis knelt down and grabbed Fiona's feet. He wrapped a rawhide loop around one ankle and pulling her legs wide, tied the leather strip to a nearby sapling.

Otis giggled again as he tugged on the other leg. "I'll hold this 'un." He ran his hand up the length of her leg to caress her thigh.

Rufus' breathing quickened as he shoved Fiona's gown above her waist and looked at her nakedness, the curves of her hips and waist, the length of her, her white skin. He pushed his breeches down to his knees.

"Danged if'n you ain't build like a fine mustang

mare. All a quiver 'cause you ain't never been rode. Sets my blood afire jest lookin' at you." He ran his hands over the curves of Fiona's body. His yellow teeth flashed in a startling grin.

Exhausted beyond measure and her emotions well spent, she experienced a strange prickling down her spine. From far off it seemed she could hear her mother telling her to be brave.

Towering over her, he lowered himself down, his hands braced on either side of her head.

Her body stiffened at the sight of his throbbing manhood. Bile rose in her throat. Desperation surged through her like ice. And then she screamed. "No!" It was a hoarse sound that tore her throat and made it bleed, and it shattered the stillness of the plains.

****

In the darkness, caution warned Bannon to advance slowly as he and Isaiah inched on their bellies toward the flickering campfire. Time stretched into infinity. A thousand thoughts raced through Bannon's head all at one time. He shook off the possibility that Fiona was dead. Then her scream tore through him piercing the deepest depths of his soul. He felt his blood curdle.

"Gawl dang, egg-sucking bastard," Isaiah hissed, "I'm gonna split him four ways to Sunday."

Rage filled Bannon, twisting his insides into a knot, tightening the muscle in his jaw, flaring his nostrils. He bolted to his feet and through clenched teeth, growled, "Move away from the girl." He brought his rifle to his shoulder.

Otis jerked around. "Holy shit...my..."

Isaiah held up the Sharps rifle. "Lookin' for this?"

A second passed before Bannon's tall figure moved into the firelight, his eyes shadowed by a fierce frown, the rifle aimed at Rufus' back. "Get off her, you bastard."

Rufus scooted back on his knees. His eyes searched the ground. A half-crazed, bellowing snarl exploded from his lips as he yanked the knife from the ground and pushed himself upright. He twisted as he drew back his arm. He was rewarded by the click of a rifle bolt that carried clearly through the darkness. The rifle's shot cracked like a whip. The knife fell from Rufus' hand.

Bannon fired again. Rufus fell forward, landing on his shoulder. His arm hung limp and useless, and while he breathed laboriously, his eyes darted in the dark shadows, insanity glowing like red-hot coals in their dark depths.

He gurgled as red sputum frothed from his mouth. "Otis, I never even got me one poke." His eyes rolled back in his head, he fell forward and sprawled on the ground.

"Sonafabitch. You done gone and kilt my brother." Even if Otis had wanted to run, he didn't stand a chance in hell of getting away alive. Fear weighed heavy in his eyes. "We was just havin' a little fun. We'd a turned her loose."

There was a peculiar expression on his face something almost like a smile in the flickering firelight as he eased his hand around to his back.

An eerie quiet had fallen across the campsite.

Fiona screamed, "Bannon, look out, he's got a knife."

Isaiah fired, the shot went wild. Otis drew back and with great skill, he pushed all his strength into the throw. The blade hit its mark, burying deep into Isaiah's shoulder.

Bannon swung his rifle up and fired. Otis grabbed his throat, dropped to his knees and died.

The killing haze that clouded Bannon's eyes lifted. Running to her, he slipped the knife from its sheath. On bended knees, he sliced through the leather throngs that bound her. "Fiona," he breathed, drawing her close and brushing his lips across her temple. "I thought I'd lost you."

She wept, hugging him tightly, her head against his chest.

"Did they...did they hurt you?" Bannon asked through tight lips.

"Not in the way you're thinking." Her voice quavered as tear-filled eyes looked at him.

Isaiah groaned, interrupting the intimate moment. Fiona turned her attention to the old scout. "He's badly hurt."

Bannon knelt beside his friend. He gripped the knife's handle. "Gonna hurt like hell, old friend."

The scout squeezed his eyes shut. "I'm a tough ole bird. Do what you gotta do."

Perspiration beaded Bannon's forehead. "Suck in a deep breath."

Isaiah nodded. Blood spread across his shirt as Bannon yanked the blade from Isaiah's shoulder. He jabbed the razor sharp instrument into the dirt to remove the blood, then he walked over and knelt down, holding the blade over the campfire's low-burning flame. "We need to cauterize the wound to stop the bleeding."

Fiona ripped the bottom of her nightgown, tearing a wide strip to use as dressing for the injury. "I'm afraid it isn't very clean."

Bannon lifted the white-hot blade from the fire. He pushed up Isaiah's shirt. The skin sizzled as he laid the knife against the gaping hole.

Fiona covered her mouth, her eyes bright with unshed tears. "While you do something with t-those bodies, I'll bind up Isaiah's wound."

Chapter Eighteen

Exhausted and hungry, Fiona immersed herself in the deepest end of the stream, allowing the water to cover her breasts. The soothing liquid cooled the chafed flesh between her legs. From this point on, she vowed to never again go to bed without wearing a pair of undergarments.

Longing for a bar of soap, she reached down and grabbed a handful of sand from the stream's bottom, and rubbed her body from head to toe. No matter how hard she scrubbed, the stench of Otis and his deranged brother lingered in her nostrils.

A half an hour later, she sat in front of the campfire, cradling a mug of coffee. "It was thoughtful of Ma Smalley to send along a dress." In spite of the warm July night, she shuddered.

"Are you cold, Fiona?" Bannon handed her a plate of fried trout.

"I-I can't seem to get those men's stink off of me." She set the plate aside, lowered her head to her knees, and for the first time since being kidnapped by lunatic brothers, run over by a horse, and nearly raped, she wept.

Bannon rose so quietly she didn't hear him leave the campfire. When he returned, he poured a generous splash of whiskey into her coffee and held the cup out to her. "There's a plant the Indians call *yerba buena*. The women use it as a medicine and as a fragrance. I'll find you some in the morning."

She smiled and nodded, but didn't drink. Bannon's voice was calm and quiet as he gently guided the mug to her lips. "Go ahead and drink, Fiona. It'll help you relax."

He leaned against his saddle, stretched his long legs toward the fire, and sipped his own whiskey laced coffee.

Fiona lifted the hem of her dress and wiped her eyes. "How soon will Isaiah be well enough to travel?"

"Tomorrow, I'll fashion a travois. If the ole buzzard is up to it, we'll pull out the morning after."

Her eyes met his. "What is a travois?"

"It's like a cart without wheels." Bannon went on to explain how the Indians hitched the device to their horses to move their belongings when they traveled from winter camp to summer camp.

"Ingenious," she whispered. She grimaced at the bitterness of the coffee. "Not as good as Irish whiskey." And tossed the bitter remains to the ground.

Firelight glimmered in Bannon's blond hair and caressed the strength of his jaw. His mouth was set in a hard line, and a vein pulsed in his neck. Certain her voice would crack if she spoke, her eyes fluttered. The effects of the whiskey coursed through her body. She yawned, taking a moment to collect her courage and cool the strange warmth that had attacked her.

"Mr. Bannon may I..." she hesitated, chewed her bottom lip.

"May you what, Fiona?"

It was so peaceful here it was hard for her to imagine that she'd survived a horrible ordeal, that Rufus and his brother were dead. Moments passed while she savored the quietude of her surroundings. It wasn't long before the answering howls of wolves shattered her thoughts.

"May I sleep next to you?" He was kind and generous, and he'd come to rescue her. Cordell

Bannon was the sort of man any woman would be proud to claim as a husband. So why couldn't she? And then she remembered—her contract, his contract—they were both honor bound by a piece of paper. She honestly would have liked falling in love with him, but she wouldn't let that happen.

She pulled the long hair off her neck and to calm her nervous fingers plaited it into a thick braid.

****

Bannon patted the place next to his saddle. Fiona stepped around the campfire and lay with her back to him. Her knees drawn to her chest, she reminded him of a small child. He pulled the horse blanket up to her shoulders, and as she sighed, he whispered, "Sleep well, Fiona."

He felt no guilt at killing the two buffalo hunters. Rufus and his brother needed to die. Sweet, gentle Fiona did not deserve what had happened to her. She was a fragrant flower, a bloom ready to be picked, and he wanted to do the picking.

Shifting to his side, he propped up on an elbow. He slowly raised a hand to stroke her cheek with the backs of his fingers. His lips tenderly brushed her forehead.

He molded his muscular frame to hers, wrapping her protectively in his arms. A fire erupted within his belly, traveling down to his crotch. Refusing to allow desire to cloud his judgment, he chased away all thoughts of sampling her fruit.

Closing his eyes, he mumbled, "I don't love you, Fiona Quinn." Angry and frustrated with his train of thinking, he shifted away, turning his back to hers.

****

Eight days later Fiona sat slumped in the saddle. Sighing wearily, she rolled her shoulders to relax the kinks in her spine. Behind Bannon's sorrel, Isaiah slept on the travois, the last glints of sunlight playing across his face. The quiet was broken only by the rustle of a breeze through the grasses all around her and the travois poles scraping against the ground.

The shadows were deep and haunting, enveloping her. True to his word, Bannon had located bunches of the *yerba buena*. She had bathed and rubbed the plant's pleasant mint fragrance over her body and through her hair, at last eradicating the malodorous scent of the men who'd dared harm her. She hadn't asked Bannon what he'd done to dispose of the bodies. For all she cared, the vultures could feast on them.

Bannon had set the buffalo hunter's badly emancipated ponies free, and for a while the horses had followed along as if not knowing what do without human contact before wandering off to join a herd of wild mustangs.

The brother's two rifles were useless without cartridges. Bannon said the weight would slow them down and had wrapped the weapons in a horse blanket and hid them inside a crevice among the rocks. The rest of what belonged to the dead men, he left for the weather to destroy. She hadn't argued.

While they rested during the heat of the day, Fiona was amazed at how Bannon used the North Star to guide them at night. They had survived off small game. Each day when they camped, she'd make a broth out of whatever Bannon provided. She'd spoon feed Isaiah and changed the dressing on his wound, using the remains of her nightgown.

The memories of that first night she'd slept next to Bannon feathered into her consciousness—his hard, male body pressed to her soft one, the sensual travels of his hands over her sensitive flesh.

The next morning she'd asked him to tell her about the name he'd whispered in his sleep.

"Was Annie your wife?"

He'd glanced up, puzzled and then angry. "Did

Isaiah tell you about her?"

She'd seen the flash of pain he'd quickly masked behind somber blue eyes. She'd shrugged. "Last night, you held me, the way a man might hold his wife and you called me—Annie."

A strange array of feelings had enveloped Fiona—jealousy, uncertainty, loneliness. "You once said that you were responsible for her death."

"Sometimes I talk too much."

"And sometimes, talking helps ease the pain." She'd wanted to touch him, to comfort him, but thought it better to appear aloof. "Oh, stuff and bother. I can't imagine you ever deliberating hurting anyone, Mr. Bannon." She gently coaxed, "Tell me about her—about Annie."

His eyes saddened. "Drop the *mister*, Fiona. Bannon will do fine."

She'd nodded while remaining silent, waiting. He'd stood, paced about restlessly. "Annie was the exact opposite of my stature. She wasn't much bigger than a minute and had a smile that could warm the coldest day. I loved her very much."

His voice was husky when he continued. "My ranch was a good ride from town. Annie's labor started a month earlier than expected. By the time Isaiah got back with the doctor, blood was everywhere." He clasped his hands over his ears. "Sometimes I can still hear her screams, begging me to stop the pain."

Anguish tore from his throat, and Fiona wiped the tears wetting her cheeks. "The doctor gave her laudanum. We waited for hours, Isaiah and me. Then the doctor came out and shook his head. The last thing he said before leaving was that big men should never marry small women because they weren't built for delivering big babies."

Bannon had stood there trembling, his hands drawn to his hips. Fiona went to him and held him

159

close. Then he'd drawn back, wiped away the evidence of his grief, saddled his horse and rode off.

After he'd disappeared she collapsed into a sobbing bundle upon the warm earth. Each night afterward, she made a point of sleeping away from Bannon and vowed to never mention his wife again.

Now at odds with herself, she looked up at the moon. She wanted to feel the warm and tender awakenings again. She had an ache in her heart that refused to go away.

Her forehead creased. *I cannot allow myself to fall in love with this man. He considers me nothing more than an alternate bride whose name is likely to be drawn from the lottery if another woman dies before we reach Oregon Territory.* She lifted her eyes heavenward. *Please don't let anyone else die.*

Fiona drew herself back to the present. "How much longer, Bannon? Isaiah's wound is festering."

He scanned the northern horizon. "We should have spotted them by now, unless Bird and Henrietta have veered off course. Maybe tomorrow."

"For Isaiah's sake, I hope you're right." The ashen pallor on the scout's face worried Fiona.

****

"Dear Lord," Fiona spoke the two words with enthusiasm as she pointed toward the bright globes of light against the darkness. "How far?"

"Mile, two at the most." Bannon warned, "Could be our wagon train—could be buffalo hunters."

"Oh." Fiona swallowed hard. The last thing she desired was another encounter with foul-smelling, sex-crazed renegades.

"Hold up, Fiona." He held up his hand signaling her to stop.

They reined in their horses. Bannon swore under his breath. He pulled the Sharps from the rifle boot and laid it across the crook in his left arm.

"If it's buffalo hunters, I'll ride on in with

Isaiah." There was a grim cast to his face. "Here's what I want you to do—hang back about a hundred yards. Don't follow me into the camp. Give me ten minutes. If I don't signal you to come in then, quiet as a church mouse, cut a wide circle around the perimeter, then put the spurs to that pony and head north." Bannon pointed toward the North Star. "Let the star guide you."

"But, I—"

"Don't argue with me, girl," Bannon hissed.

Fiona wordlessly nodded. She nudged the pinto forward at a slow walk, lagging behind Bannon's sorrel.

They approached the camp, and when close enough, Bannon called, "Hello the camp."

Fiona heard the ominous click of a rifle bolt that carried clearly though the darkness. "Bannon?"

"I heard it."

A woman's voice demanded, "Who goes there?"

Ten minutes later, Fiona found herself surrounded by the jubilant faces of the women at the wagon train.

With hugs shared all around, Fiona extracted herself from the weeping figure of Althea. "Isaiah is badly hurt, Ma Smalley."

"You and Bannon look plumb tuckered out." Althea shouted orders. "Henrietta, ride out and bring Bird LeBlanc in. I'll need her to assist me with the doctoring. Mercy, don't just stand there gawking like you got nothing else to do. Get my box of medical supplies." Althea shifted her gaze. "Gerda Olsson, where are you?"

"Ja?" The Swedish woman stepped forward.

"These young'uns look pert near starved to death. Get your ladies to fixin' up some vittles, and make a good strong broth for Isaiah." Althea huffed out her commands like a drill sergeant."

Louise Schultz said, "What can I do?"

Amused as he was at the way Althea had taken charge, he said, "Bird the only one standing guard?"

Lou winged up the corner of her lip. "You can't see 'em, but we've got women on all points." She grinned. "Didn't know who you were 'til you hailed the camp, but we had you spotted."

Bannon clicked his tongue as he stood quietly in the circle of women. "It's been a long ride back. I thank you for looking after Isaiah." He tipped his hat. "Soon as the horses are tended, I'll be back for a plate of vittles."

The flickering glow of campfires reflected in his eyes as he quietly studied Fiona—disheveled, stoic, beautiful.

She whispered, "I'm sorry to have been the cause of so much trouble."

She reminded him of a child needing comfort and wanted to enfold her into his arms, to assure her that time healed all wounds. Yet, he knew he was being hypocritical for time had not healed his.

He brushed his hand across her hair and looked down at her. "No trouble, Fiona. I would have come after you, no matter what. You're worth saving," came his husky response.

"I thought that..." Her breath caught and she shrugged a shoulder, "you—"

Instantly, he cut her off. "Miz Smalley, Fiona needs the healing attentions of a woman. See to her, if you will."

He laid a hand on Fiona's shoulder and stood there for a time. "Rest well, Fiona. Tomorrow's another day."

The sky had never seemed so big, the dark had never seemed so thick. After seeing to Isaiah's comfort, tending the horses and sating his appetite with fried ham, beans and coffee, Bannon leaned back against a tree and tried to get comfortable. Even though, Fiona had assured him that neither brother had satisfied their animal urges inside her, he felt a cry of outrage rising in his throat.

****

Fiona was grateful for Althea's and Henrietta's help as she bathed. They had a quart of warm water left over from dinner and saved in a stone bowl. The rest was cold water out of a bucket, but the kindness and concern that went with it caused Fiona to weep. The women touched her scratches and rawhide burned wrists and ankles with a healing ointment, held cold wet clothes to her bruised face, while Mercy combed sand and trash out of Fiona's long auburn hair.

"I hate to cry," she muttered irritably to herself and scrubbed at her wet lashes.

"Fiona," Mercy smiled at her. "It's going to be all right. Trust me, I know."

Fiona held on to Mercy, and Mercy held on to her, giving comfort for the secret they shared.

At last Fiona lay on her cot in the warm darknes—wide awake. Her still distraught mind fed back over what the buffalo hunters had done to her, and again she felt the loathsome, indecent proddings and cuppings. The recollection shamed her. When Mercy had related how Blackie Sledge and his men had raped her, Fiona had empathized but hadn't fully understood what the girl had suffered. She still could hardly conceive how men could be so evil-minded, so cruel.

The night wore on. Slowly an inner warmth reached Fiona's heart. Gradually, she realized her living nightmare was over. Still the uneasiness she felt annoyed her because it was totally unfounded.

She was safe.

They were all safe—weren't they?

Chapter Nineteen

Bright sunshine intruded rudely upon Fiona's sleep when Mercy flung open one of the wagon's canvas flaps the next morning. Groaning her disapproval, Fiona rolled onto her stomach and buried her head beneath the pillow, closing out the light, and muffling out the girl's cheery greeting that it was indeed a beautiful sunrise and Fiona shouldn't miss it. Little did Mercy know Fiona had already seen the early markings of dawn and had just now managed to fall asleep. She'd spent the entire night tossing and turning in bed, all of which had failed to distract her thoughts away from the ugly leering faces of Rufus and his brother, Otis.

Fiona released a long sigh as she pushed the mop of curls from her face. "We're moving."

"Of course, silly." Mercy shoved a mug of coffee and a slice of corn pone toward Fiona. "Been moving for nearly an hour. You were sleeping so peaceful like Ma Smalley said to let you be. 'Specially after what you'd been through and all."

Fiona's eyebrows gathered in a perplexed frown as though a thousand muddled thoughts were pulling together within her brain. She thanked Mercy for the meager meal, and still hungry from days of measly rations, devoured the cornbread sweetened with honey.

"Stuff and bother. 'Tis for sure I can't be moping in the bed all day. What's done is past. I still own my virginity, and I'm no worse for wear." She swallowed the last dram of coffee, and as she handed the cup to

Mercy, noticed the bump at the girl's waistline.

Seeing the direction of Fiona's eyes, Mercy placed her hands over the small swell. "I can't hide it much longer, can I?"

Fiona didn't miss the dark desperation in Mercy's eyes. She reached out and took the girl's hand and held it. "Don't you worry, Mercy. If Mr. Henry Filmore won't accept you, I'll take care of you."

"Oh, Fiona, you would do that for me? But, how?"

Fiona pondered the question. "I still have my fifty dollars from the bride's money. That will last for a while, and surely, there are jobs to be had in Glory. Maybe a newspaper office where I can draw pictures of ads." Fiona sounded hopeful, even to herself. "Besides, my father always said things have a way of working out."

Mercy favored her with a sad smile. "I'm sorry to be such a pickle puss."

Fiona scooted off the bunk. She shed her nightgown and dressed in a drab green frock, slipped on her brogans, and said, "Never be sorry for something that isn't your fault. But you should be telling Ma Smalley, Mercy."

"I will, but not today." Mercy's eyes pleaded for understanding.

Fiona patted the girl's shoulder. "I'm going to check on Isaiah. Is he in the supply wagon?"

Without waiting for an answer, she unhitched the chains that held the wagon's end gate in place and lowered it. Sitting down and swinging her legs back and forth until she was in momentum with the movement of the wagon, she hopped to the ground without missing a step.

"It's a beautiful day, Mercy." Fiona stepped out of the way of the on coming wagon. She lifted her hand and waved. "Mornin' to you, Mrs. Gaffney."

The woman driving the mules returned the greeting. "Good to have you back safe and sound, Fiona."

Fiona called to each woman as their wagons passed. When the supply wagon came in sight, she stopped and waited. Bird LeBlanc slowed. "*Kwé Kwé*, Fiona."

"And a good morning to you, Bird. May I ride with you?"

The Iroquois woman slowed the wagon, and with deftness Fiona stepped on the wheel hub and swung up to the seat. "I've come to check on Isaiah."

The old scout, hearing his name, called out, "I'm fit as a fiddle, lass, jes' not quite ready for the dance."

A smile turned the corners of Fiona's mouth up as she winked at the Iroquois woman. "I'd say that whatever medicine you and Ma Smalley gave Isaiah is surely working its magic."

Bird clucked the mules to hasten their dawdling pace. "Him better. Be riding his horse soon. I like ride horse, too." She turned dark smiling eyes toward Fiona. "You drive wagon, I help Bannon scout." She handed the reins over to Fiona and jumped to the ground.

Isaiah climbed to sit beside Fiona. She spied the sling that cradled his injured arm. "You shouldn't be up and about. The fever might take hold again."

"Never felt better in my life. Like Bird said, in a day or two, I'll be riding that pinto pony of mine. Fine woman, that Bird LeBlanc."

"Were you ever married, Isaiah?"

He waggled bushy eyebrows at her. "Rascally feller like me, nah. Never felt much like settlin' down."

"What about now?" She'd not missed the inflection in his voice when he'd said Bird was a fine woman.

"You proposing, Miss Fiona?" He chuckled and gave her a wink.

She joined his good humor. "You're a fine figure of a man, Isaiah, but I was thinking more in terms of a certain French and Iroquois woman."

He harrumphed. "I'm a grizzled ole buzzard past his prime—even if she was available." He scratched the side of his nose. "Which she ain't."

Fiona smiled across at him. "How old are you, Isaiah?"

He scratched his chin. "Danged if I rightly know."

She listened to his muted calculations as he used his fingers to add up the years. He cleared his throat. "Best as I can calculate, I've seen fifty-six winters."

They rode along in silence for a while as if no more words needed speaking. Fiona sat on the hard seat, her thoughts running topsy-turvy through her brain, her fingers tightly looped through the broad leather reins, a painful emotion tugging a tidal wave within her. "I'm beholding, Isaiah. You almost lost your life saving mine."

His gray bushy brows pinched together. "If'n it weren't for your tendering touch on the trail, I'd a give up the ghost for sure. I'd say that makes us 'bout even."

He patted her arm. "Find myself gittin' a little tired." He climbed over the seat. Before disappearing inside the wagon, he said, "Cordell was like a bloodhound, Fiona. He would'na stopped 'til he found you. I ain't never seen him in such a fit as when Miz Smalley come a runnin' telling us you was gone." Then, as if knowing he'd said more than he should, he shrank back in the dim interior of the wagon.

"Thank you for telling me, Isaiah." She spoke the words softly. Drawing in a deep breath, she soothed her emotions by assuring herself there would be no more tragedies along the trail, that she would arrive in the town of Glory a free woman, and she would do everything within her power to win Cordell Bannon's heart.

Fiona relaxed against the wagon seat's backboard, listening to the steady rhythm of the mules' hooves and the hum of the wheels as they clattered across the hard packed earth.

Then realization smacked her as if being struck by lightning. *When had she allowed herself to fall in love?*

****

The endless days of travel across the prairie caused Fiona despair. The traveling was pleasant. Hickory, elm, and cottonwood trees provided shelter from the heat of the day. Isaiah's shoulder had healed, and he'd resumed his duties as scout, returning to camp each night with strings of quail, rabbit, and squirrel, enough for all.

Fiona helped Bird set out fishing lines, while Althea and Henrietta gathered herbs, berries, and edible roots. It wasn't the work that created Fiona's gloom. She needed sleep, but each night she tossed wakefully.

When at last she slept, she often had dreams in which her kidnappers dwelt roaming their hands over her body. She would waken in a profusion of sweat. She had reached such a point of agony that she often cried out in her sleep.

A gentle hand shook her awake. Fiona stared, wide-eyed and confused. She blinked. "Is something wrong?"

Althea handed the trembling girl a damp cloth. "You cried out. Were you dreaming, again?"

"I can't seem to get their faces out of my head."

"To have such a thing happen is a terrible shock, child. The best way to rid yourself is to write it all down in your little book. Don't leave out any details.

Include every frightful emotion you felt—hatred, and remorse. Write it all down." Althea smoothed a hand across Fiona's forehead. "And if it helps, draw their ugly mugs. Those men are dead, Fiona. Dead and buried. They can't hurt you or anyone else ever again. Only the memories can hurt you—if you allow it."

Fiona clasped Althea's hand to her cheek. "Bannon hasn't spoken to me in weeks. He was there and stopped those men before they...before they..." She couldn't bring herself to say the word rape. "Do you think he blames me?"

"No, child." Althea laughed half-heartedly. "It's more likely he blames himself for not protecting you, for not being able to keep you from being disgraced. Thankfully, he got there in time. Still and all, he's a man of strong principal. Killing is never easy—even if those low-down skunks deserved killing. Bannon needs time, just the same as you."

"What month is it, Ma Smalley? I seem to have lost track of time." Fiona spoke in whispers.

"If my calculations are right, we're about the middle of August." Althea sighed deeply. "Close your eyes and think sweet thoughts. Morning will come soon enough."

Fiona bade the older woman goodnight. When soft pattering snores filled the darkened interior, Fiona gathered her shawl, donned her shoes and slipped from the wagon.

She saw him down by the water's edge. He rose and began to fling off his clothing. It was the second time she'd seen him standing naked. Bathed in moonlight from his feet to his neck he was the powerful male, broad shouldered, slim hipped, long muscular legs. An ache grew in the pit of her stomach, her heart fluttered, and breathing became ragged.

Feeling confused by her emotions, she moved

forward. For once in her life she wanted to act as if life were made just for her.

****

A little moon had disappeared behind the hills, westward. The night was fragrant and still. Bannon stood at the water's edge. An unexpected yawn caught him off guard. Tugging his shirttail free, he pulled it over his head and dropped it to the ground. He'd slid out of his breeches when a strange feeling assailed him, a sense that from somewhere in the dark a pair of eyes watched his every moved. He inched his hand down and wrapped it around the hilt of the knife, slipping it from its sheath. His attention was keen as he quickly surveyed the night, every muscle in his tall frame rigid.

"Whoever you are, I suggest you move very slowly," he warned.

"Bannon, it's me," came the tiny frightened voice.

"Fiona?" Moonlight fell across her face and spotlighted her in its ashen glow, a vision that nearly took his breath away. Gathering his composure, he stepped into his breeches, and pulling them over his hips, he scolded, "Of all people, you ought to know that traipsin' around in the dark, alone, is dangerous."

"Don't be angry, please."

He laughed, but it was a torn, hurting laughter. It took a while before words reached him. "What are you doing out here?"

She gave him a damning look. "It's a free country. I can go anywhere I desire."

He gazed over her as he took a step closer. "So you can." He envisioned the two of them locked passionately in each others arms. He reached out to touch her lips with his fingertips. He moved within an inch of her, deliberately holding back though his arms ached to embrace her.

"Did you know your eyes turn the color of emerald when you're angry? And your hair..." he paused to twist a shiny lock around his finger. "It reminds me of the setting sun."

He wanted to tell her that there wasn't much about her that he didn't love. *Damn the contract all to hell...damn...damn!*

"I've tried so hard to stay away from you." A frown played across his face, and then he smiled. "You're a sweet Irish witch, Fiona Quinn, who's beguiled me. I love to hear you laugh, I love to watch you...writing in your journal of yours...picking wildflowers...standing here in the moonlight."

When she looked up at him, a tear caught in the corner of her eye glistened in the moonlight. "No man has ever said such wonderful things to me. Somehow, I feel unworthy of your praise."

"It isn't praise; it's the truth." A flash of white teeth showed with his warm smile as reached out to take her in his arms.

He read the invitation in her eyes as she gazed up at him. He bent toward her. She lifted her lips without question. His arms and her own rush of emotion pressed her to his clean, man-smelling skin. Their lips moved upon each other's, parted. Bannon sought with his tongue; she answered. Waves of gut-wrenching desire swept over him. Her shawl fell from her shoulders and he felt the hardening of her nipples through her thin nightshift. Her arms wrapped around him and returned his embrace.

When at last he released her, the moonlight showed her shining eyes, and he saw the flush of desire on her face. She was a woman ripe and ready for the taking, and he felt his own need growing hot and hard. He drew her into his arms again.

Bannon let her go and took her hand, kissing her palm in a way that sent her heart skittering.

He squinted down the river, his face changed.

He seemed to draw into himself. Something bitter came over him. "Get the hell away from me, Fiona. Go back to your wagon."

"But I-I...but why?" she asked, bewildered.

She flinched as the strength of his fingers bit into her arm. "Because of the damned contract, because we still have over a hundred miles before reaching Oregon Territory, because we still have another river to ford...because there's still the damned lottery..." The words came in angry bursts. "Take your pick, Fiona. I'm not God, and I can't control what He's ordained."

Chapter Twenty

The morning dawned hazy and hot, and the sun had barely broken the sky. Fiona didn't talk much during the day and even less at night. She tired of the women's conversations, which consisted mostly about meeting their new husbands, how they would furnish their new homes, and having children.

During the day she would search for sight of Bannon, and during the night she'd wrap herself in the sweet words he'd spoken to her that night at the river. He was a man who needed loving...needed a wife and children...and grandchildren.

Inside her journal, she created a calendar, tracking the number of days left before arriving in the town of Glory. Each day she crossed through brought another day's hope that she would arrive as a free woman to become Bannon's wife.

They followed the course of the Snake River along the forested bank, and the traveling was pleasant. The tall bluestem grass was plentiful.

At twilight Bannon rode to the lead wagon and held up his hand. "We'll make camp here, Fiona. Circle up."

Fiona pulled reluctantly on the reins. There was another hour of daylight and she didn't want to stop.

He raised his booming voice to be heard as far back as the fourth wagon. "We camp here tonight," he called as he urged his horse down the line of wagons.

By the time the women had taken care of their teams and made their camps, almost an hour had passed. Fiona watched timid Mercy Anders stroll away from the camp. She turned and waved at Fiona. "Time for a little privacy."

She was only a few feet away when Fiona noticed something odd about the shadow in the tall grass. A second later she knew what it was. She had barely broken into a run before hearing the ominous whirring and Mercy's scream.

"Don't run, Mercy," Fiona demanded in shrill alarm. "You'll only cause the poison to spread faster."

The frightened girl didn't listen. "A snake...I'm bit." Mercy screamed as she ran.

Fiona felt as if a cold hand squeezed her heart. She flung out the words, "Bannon...Mercy...rattler." She pressed a knuckled fist against her trembling lips as Bannon threw down the ladle of water and lunged into a sprint.

Someone shouted, "Kill it...kill the filthy serpent."

Closer than Bannon, Isaiah grabbed his shotgun and raced to where a six or more foot long rattler laid writhing and coiling on the ground. The shot echoed inside Fiona's skull.

Bannon scooped Mercy into his arms. With long strides he raced toward the encampment. Sweat made muddy rivulets on her forehead and cheeks, and her breathing was quick and shallow as he settled her on the ground beneath the shade of the wagon's canopy.

Fiona knelt by the girl. "Lie still, Mercy...just lie still."

Wide-eyed with fear, Mercy nodded as Bannon cut a rent up her stocking leg with his skinning knife. "Fiona, I need a strip of cloth," Bannon said, revealing an angry red wound on the calf of Mercy's leg.

Quickly, Fiona bent to lift the hem of her skirt

and tear off the bottom ruffle of her petticoat. She handed this to Bannon and watched as he tied a tourniquet around Mercy's leg. He glanced up. "Miz Smalley, get some whiskey," he ordered, but he was already cutting an X-shape on Mercy's badly swollen leg.

When crimson blood beaded on the lanced skin, he bent and put his mouth to the girl's flesh. He sucked hard, turned his head and spat, sucked again. Mercy cried out, her face was contorted with pain and fear.

The process continued for several more minutes, with Bannon loosening and tightening the tourniquet at intervals. Finally, Althea brought the requested whiskey. She poured the amber liquid into a cup and handed it to Bannon. He reached under Mercy's shoulders and lifted her. "Drink this."

She choked on the gulp, turned her head and threw up. "I-I'm sorry."

Fiona hushed the girl as she laid a damp, cool cloth over her forehead. "Hush, now. You've nothing to be sorry for."

Bannon filled his mouth, spat into the dirt, poured more whiskey past his lips, and swallowed. Then he shoved the bottle at Fiona and without looking at her, again loosened the cloth around Mercy's leg. His face was unreadable as he lifted the girl into his arms, carried her inside the wagon to her cot.

Before closing her eyes, Mercy said, "It hurts."

"I don't doubt that," he said. "Shut your eyes, and do your best to relax."

Worried faces greeted him as he stepped down out of the wagon. Fiona twisted her hands together. She whispered not wanting Mercy to hear her question. "Will she die?"

Several of the others drew closer to hear his answer.

He shrugged his shoulders. "I've drawn out as much poison as I can. Now's the hardest part—the waiting."

"It happened so fast," Fiona murmured with fear-glazed eyes. "Mercy is deathly afraid of snakes. That's why she rode mostly in the wagon instead of walking."

"I'm pretty sure I sucked out most of the venom from Mercy's leg. Still, when I touched her she was hot as an oven brick, and that's not a good sign" Bannon glanced around. "Where is Bird LeBlanc?"

Henrietta said, "She's making a poultice of charcoal."

Fiona's eyes seemed to beg. "Will it help?"

"Fiona—" he began. She was a vulnerable young woman, and the prairie was a dangerous place. He wanted to brush his lips across hers, to reassure her. "It can't do any harm."

Althea Smalley huffed up to the crowd of women. "Shoo, get on about tending your business, the lot of you. Good heavens, it's a wonder poor Mercy can breathe, what with all of you standing so close, gawking and sucking the air right out of the wagon."

Still Bannon just stood there, staring at Fiona and she at him like a couple of fascinated strangers. It was Bird who broke the spell.

"Fi-on-nah, you help."

Fiona pushed the lump past her throat. "Of course."

"Bring water."

She ladled water into a basin and followed the Iroquois woman into the wagon. Fiona touched Mercy's forehead and forced herself to smile.

While Bird bound the poultice around Mercy's leg, Fiona bathed the girl's feverish brow.

Mercy opened her eyes. "I can't die." She wrapped her hands protectively around her abdomen. "I thought I hated it, but it's not the baby's fault what happened, is it?" Her eyes seem to plead with Fiona.

"No one should ever fault a child." She had to turn her head for a moment, so Mercy wouldn't see the tears shimmering in her eyes. "Don't worry, Mercy. You'll be fine," Fiona insisted.

When the two women had done all they could to make the girl comfortable, they stepped outside. Fiona laid her arm on Bird's. "Will she live?"

"Not know." The Iroquois woman made the sign of the snake's fangs with her fingers. "Plenty big snake—much venom for so small a woman," she said honestly, because to mislead was not the Indian woman's way. "She is with child."

"Yes, I know," was all the answer Fiona offered.

During the night Fiona listened to Mercy's distorted ramblings, her words were no longer coherent as she thrashed back and forth on the bunk bed.

Exhaustion tugged at Fiona. She had lain awake for most of the night, and now for most of the morning she'd knelt beside the cot as Althea tended Mercy. There were big dark circles under the young woman's eyes, and her skin was bluish-pale, like thin milk.

"She's in pain, isn't she?"

Althea gingerly removed the poultice from Mercy's leg. She sucked in an audible breath. The bite was still angry, the leg severely swollen. "Merciful heaven, the swelling is getting worse and there's signs of infection."

"Tell me what to do, Ma Smalley."

"Brew some hot water with molasses and add a shot of whiskey. It might dull the pain a little."

By the time Fiona had brewed the concoction, Mercy was completely delirious. She laughed and cried, talked about everything from marrying Mr.

Henry Filmore and raising her baby, to pleading with Fiona not to let her die.

Althea lifted Mercy to a sitting position while Fiona spooned up the homemade elixir. "Drink, Mercy. It'll make you feel better."

Mercy wrinkled her nose and scrunched up her face.

"Drink it," Fiona commanded.

She allowed Fiona to place the spoon between her lips. She sipped, coughed. Fiona lifted another spoonful. Mercy pushed her hand away, spilling the liquid.

Fiona refilled the spoon. "I can be just as stubborn, Mercy." She put the spoon to the girl's lips. "Drink."

Reluctantly, Mercy accepted the potion and swallowed. After two more sips, she said, "I'm so tired." A smile wobbled on her face, then disappeared. "Fiona, Ma Smalley—my dearest friends."

When Mercy closed her eyes, Althea bent over, her ear to the girl's chest and listened. "It's okay, she's sleeping." With Mercy quieted down and sleeping, Fiona assisted Althea in cleansing the snakebite. Althea bandaged the leg with strips of cotton torn from a bed sheet.

Fiona whispered, "Do you think she'll survive?"

"It's as bad as I've ever seen. If she makes it through the night...maybe." Althea smoothed her hands down the front of her apron. "Did you know she was pregnant?"

In spite of the sweltering August night, Fiona shuddered. "Blackie Sledge. It happened one night before the meeting at the church. Mercy's not to blame, Ma Smalley. She didn't ask to be violated."

Althea frowned as she tied the bandage. "I reckon men like Blackie Sledge are spawned by the devil, himself." She looked at Fiona with bleak eyes.

"For the time being, we've done all we can do. Let's go see if Henrietta has some coffee brewing."

After a brief meal, Fiona excused herself from the group. Before climbing up on her bunk, she remoistened the cloth on Mercy's forehead. The lantern light showed flesh that was the waxy color of death, and her breathing was so shallow that her chest barely moved.

Fiona settled in her bunk and offered up a prayer of healing for her friend. She blinked back tears. Sadness settled in her throat. If there was one thing she'd learned in her youthful life, it was that sometimes all a person could do was just continue putting one foot in front of the other.

The moon's bright yellow shafts pierced Fiona's eyes. She struggled in her sleep. Something was wrong. She needed to awaken.

"Mama!" Mercy's scream rent through the wagon. "Mama, where are you?"

Fiona nearly tumbled from her bunk as she swung her legs over the side to slide to the floor. Althea Smalley said, "Merciful heavens."

Henrietta flung back her sheet and sat up. "Scared the living daylights out of me."

Fiona gathered Mercy into her arms much the way one would do to a child frighten by a nightmare. "I'm here, Mercy."

The faintest smile touched Mercy's lips. "I've missed you Mama."

Fiona cut her eyes toward Althea Smiley who answered with a slight nod. Fiona's voice was tender when she said, "I've missed you, too, Mercy."

"Don't worry no more, Mama. I'm coming home." A sudden strength seemed to seize Mercy as she sat up and reached out with both hands.

Just as a cloud passed over the moon, blotting out its light, Mercy Anders drew her last and final breath. Murmuring a brief prayer, Fiona wept.

Fiona insisted she help Althea and Henrietta wash Mercy's body. They laid small flat pebbles on her eyes to hold them shut, combed her hair, and clothed her in the pale pink dress that was to be her wedding gown.

"The funeral?" Fiona asked Bannon, her voice barely more than a whisper.

"This evening, soon as it cools off a little," he answered, sighing and pushing a sweat-soaked tendril of hair back from her face. His touch was comforting.

She was half-blind with fatigue and despair. She turned toward the wagon where she intended to splash her cheeks and throat with tepid water before stripping and washing the bedding from Mercy's bunk.

"Look at me, Fiona," Bannon said.

She had no strength left, so she met his gaze and saw that he was regarding her gently. "Don't bother with the chores," he ordered her quietly. "Get yourself something to eat and lie down and rest."

She nodded dumbly, and her distracted gaze wandered to the hole that Bannon and Isaiah had dug. When she reached the wagon, she didn't want to go inside. She yearned to stretch out in the cool, fragrant grass under the birch trees and close her eyes and not have to deal with another painful thought for years and years. She was sitting cross-legged on the shady ground when Bannon brought her a cup of cool water.

"Come back to the wagon, Fiona. You're exhausted."

"If I go to sleep, I'll miss the funeral."

"Don't fret, so, Fiona. I'll see that you don't miss the service." He took the cup gently from her hand, his voice low and quiet.

"Poor Mercy." Fiona's eyes fluttered shut.

Bannon held her close in his arms. She leaned

her head against his chest and weary to the bone slipped into a sound and desolate sleep.

****

Fiona stood with the other ladies, a small bouquet of wildflowers in her hand. All of the mourners stood clad in their work dresses.

Although she would not have thought to lean on him, Fiona took assurance from knowing Bannon was standing directly behind her, as solid and well-rooted as an oak tree.

She looked on, dry-eyed and oddly distant from the proceedings, while Althea read from the Bible over Mercy's grave.

Women all around her wept softly, and Fiona wondered if there was something missing in her own spirit that caused her to look on stoically. She despaired if this was all there was to life—you lived and then you died. She wondered if anyone had a right to hopes and dreams.

She looked up at the pink and gold sky searching the feathered clouds and wondered if heaven really existed, and if Mercy had gone to rest in that beautiful place like Althea Smalley proclaimed.

Althea's words filtered through Fiona's seared emotions. "Ashes to ashes, dust to dust, we return this sweet, innocent soul, Mercy Anders, to the earth."

One-by-one the women followed Fiona as she laid the little bunch of blue flowers on top of the rock-piled mound and whispered her final good-bye.

Her feet dragged as if weighted with lead as she walked back to her wagon.

The wagon springs creaked as Fiona climbed up into the dim interior. She wearily settled on top of her own bed and closed her eyes, glad to see the last of the wretched day, but a grim kaleidoscope of scenes blossomed in her mind, driving away any hope of sleep.

Before retiring for the night, Bannon had gathered the women and announced that there was no need to delay, that it was time to hold the lottery.

Chapter Twenty-One

Bannon sighed dispiritedly. There was one in two chances that Fiona's name would be drawn to assume Mercy Ander's bridal contract.

Isaiah sidled up to stand next to him. "Cain't you buy Fiona's contract, Cordell?"

"Who says I want to?"

Isaiah spat a stream of tobacco, drew the sleeve of his shirt across his mouth. He rocked back and forth on the balls of his leather moccasins. "Ain't nobody said it. Leastwise, not in words."

When Bannon didn't respond, Isaiah said, "I ain't blind, you know. I see the way the way you look at her and her, you."

Bannon's throat felt tight. "The document states if I so choose, I am free to select and wed, upon safe arrival in the town of Glory, any alternate bride who isn't bound by contract."

The scout patted Bannon on the shoulder. "Well, c'mon. Might's well get it over with."

At Bannon's command the two women gathered, while the other ladies drew around them to see who would be the next chosen. He handed Fiona the journal. "You know what to do, Fiona."

His heart felt as bleak as the nod she offered when she accepted the book that held all the names of the brides and their prospective grooms, the accountings of the journey, the names of those women who had died and brief descriptions of their burial sites.

He dropped the remaining names printed neatly

on brown butcher paper into Isaiah's hat, and watched as the grizzled scout tossed the hat up and down as if making sure the slips of paper were equally distributed.

"Bird?"

The Iroquois woman stepped to the front of the waiting group. She looked only at Bannon, the expression on her face solemn. "I know what to do."

He nodded an acknowledgement, held his tongue. He couldn't think of anything he wanted to say.

She reached into the hat, hesitated, withdrew a folded slip of paper and thrust it forward. Bannon stood unsmiling. His jaw clenched as his eyes settled on the name. He glanced over at Fiona and gave her a slight, distraught smile.

Esther Gaffney said, "Who is it, Mr. Bannon? Whose name did you draw?" She clasped her hands together, expectantly. "Oh, please let it be me."

His words were spiritless. "The alternate bride who will assume the contract of the deceased, Mercy Anders, and who is now legally betrothed to Henry Filmore, is—

****

Rubbing her aching temples, Fiona sank back on her blankets. She tried to sleep, tried desperately, but as the hour grew later and later, she could no longer deny what was true. It was she who would wed Mr. Henry Filmore.

The hurt was almost more than she could bear. Presently, she turned onto one side, watching through tear-blurred eyes as stars twinkled above the moon-washed prairie.

She vowed by all that was holy no one would ever guess how deeply the pain of her name being selected to replace Mercy's pierced her. Especially not Bannon.

The next morning, Fiona rose before the sun, as

usual, and the instant she opened her eyes, the hopelessness was there to greet her.

Breakfast was well underway, and the women were finishing off the second pot of coffee, when Bannon arrived. He was clean and dressed in fresh buckskins, and it was as if he silently dared Fiona to look at him.

She didn't.

She walked to edge of the stream, stooped and splashed cool water over her face and arms. She dreamed into the reflections of her face. She was gowned in white, a bouquet of yellow daisies in her hand, she'd turned to allow the man at her side to lift the veil, she'd kept her eyes open, waiting for his lips to press against hers, but the face leaning toward her was indistinguishable.

Angry with wasteful daydreaming, she picked up a sizeable rock and chunked it into the water, watching the ripples carry the dream away. She let loose a string of curse words that she thought she'd forgotten, then lifted her skirts and strode to the remuda. She ranted softly to the mules.

"Who am I but a poor wretched Irish lass wishing for naught more than she deserves? I signed the damned contract. And 'tis a proper wife I'll be to Mr. Henry Filmore."

She slipped the bridle over Jonah's large floppy ears. "But I won't be lovin' him." She stamped her foot. "I'll cook and scrub and sew, but no, for certain, I'll not give my heart to him."

As if understanding her words, the larger of the two mules rubbed his head against her shoulder, and made little grunting sounds. She patted his broad forehead. "You're a good laddie, Jonah."

True to his cantankerous nature, Rufus rolled his eyes and snorted. Knowing what was coming Fiona slapped his nose before he could reach out and nip her. "You're a stubborn, disagreeable mule,

Rufus." Then an unpleasant thought struck her. "What if Mr. Henry Filmore has a temperament like you?" An impish smile tugged at her lips as she buckled the bridle's chin strap. "Why, I'll just box his ears. Yes, that's what I'll do."

Then came another thought. This one more distasteful. "Oh, stuff and bother. He'll be wanting to bed me for certain." A hot flush crept up to her cheeks. She leaned her head against the mule's broad brown neck. "But it isn't Mr. Henry Filmore's bed I'm wanting to snuggle up in."

The sun played hide and seek with the clouds in the bluest skies. Even the eagles seemed to watch benignly as they circled and glided above her.

She'd deliberately avoided Bannon all morning. But somehow, when she looked toward him, she found that something had impelled him to look at her.

Gathering up the lead ropes, Fiona led the mules to camp and set about harnessing them to the wagon.

****

Bannon had not slept that night. He'd sat up until all hours, jawing with Isaiah about improvements he wanted to do at the ranch once the women were safely delivered. Then he'd gone to the stream to have himself a bath and lie tossing and turning in his bedroll until dawn broke.

He'd half hoped Fiona would come to him, but she hadn't. For the rest of the evening, she had treated him as if nothing had happened. Hell, she'd hardly batted an eyelash.

The day began soon after he'd handed his empty plate to Althea Smalley. He listened to Fiona's sweet voice crooning a lullaby to the mules as she hitched them to the wagon. The need of Fiona and the comfort she might have lent echoed within him like a night wind caressing the treetops.

The day carved a groove into which the future flowed. Bannon made up his mind. After he delivered the women safely to town, he wouldn't hang around to watch Fiona exchange vows with any man.

A sudden urge to hear the lowing of cattle and share a nightly poker game with his ranch hands at his Lone Tree Ranch gripped him.

A pang of compassion stirred within him as he thought of the misery Fiona must have felt when he'd read her name. A long sigh slipped from him as he flung an arm over his head and turned his face away from the camp.

Chapter Twenty-Two

A muddle of emotions simmered and stewed within Fiona—anger at Bannon for ignoring her, sorrow at Mercy's dying, and gloom of marrying a man whom she knew only by an image in a daguerreotype and a short missive he'd written. She sniffed once and gave the sheet of paper a nearly imperceptible snap before reading it.

Dear Lady,

My name is Henry Filmore, and I have lived thirty-one years. I am a plain man who does not believe in frills or extravagance. On occasion, I enjoy a mug of beer with the crew on a Saturday night and a hot toddy to ward off winter chills. Like most of the men in Glory, I work for the timber company. I am a cutter. That means I saw down trees. Being a company man, I live in crew quarters, but will do my best to have a one-room cabin built by the time you arrive in September. My demands of a wife are simple. I expect good meals on the table each evening, a clean house, church one Sunday per month, and your willingness to perform other wifely duties.

Fiona sank back against the wagon wheel, and gazed out across the grassy expanse. She carefully folded the page, returned it to its envelope and then rose to climb inside the wagon. She knelt to grope under the bottom bunk, pulled out the leather valise that held all her earthly belongings and unbuckled the straps. Her first inclination was to wad the letter up and toss it into the cook fire. Instead she tucked the envelope beneath her mother's wedding dress.

When she turned around, she caught Althea watching her with a thoughtful smile.

"What was in the letter that put such a dour frown on your lovely face, child?"

Fiona pressed her lips together, smoothed the skirts of her gingham dress. She stepped down from the end gate and used one hand to shade her eyes from the sun.

"He's a plain man who likes beer and whiskey and expects wifely duties in the bedroom." Fiona stamped her foot.

Althea expelled a hearty laugh. "Merciful heavens, is that all? Why child, he sounds no different than most men."

"'Tis no laughing matter, Ma Smalley. 'Twas the way he said it. Mr. Filmore sounds like a stingy miser who expects everything of a wife while he himself gives very little in return." Fiona placed her hands on her hips and kicked a clod of dirt. After a moment, her lips turned upward.

"What kind of Irish devilment is floating around in that head of yours, Fiona? Don't deny it. I see it in your eyes."

Fiona shrugged a shoulder. "Esther Gaffney is anxious to wed. Perhaps she will buy my contract— no, I'll give it away for free. And I'll add Mercy's bride's money to sweeten the deal."

Althea watched her intently. "How old is Mr. Filmore?"

"His letter said, thirty-one."

"Hmm. I don't know all the rules about the contracts. That's something we'd have to ask Bannon, but it won't do, Fiona."

"And why not?" Fiona's voice was incredulous.

"Because a young man desires a young woman who'll bear him children. Esther is the right age and a widow. I overheard her confide that after two years of marriage, she'd never conceived." Althea seemed annoyed as she fanned away a bug that buzzed around her face. "You signed a contract, Fiona. You weren't ignorant of the fact that something like this might happen." And then she smiled. "Do I dare ask what's got you so dead-set against entering this union?"

Not wanting to meet the older woman's intuitive eyes, Fiona hung her head. "Nothing...nothing at all. It's just that Mr. Filmore doesn't sound much to my liking."

"Uh-hmm. Not as much as a certain wagon master is my guess."

Fiona's eyes widened. She sidestepped a response by asking, "Aren't you the least bit apprehensive about wedding a man you've never met?"

Althea bent over the cook fire and using the hem of her apron grasped the coffee pot's handle. Fiona held out two mugs while Althea poured. Taking their cups of coffee, Fiona followed as Althea ambled over to upturned buckets and sat down.

After a moment of pensive quiet, Althea said, "I loved my first husband, and I liked my second husband more than I loved him. As for marrying Mr. Otto Hackett, he's a store owner, and what he said in his letter appeals to me. Now Fiona, at my age I'm satisfied to know that I'll have a roof over my head, food on my plate, and companionship to scare away loneliness. To a young woman, like yourself who's looking for starry-eyed romance, sometimes friendship grows into love." She swallowed the last swig of coffee and patted Fiona on the shoulder. "It'll all work out, girl. Trust me. I know about these things."

Fiona sighed. "I hope you're right."

****

Fiona sat hunched forward on the hard seat. Her knees supported her elbows. She clucked the mules to speed up their plodding pace. The sun seared down in burning rays, and she thought she could hear her skin sizzling. In spite of the heat, she shivered.

"Cold, Miss Quinn?" Bannon drawled, his eyebrow lifting in a way that infuriated Fiona.

"My, aren't we being formal?" She glared at him. "Yes, thank you. It's quite nippy out here for the first of September, don't you think?"

Shrugging, Bannon dropped his gaze from her glare to the damp stains on her blouse. Fiona could feel perspiration trickle between her breasts and barely controlled the impulse to glance down to see if it showed.

Of course it didn't show. Why was the scoundrel trying to make her self-conscious? She slapped the leather reins against the mules' dusty backs. "Stop dragging your feet, Jonah. Get along, Rufus." The mules lifted their heads and brayed their protest.

Though she didn't turn around to look, she felt Bannon's gaze boring into her back. At least he didn't follow along beside her.

Choking on the dust stirred up by wind and the mules, Fiona had finally come to terms with the idea of marriage. "I wish I was a man."

"Would you now?" Bannon chuckled.

"I-I thought you were gone."

He let his gaze roam over Fiona's flushed face. "You didn't answer me. What would you do if you were a man?"

"I'd give you the beating you so richly deserve."

His eyes widened in mock surprise. "And just what is it that I've done to earn such wrath, Miss Quinn?"

"Stop calling me, Miss Quinn. For a thousand miles you haven't minded using my given name."

A mocking smile curved the harsh line of his mouth as he nodded. "All right, Fiona, but you didn't answer my question."

Her fingers tightened around the reins, and her heartbeat quickened as she recalled how his lips felt, the way he had stirred a long-slumbering response from her body. Had this need to be touched, to be kissed and caressed even when she knew better, always waited there, hidden away in some private part of her? Deep inside, she still yearned for the unquenchable fire of feeling the hard pressure of his body against hers.

Trembling, she did the only thing she could do. With quiet dignity, she turned her face away and stared over the backs of the mules. "Go away, Bannon. I'm a betrothed woman. Leave me be."

Her shoulders sagged dispiritedly. Angry tears pricked her eyelids. Fiona blinked them away, wiping her eyes with the back of her hand.

A hot breeze whipped up a froth of dust, and the late afternoon sun backlit Bannon's head as he spurred his sorrel and rode ahead of her wagon.

She gazed off into the distance where the hills rose against the purpling sky. The ridges glowed with a bluish color as the sun cast long shadows across them. Wind moved through the trees bringing a unique fragrance that reminded Fiona of perfumed soap. In spite of the heat, there was a crisp feel to the air. She thought it lovely.

"Fiona...Fiona?"

Lost in some nether land of dreams, Fiona blinked as she looked down at Althea striding beside the wagon.

"Bannon said we'd camp for the night up there."

Fiona craned her neck in the direction Althea was pointing but saw only a flat stretch of land broken by a line of trees.

"By the trees?"

"By the creek."

Fiona stared. "I don't see a creek."

"He said it was there."

Fiona slowed the wagon. "Hop up. No sense in walking when you can ride."

Althea settled next to her, and Fiona was surprised when they neared the banks of a slow moving creek that wound through the dust and trees. It was shallow, gurgling gently over smooth, round rocks on the creek bed.

****

Bannon rode up and stepped down from the saddle. He tied the sorrel's reins to the wheel of Fiona's wagon. "There's plenty of dry wood on the ground, ladies. Easy pickin's."

He watched Fiona's lithe body as she stepped down from the wagon. Althea stretched and placed her hands to the small of her back.

"I'll take care of the mules, if you'll collect enough wood for the fire, Fiona. I'll set Henrietta to scraping potatoes," Ma Smalley said.

Fiona's hair tumbled around her shoulders, framing her face in a silken mass of red tangles. The loose blouse and skirt did little to hide the gentle swell of her hips and thrust of her breast from Bannon's too-sharp memory. He could supply all the details of what the garments hid and cursed himself for it. This damnable lust for the girl was clouding his judgment, lingering in his mind when he should be thinking about his ranch and improving the breed of his cattle.

On soft feet he followed her into the forest, but she saw his approach. Fiona's fingers tightened around the stick of wood she held. Bannon took several deliberate steps forward. There was an undercurrent of tension just beneath the surface of his calm, an air of purpose that seemed to transfer to Fiona.

"Don't come any closer," she warned in a shaky voice.

"What do you plan to do, Fiona, beat me to death with a twig?"

She glanced down at the small stick in her hand. "I don't know what's the matter with you, but keep your distance."

"You know damn good and well what's the matter with me."

"No." Shaking her head and backing away, Fiona huffed, "I don't. I don't have the foggiest notion what's fluttering around in that pea-sized noggin of yours."

Still advancing with slow, measured steps, Bannon scratched the rough whiskers on his chin. "I can't seem to get you out of my mind."

When he reached her, he plucked the stick from her hands and tossed it away. He stared down into her sea-green eyes. It seemed only natural to reach out and pull her into his embrace, to lower his head and kiss her with urgent desire. Fiona gave a slight shudder, and he felt the tremors rack her body. Since their first meeting, there had been a spark of physical attraction between them. All he wanted was to lose himself in her.

His fingers fumbled with the buttons on her blouse. There was a fierce urgency to undress her. To claim her, to put his mark on her, to make her his.

Fiona closed her eyes and moaned, yet she pushed her hands up between them to break Bannon's embrace. "No...stop, now." Her hand snaked out and before he could react, his head snapped sideways with the impact of the stinging slap against his cheek.

She pushed away and with trembling fingers buttoned her blouse. Her words came in breathy spurts. "Have you no decency? You have no right to take what isn't yours." The dark sweep of her lashes lifted. Her chin quivered. "Why...why..."

As he watched her struggling emotions, her next words were like dumping an avalanche of snow on smoldering embers.

She lifted her chin, and her bright green eyes fixed on Bannon's face. "The only difference between you and those two insane animals that kidnapped me is that you smell better."

The venom in the words of her insult shook him. With a grimace of contempt at himself, he backed away.

She raised her eyes—they glittered with tears—all she had left now was defiance. "When I go to Mr. Henry Filmore's bed on my wedding night, I will go as a virgin." Her chin jutted to a down-right mulish angle as she bent and lifted a tree limb the size of her arm and held it as if to ward off an enemy. "If you'll excuse me, *Mr. Bannon,* I have wood to gather."

The sun was just peeking over the horizon of whispering pines, pushing back the shivery chill of the night. Abruptly, Bannon's frown sharpened into one of pure anger. "My apologies, Miss Quinn." He looked at her a moment longer and uncomfortably moved away. And then as silently as a wisp of fog, he left her standing there.

Chapter Twenty-Three

The rain came in a pounding deluge. It thundered against the canvas bonnets of the wagons. Spiny fingers of lightning danced across the sky illuminating the night with an eerie clarity.

The lantern hanging from the wagon's center rib swung back and forth casting shadows across the faces of the women huddled in their beds. Fiona sat propped against the back of the bunk, a blanket tucked around her to ward off the chill. Her head was lowered as she focused intently on the words she wrote.

September 3, 1847

We crossed the Willamette Valley, today. It was a deep mountainous terrain and quite spectacular with its formidable cliffs. Thankfully, every wagon made it across without further mishap. Isaiah says it's only thirty miles to the town of Glory, and if the weather holds we'll arrive in two days.

I am both excited and apprehensive about reaching our destination—excited to put an end to this long arduous journey and all the tragedies that have followed us, and nervous as to what the future holds for me.

Since my forthcoming marriage isn't an especially happy occasion, I have decided I will not wear my dear mother's wedding gown. Instead, I shall wear the green dress I keep for church.

Her spirits were heavy as she turned to a blank page and sketched a picture of a tall man with broad shoulders holding the hand of a woman dressed in a white gown with a long flowing veil. The couple faced a minister who stood behind an altar. Using small intricate movements of the pencil, she drew images that at a glance resembled flowers. Only a discerning eye would see that the leaves and stems and petals spelled—*Bannon's Bride.*

****

Thoroughly drained of his energy, Bannon waited out the storm inside the supply wagon. Propped against his saddle, he tucked the blanket tighter around his body. Casting a sideways glance at Isaiah, he said, "We'll arrive at the Long Tom tomorrow. It'll be a good place for the women to rest. They'll have plenty of fresh water for bathing and cooking."

"Yup, for what they've gone through, they deserve a few days relaxation before the big shindig." Isaiah drew a long puff on his pipe and released a curl of smoke. "Gotta admire every last one of 'em. Don't know many greenhorns that would've survived what these ladies have been through. Yep, good women all 'round."

An involuntary shudder wracked Bannon's body. "Yeah, good women."

Women needed proper things in their proper places to give them assurance, a sense of rightness and stability. These were things Bannon's wife had told him, things he'd forgotten.

He knew the trail had often been bleak and uncertain for the women, and the mules could not last much longer.

Exhausted, his back aching, he shifted to a more comfortable position. He stared up at the underside of the canvas roof, listening to the patter of rain, and wished Fiona was there beside him, his to hold.

Blasted woman.

With a deep sigh, he closed his eyes, and in the next instant he was asleep and dreaming. Her

197

mouth easily surrendered to his. He felt the heat of the kiss lingering with him, and the force of the emotions raised by her response vibrated through his very bones.

When Bannon awakened the next morning, the air was golden, scrubbed clean by last night's storm. He tugged on his boots, tucked his shirt, strapped the gun belt around his waist, and stepped outside, arms loosely folded in front of him. He watched the activities solemnly for a few moments, scratched the back of his head, and narrowed his eyes to a squint.

The smell of breakfast was in the air as dawn approached, and while the women bent to their duties, he knew they as well as the mules were exhausted from their travels. Even though he was hungry as a bear, Bannon didn't intend to eat, and he didn't speak to Fiona—not directly.

"Ladies, grab a cup of coffee and gather 'round." He sighed, clasped his hands together, unclasped them, took off his hat and put it on again. He let out his breath in an impatient huff. "In about four hours, we'll reach the Long Tom River. That puts us a mile or so outside of Glory."

Loud cheers, hands clapping and whistles went up from the group of tired women.

"Settle down." Bannon's voice boomed with authority. "There's plenty of cool water and shade and good fishing. It's a safe place for you to rest and make yourselves ready for your big day." He shifted his weight from one foot to the other. "Isaiah and I will ride on ahead and let the town know when to expect you."

"How long you giving us, Bannon?" Althea wanted to know.

"Will a week be enough?"

"Plenty of time for us to soak our weary feet in cool water, air out our good gowns, and scrub ourselves clean. Yes sir, a week oughta do just fine."

Althea clapped her hands together. "Well ladies, let's get a move on."

"Isaiah and I will ride on ahead and point the trail." Bannon glanced around the group. "Bird, you and Henrietta take the lead." He briefed the two women on directions. "We'll mark the spot where you're to set-up camp. Barring no troubles, you should arrive by noon."

Bannon watched Fiona move away from the group. He thought he saw sorrow and dread in her eyes. And he felt a yearning deep inside himself that didn't want to let go.

After some casual talk and a few questions, Bannon and Isaiah excused themselves. They walked to the supply wagon, grabbed their saddles and toted them to the remuda.

Slinging the saddle in place, Bannon reached under the belly of his sorrel and grabbed the cinch strap, drew it up and tightened it in place. He slipped the bit between the horse's teeth, settled the bridle and buckled the cheek strap. He did all of this without passing any morning pleasantries.

"Something eatin' at you, Cordell?" Isaiah completed the task of saddling his pinto.

"Nope." Bannon set his foot in the stirrup and rose up into the saddle.

"Yeah, and a skunk don't smell its own stink neither."

"What the hell is that supposed to mean?"

"Nothing, Cordell. Not a damned thing." Isaiah swung into the saddle. "When we get to town, I'm gonna belly up to the bar at Jake's Place and drown myself in a mug of cold beer."

Fox squirrels chattered in the overhead ceiling of trees. Bottom limbs of the great sequoias reached far above them in this forest of ancient growth.

The men rode side-by-side to the camp. Bannon's eyes swung toward Althea. "Look for our return in four or five days. It all depends on how long it takes to get word to the lumber camps and gather the men to town."

"We'll be ready." Althea beamed up at him.

He touched the brim of his hat and turned his horse in the direction of town.

****

Fiona stepped down from the end gate of her wagon. She shaded her eyes from the morning sun while watching the two men disappearing down the trail. "I love you, Cordell Bannon." She sobbed and tears coursed freely down her cheeks.

After greeting her friends with a rather fragile smile, Fiona said, "I feel like walking, Ma Smalley." Fiona caught up her skirts and without another word turned away and hurried ahead of the mules.

"Suits me," Althea called. She flapped the reins to get the mules started. "Get on up there you flop-eared jackasses."

Blinded by frustration, Fiona raced ahead unmindful of the direction she had taken, only that no matter how far she walked, it wouldn't be far enough.

Something rustled in the dark bushes beyond her, a stone grated as it was kicked aside by a small scurrying creature. She veered off to her left and sought the cover of trees. She needed to be alone, to have time to make sense of her emotions.

Dense foliage, prickly bushes, and decayed tree branches hampered her steps. She stumbled several times, falling painfully to her knees and snagging the skirt of her brown dress. Yanking it free, she ignored the sound of rending cloth and continued until her strength had waned and sheer exhaustion brought her to a staggering halt at the base of a huge sequoia tree. Sliding down along its trunk, she collapsed in tears onto the ground.

Her rage wanted to claim Bannon had planned

to take advantage of her. Was it his plan to make her fall in love with him, knowing the two of them could never legally be together?

Her agony weighed heavily against her chest, and she struggled just to breathe. "Maybe Ma Smalley is right. Maybe it's the necessary comforts like a roof over my head, clothes on my back, and food on my plate that are more important than love. Who knows? In time I may even come to admire Mr. Filmore."

She paused and listened to the silence. It was as if the birds and forest creatures had stopped their chattering and scrapping to listen to her one-sided conversation.

She rose from her resting place and smoothed the sticks and brush from the backside of her skirt. "Oh stuff and bother, Fiona Quinn, stop this weak simpering. You're Irish and don't you forget it. And to hell with you, Cordell Bannon."

Turning in a circle to get her bearing, she mused, "Well, lass, you might be Irish, but I think you've gone and got yourself lost."

Frantically, she turned to the east, and the south, and the north. She stumbled a few steps forward, searching for signs of broken twigs, anything that would point her in the direction of the trail and the wagon train.

Her heart pounded desperately, wildly, but the signs weren't there.

Relief washed through her like warm bath water when a voice called out, "Fi-on-nah!"

"Over here, Bird. I'm over here."

"Keep calling—so I find."

After several minutes, the Iroquois woman rode into sight. She extended an arm and helped Fiona swing onto the back of the horse.

"Spotted big black bear. We worry 'bout you."

Fiona shivered at the prospects of being

attacked. "It was foolish of me to stray from the trail. Thank you for finding me, Bird."

The river sounded close, whispering and gurgling, and the tree frogs were humming an erratic chorus.

Althea ran forward to greet the women.

Fiona slid from the horse's back. She took in the frown on her friend's face. "Please don't scold, Ma Smalley." She glanced at her surrounding. "It's like something out of a picture book."

Not giving the older woman an opportunity to issue a reprimand, Fiona rushed to the wagon intent on sketching the scenery inside her journal.

Later in the evening, at Fiona's fire, supper was supplemented with fried fish, wild mushrooms, and stewed dandelion greens.

"We made it," Althea said as she poured hot water into a basin.

"Tomorrow, I think we should string up a clothesline of sorts so we can hang our dresses to air and to let the wrinkles drop out of them." Henrietta gathered up the plates to help with washing the dishes.

"Good idea, Henrietta."

Fiona listened to the idle, but cheerful chatter as she dipped a cup of grain into two feedbags. Voices rose in song and other voices joined. The women came together around one campfire. The long treacherous journey over a thousand miles of prairie was over. In a few days each would begin a new journey.

The mules greeted her with expectant hee-haws. She laughed. "Ah, me good laddies, you know 'tis time to tie on the feedbag."

She slipped the bags over their ears and gave each mule a gentle slap on the neck. "I put in a little extra grain for you, tonight."

Only the soft munching and grinding of teeth

answered her.

She turned on her heel and started toward camp, and then looked back. "I hope wherever you go next you're treated kindly."

Chapter Twenty-Four

It was a bittersweet moment as Bannon rode down the center of town. He'd lived up to his end of the bargain. In five months, he'd pushed a group of women harder than he'd ever pushed his own ranch hands.

"Looks like the town's growed some since we left." Isaiah observed as his pinto plodded along side Bannon's sorrel. Isaiah pointed at a large wooden pavilion that had all appearances of being new. "Look yonder, Cordell. Reckon that's where the shindig's gonna take place?"

Bannon drew up on the reins in front of a hitch rail and dismounted. Opening the saddlebag, he withdrew an oilcloth packet that held his journal, the letters and tintypes of the women. "Your guess is as good as mine, Isaiah."

The men stepped up on the boardwalk. The sign on the door read—*G. W. Daggert, Esq., Attorney at Law.*

Bannon sucked in a breath, clasped the cold brass knob and turned. A smallish man with a face that reminded Bannon of an owl glanced up from his paperwork. "May I help...*Mr. Bannon.*" He rose from his chair, nearly knocking it over. He rushed to a closed door, rapped once and then opened it. "It's Mr. Bannon and Mr. Thomas, sir. They're here...right here."

"Well, don't just stand there gawping, send them in, and put on a fresh pot of coffee." A pudgy man wearing a white goatee rushed around his desk, banging his hip in the process.

"Bannon...Isaiah...welcome back." He shook hands with both men. "Sit...sit." He opened a cabinet door and withdrew a bottle of brandy and three glasses. "The women?"

Bannon laid the bundle of information on the lawyer's desk. "Got 'em camped out on the Long Tom."

"*Good...good.*" Daggert handed each man a glass. "A toast, then, to a successful journey."

Bannon slugged down his drink and grimaced. "G.W., I want your word to keep the whereabouts of the women quiet."

The lawyer frowned. "Is there a problem?"

"No problem, except they're plumb wore to a frazzle and deserve a good rest." Bannon leaned forward offering his glass for a refill.

"You have my word. And the contracts?"

Bannon nodded toward the packet. "I've kept a complete record of the deaths along the trail, and the names of the men that the women matched themselves up with, and my expenses."

The lawyer settled back in his chair, his hands resting on his belly, fingers laced together. "How long?"

"If you mean how long for the women, I gave them my promise, one week to rest and make themselves ready. Besides, I figure it'll take most of that time to get messages to the timber camps." He leaned forward in his chair, his eyes serious. "I have a few words to impart on the soon-to-be husbands...before they meet their brides.

"And something else, G.W., these women deserve the finest barbeque with all the trimmings you can furnish, lemonade, cakes and pies, and a band with good music, like waltzes and reels."

The lawyer's kindly eyes crinkled. "Reverend Harris and his wife are in charge of the planning committee. We've met on a regular basis. You can rest assured this will be the biggest and best event Glory has ever seen." He pulled a folder from his desk drawer. He ran a finger down the list of names. "The timber workers are contained to two camps. Except for three who are ranchers, the remaining five men own businesses here in town." He called out, "Hadley—"

The clerk stepped to the door. "Sir?"

"Go to the church, and tell Reverend and Mrs. Harris to come to my office, post haste." Daggert placed a finger to his lips. "Not a word to anyone else about our news—understand?"

"Yes, sir—not a word." The bandy-legged clerk grabbed his jacket and disappeared out the front door.

Daggert directed his attention to the seated men. "As soon as Hadley returns, I'll send him out to the camps. The reverend can notify the men in town. That leaves the ranchers."

Bannon and Isaiah looked at each other and shrugged. Bannon slapped his buckskin breeches, sending up a cloud of dust. "We're both saddle weary, G.W., and our horses are footsore. I plan on a long soak in a hot tub, a juicy steak, a soft bed, a clean suit of clothes, and two days of undisturbed sleep."

"Same for me, Cordell." Isaiah winked.

"Send someone else out to notify the ranchers." Bannon rested his hand on a crossed knee.

"He won't like it, but I'm the boss. I'll send Hadley."

****

Three days later, men of all ages, sizes and shapes gathered inside the pavilion. Seated on the band platform were G. W. Daggert, Reverend Harris and Isaiah.

Bannon stood legs apart, arms folded across his

206

broad chest. His eyes wandered across the faces staring up at him. Some were friends, good men. He trusted them to do right by their new wives. Some he was merely acquainted with, others he didn't recognize. A mental count showed there were three too many men. He'd let them work out their matchmaking.

Daggert stood and spoke first. "Men, almost a year ago you came to me with a request for mail-order brides. Mr. Bannon and Mr. Thomas were hired to represent you and traveled to Philadelphia, Pennsylvania to select a group of available women. As you can see, he has returned. We indulge your patience as he speaks a few words to you." The lawyer returned to his chair.

Bannon cleared his throat. "Gents, several of these ladies are widow-women. Those who are were instructed to say so in their letters. I'm only telling you this because I don't expect to hear any complaints about used goods."

A few guffaws went up and then silence.

Bannon continued. "Knowing to expect deaths, we contracted thirty women as brides and selected ten additional women as alternates to replace the ones who didn't make it across the prairie. Thirty-one women arrived from a trip that would have caused most men to fold under. These women have survived floods, forded raging rivers, fought off Indians, braved lightning storms, heat-scorching sun, rattlesnakes, and swarms of biting insects.

"To avoid a massacre from a band of rampaging Oglala warriors, the women looked death in the face and drove their wagons in and amongst a herd of buffalo."

An awed murmur rose up from the seated men. Bannon lifted his hand to quiet them.

"As I was saying, I've stood with them when they buried friends, then drove their wagons over the unmarked graves to destroy all signs of burial to keep varmints and scalp hunters from finding the spot. And this, the women did it without complaint."

A bird flew inside the pavilion and perched on a high rafter. It chirped a happy little song. A muffle of released tension seemed to filter through the audience.

"Where are the women, Bannon?" A voice called.

"They're resting." A veiled threat tinged Bannon's answer. "These ladies have crossed a thousand miles of rough terrain, but mostly they've walked to get here. They're sunburned, exhausted, and need to rest. And like all women, they need time to make themselves presentable.

"I'll bring them in at the end of the week." He stepped forward and sent a challenging glare toward the men.

"I expect every man jack here, to show up on Sunday, bathed and smelling good. If you need a haircut, get one. If you need a shave, do it, and if your beard needs trimming, take care of it.

"If you don't own a good suit, go over to the general store and buy one. And while you're there, pick out a nice gift and have it wrapped."

"What kind of presents should we get?" Levi Sims, the blacksmith, asked.

"Perfume, comb and brush, a shawl, hell, I don't know. Get Mr. Hackett to help you. He owns the general store and will know better than me. Just get something nice."

Isaiah stood. He crossed his arms over his chest and scowled at the men's expectant faces. "Don't mean to interrupt you, Cordell, but I got a few things to say. Don't none of you nob-heads show up with likker on your breath, and leave the bottle at home. These here are ladies, not dancehall saloon floosies. Cordell said to bring a gift. I best see you with a bouquet of flowers, too. If'n you don't you'll answer to me." He rubbed his nose. "That's all I got to say." And he sat down.

Bannon, again, took up the rhetoric. "If word ever gets back to me that any one of you has mistreated or in any way neglected or abused your wife, I'll come callin' with my black snake and peel your hide off right down to the bone." His hand reached for the whip fastened to his belt. His blue eyes darkened to black as he let the challenge sink in. He stepped back and sat down.

Lawyer Daggert stood. "You timber men that live in company housing, you've had most of a year to build and furnish cabins. Reverend Harris has kept an accounting of this." He turned and looked at the minister, who gave a barely perceptible shake of his head.

Daggert continued, "While all of you have complied there's one or two whom we've put on notice that one room isn't enough. I needn't call any names—you know who you are. We'll make another inspection in October. Two rooms before the first snow, or expect to pay a hefty fine." He cleared his throat. "Uh, yes, now we'll hear from the reverend."

A tall man who looked as if he needed several good meals stood. "Mr. Bannon tells me the women looked at your tintypes and made their own matches. Likewise, they have sent along their photographs and written their own letters. As I call your name, please come forward. "Otto Hackett, Althea Smalley has chosen you as her groom."

Hearty laugher filled the pavilion. Men patted the store owner on the back as he walked forward. Hackett looked at the tintype of Althea. He turned and smiled as he held up the likeness. "She is a handsome woman for such an ugly old bear like myself."

Another name was called. "Jacques Medoro."

The Frenchman puffed out his chest as he

strutted forward and accepted his packet. His eyes widened. "*Mon Dieu*. She is—" He lifted his eyes toward Bannon. "My good friend, what tribe is she?"

"French and Iroquois, Jack."

"Bannon, you have brought me a beautiful treasure." The Frenchman gazed at the image of Bird LeBlanc.

"She's smart, too, Jack," Isaiah said. "Why when I was wounded, she took my place as scout. She can fish and hunt, knows berries and herbs, and can fashion a poultice for most any ailment."

The Frenchman's grin widened. "Such a woman, I never guessed to have."

The minister called, "Levi Sims, Henrietta Hightower is your chosen one."

The burly blacksmith smiled a sheepish grin. He accepted the packet. "Bannon, I am a big strong man. Is she...she isn't...tiny is she?"

"Give or take an inch, I'd say she'll match your six feet. And she's a good cook, too."

The blacksmith offered another sheepish grin. "I'll be good to her. You know I will."

"Arn Johansson, are you here?"

With the aide of two crutches, a brawny Swede struggled to his feet and made his way forward. "Ja, Reverend, I am here."

Reverend Harris said, "Seems that you and Miss Gerda Olsson have something in common, Arnie."

"Gerda Olsson...by yumping yimney, she is Svedish, too. We make fine blue-eyed, blond sons together, I tink."

The men in the crowd cheered and stamped their feet sharing in the Swede's good fortune.

The blond man held up a crutch and yodeled. His blue eyes grew serious. "Doctor say, 'Arnie no more log rolling for you'. So, now, I make fine furniture like in old country, have my own shop. You tink the *kvinna* vill be pleased?"

The minister said, "I'm certain of it."

With each name called, the muscles in Bannon's stomach tightened. His knuckles whitened as he gripped the chair when the lawyer called, "Henry Filmore, step forward. You will wed Fiona Quinn."

Bannon cut an eye toward Isaiah. The scout shook his head giving the silent answer that he didn't know the man.

The reverend's voice drew Bannon's attention. "Henry Filmore, what do you say for yourself?"

The man snatched his cap from his head and wadded it against his chest. "I have framed up the second room. With the help of my new wife, I'll get it finished before—"

Bannon leapt to his feet and growled. "The hell you said. Miss Quinn wasn't brought here to be your mule." He glared at the timber cutter. "You'll pay for Miss Quinn to live at the boarding house until you *completely* finish the cabin and it passes *my* inspection."

Lawyer Daggert stepped forward. He placed a hand on Bannon's arm. "Henry, you agreed to the terms of the contract that a solid, weather-fit structure with two rooms—one for cooking and sitting and one for sleeping—was to be finished and furnished by September."

Arn Johansson's loud voice boomed. "When I break leg, I ask friends to help with der building of my house. Dees men, the loggers, they come, help Arnie build nice house for his new wife. Shame on you, Henry. Why you no ask for help?"

Filmore glared at the Swede. He stomped forward and snatched the packet containing Fiona's picture and letter from the minister's hand. Jamming the cap on his head, he strode down the pavilion steps, mounted his horse and galloped from town.

A muscle under Bannon's eyes ticked. He

seethed inside.

With the last of the names called and packets handed out, Bannon once more addressed the men asking if they had any questions.

Men surrounded Bannon and Isaiah asking for details about the women who were to become their brides. Bannon noted some read and reread their letters, while others hustled over to the general store to select gifts and purchase new suits.

Chapter Twenty-Five

A cloudless blue sky, warm sunshine, and soft breezes filled with a hint of sea salt from the Pacific Ocean marked the long awaited wedding day for the mail-order brides. Fiona hoped it was an omen, that the beauty of the day meant God approved of all the matched marriages about to take place.

Coppery hair that normally hung in a long braid down her back was now confined in a neat bun on the nape of her neck. She fumbled with the row of buttons lining the front of her green dress.

"Such a shame about your mother's gown. I know how much you looked forward to wearing it on your own wedding day." Althea fussed over last minute adjustments to her own gray taffeta dress.

Fiona forced her lips into a thin smile. She hadn't shared the letter the timber-cutter had written with anyone. If she had wrongly pre-judged the man, she didn't want anyone to know. While on the inside she was elated that yellow age streaks stained the creases of the dress and gave her an excuse not to wear it, she was really unhappy. She wanted to wear white and too look beautiful for only one man—a man she could never have. She forced a huge sigh. "Do you think Mr. Filmore will mind I'm not gowned in white?"

"How could he object when he's getting such a beautiful bride?" Henrietta smiled as Fiona lined white daisies inside the coil of her friend's brunette braid making it resemble a tiara.

"Oh, Henrietta, the pale yellow makes your skin

213

glow like sunshine. And Ma Smalley, your gray taffeta becomes the color of your salt and pepper hair." Fiona smoothed the skirt of her own dress.

In the close confines of the wagon, Henrietta twirled around. "Do you think Mr. Sims will mind that I'm not a...you know." Her face reddened. "Anyhow, I didn't think white for a second marriage was fittin'."

Fiona touched her friend's cheek. "From what you've shared of his letter, I'm certain Mr. Sims is a kind and understanding man."

Henrietta said, "The three of us have become as close as sisters." Her eyes misted. "Let's make a pact to always remain friends, and to always be there for each other, the way we've been on the trail."

Althea lifted the clean hankie to dab the corner of her eye. "In a few hours my name will change to Althea Hackett—Mrs. Otto Hackett. I'll no longer be Ma Smalley, so I'm thinking the two of you should start calling me Althea."

"In a few hours, all our lives will change." *I hope for the better.* Fiona's heart thudded furiously.

"Oh, merciful heavens, we can't be crying on our weddin' day." Althea swiped at another tear.

At the sound of hooves, the three women lifted their skirts and stepped from the wagon. Bannon and Isaiah rode into the circle of wagons and dismounted.

Bannon sought out Fiona. Their eyes met. Her spine stiffened as she recalled the times he'd brought her to the pinnacle of desire only to reject her like a piece of undesirable meat. Two pink spots appeared on her cheeks, and she offered him her sweetest smile. *I promise to never speak to you again.*

He smiled, and Fiona thought he was mocking her.

"Well, ladies, this is the last time I'll be askin' you to gather 'round." He chuckled. "The grooms are eagerly waiting for your arrival, and a handsome lot they are." His tone grew serious. His glimpse lingered over the smiling faces. "I'm proud to know each of you. You're all brave women." He touched his fingers to the brim of his hat and stepped up into the saddle. "Isaiah will escort you into town."

A stab of panic struck Fiona. This was it, the last time she'd ever see him. All her resolve to hate Bannon melted.

A murmur sifted through the group like wind echoing through a pine-needle forest.

Althea stepped forward. "I was hopin' to get at least one dance with you, Bannon."

He grinned his appreciation. "Another time, Miz Smalley. Right now urgent business at my ranch requires my attention."

His eyes narrowed, slightly. "How long you planning to stay in town, Isaiah?"

Dressed in a new blue shirt, brown chinos and wearing a new slouch hat, the grizzled scout squinted up at his friend. "Soon as I'm satisfied all these ladies are proper wedded, and I wet my whistle a few times, and fill up my innards with some of that fine barbeque, I'll be on. You can look for me when you see me comin'."

Bannon shifted in the saddle. "Fiona, Miz Smalley, Henrietta, Bird, the best of luck to all you ladies. Been good travelin' with you."

****

Fiona's muscles were strangely uncooperative as she climbed on the wagon seat. She slid to the middle and gathered the reins. Flanked on either side by Althea and Henrietta, she waited for them to settle their skirts, then flapped the reins urging the mules forward.

"One mile." Althea sighed.

Henrietta fussed with a strand of hair. "What time is it, Althea?"

"My timepiece says seven o'clock straight up." Althea lifted the pendant watch attached to her dress.

Fiona nodded. She didn't want to talk. She forced herself to loosen tense muscles.

At the edge of town, Isaiah turned his pinto and rode up alongside Fiona's wagon. "I'm gonna ride on in and let 'em know to strike up the band. Fiona, there's a large field behind the pavilion. After you circle up the wagons, get the rest of the ladies and hustle on over."

She nodded her understanding. "Where will you be, Isaiah?"

He grinned. "I'll meetcha at the steps."

Sunlight filtered in a shimmering haze over the broad streets of the small town. A huge banner stretched from one side of the street to the other. Large blocked letters printed in red blocks read, *Brides—Welcome to Glory!*

Fiona spotted a young boy who lit out running as fast as his feet would carry him the minute he spotted her wagon. Moments later, music greeted them. Her eyes darted back and forth. "There's the pavilion."

A fusillade of fireworks erupted, like fireworks on the fourth of July. Fiona tightened the reins and spoke stern commands to the frightened mules.

"Merciful heavens, would you look at all those people." Althea patted her hair. "How do I look?"

"I don't think I was this nervous at my first wedding," said Henrietta.

Fiona merely nodded as she tugged on the reins, guiding the mules to the left while the other wagons followed to form a circle.

After stepping down and shaking out their skirts, Fiona gathered hands with her two friends while waiting for all the ladies to set the brakes on their wagons and join them.

She admired the array of finery, from straw hats adorned with dainty flowers, to colorful shawls, white wedding gowns, to dresses in the palest of pastels. With a full week of relaxation, adequate sleep and no worries over what dangers lurked around the next bend in the trail, the women had transformed from a sun-browned bedraggled group to a picture of beauty.

"Ma...ummm...Althea, Henrietta, look at Bird. Isn't she beautiful?" Fiona marvels at the way sunlight cast a blue glint off the Iroquois woman's straight black hair. She wore a white doeskin dress, with a fringed hem, the bodice adorned with intricate beadwork, and knee-high moccasins that mimicked the same fringe and beading. Draped over her arm was a colorful blanket. She greeted her friends with a smile.

Fiona commented on the outfit. "Your dress is lovely, Bird, and so are you."

If it were possible, she thought the Indian woman blushed. "I have brought marriage blanket for Monsieur Jacques Medoro."

"Did you weave it yourself?" Henrietta wanted to know.

The conversation was more to calm twittering nerves while waiting for all the ladies to gather. Fiona blew out a breath. "You're the official leader, Althea. We're all waiting on you."

"Gather round ladies. This calls for one last group prayer." Althea clasped hands with Fiona, and the women formed a circle and bowed their heads.

"Lord, you've seen us through some terrible times. You've given us bravery in the face of the enemy, and given us hope when we figured there wasn't any left. We mourn the loss of those we buried and left behind. Today we celebrate a new journey, and ask you to remain with us as we travel our separate roads to begin new lives. Amen."

Fiona sniffed and wiped a tear. "That was beautiful, Althea. Thank you."

Althea squared her shoulders. "There's Isaiah waving at us. C'mon ladies. No need keeping the grooms waitin' any longer than we have to."

Isaiah snatched off his hat as the women stood at the bottom of the pavilion steps. "Fiona, Miz Smalley...ladies, you could put a patch of wildflowers to shame."

Fiona smiled at the scout's awkward compliment.

The minister stepped forward. "Welcome to the town of Glory, ladies. I trust you brought the tintypes of the grooms you've selected?"

At a round of nods, he said, "Good...good. Please hold them in front of you, and stand far enough apart so the men can easily match themselves to you."

Fiona and the women followed the minister and his wife to the east side of the domed building that was festooned with colorful draped banners. An arched arbor was decorated with fragrant pine boughs and wildflowers. Someone had fashioned wedding bells from white paper and hung them from the center of the arbor. Inside the arbor's archway was a podium, and on top of the podium laid an opened Bible.

Long tables with white linen tablecloths lined the grounds next to the pavilion. Mixed aromas from venison, beef, and smoked fish filled the air.

Fiona had never seen so many delicate cakes, pies and baskets of bread all in one place.

After miles of wearing brogans, her feet felt pinched in her Sunday shoes, and though the day was cool, moist patches collected beneath her armpits.

She swept her gaze across the pavilion where men dressed in suits stood, then up to the bandstand. She searched each face in the crowd. Her heart faltered. Bannon wasn't there.

What did I expect—that he would come charging up on his horse and rescue me. Aggravated with herself, she wanted to stomp her foot. *This isn't a fairytale, and Bannon 'tis no prince.*

A voice interrupted her thoughts. "Ladies, my name is G. W. Daggert, welcome to Glory. As an attorney of law, I tend to be a little longwinded. The grooms have requested that I keep my speech short."

A peal of laughter rose from the crowd.

The lawyer held up his hands to signal silence. "Brides, the grooms will come to you. Hold the tintypes high enough for them to see. As soon as a match is made, form a straight line with ten to a row in front of the wedding arbor. When all matches have been made, Reverend Harris will perform the ceremony. As he speaks your names, Mrs. Harris will fill in the marriage certificates. Make sure you sign it before the day is out." He clapped his hands together. "Grooms go and meet your brides."

Cheers and applause went up from the spectators. With flowers in one hand and a wrapped gift in the other, the men reminded Fiona of shy boys as they slowly approached the waiting group. She shifted the photo from one hand to the other while she reached behind and wiped a sweaty palm on the back of her skirt.

By sheer will of force she put the starch back into her knees and stood stiff as a fire poker. All around her were shy introductions as couples paired up. She listened to their conversations.

"Oh, Mr. Hackett, the cameo is beautiful." Althea asked him to pin it in place.

"A husband should be known by his first name," he'd replied. Fiona watched his nervous fingers pin the broach above Althea's heart, his voice gentle, "Please, I am Otto, and you are Althea."

She listened to Gerda's happy exclamations over the beautifully crafted cuckoo clock given by Arn Johansson.

She watched the French trapper dressed in new buckskins claim Bird LeBlanc. After he had handed her flowers and kissed her hand, he led her to the railing and pointed. "You see the black horse with white ribbons in its mane. She is a fine mare and my gift to you."

A smile on her face and a lilt in her sing-song voice, Bird said, "She is a gift of great value." And then she handed her groom-to-be the wedding blanket.

And so it went with happy couples holding hands and quickly taking their places before the podium beneath the decorated arbor. As the matches were made and the number of women next to her dwindled, Fiona placated herself that perhaps Henry Filmore had gotten cold feet and decided not to come, or maybe—she brushed aside the thought he'd met with a fatal accident while on the road to met her.

Her hand flew to her mouth. "Oh dear," she murmured through her fingers. The man stumping up the steps reminded her of a garden scarecrow, and she determined in a few years his thinning hair would leave him bald.

She glanced around and found she stood alone. This was Henry Filmore and he was coming to claim her. Forgetting about holding up the tintype, her hand dropped to her side.

He stopped in front of her. "Since you're the only one left, I take it you're Fiona Quinn."

"And you are Henry Filmore?"

"If I wasn't, I wouldn't be standing here, now would I?"

The serious tone of his voice made her uneasy. Fiona glanced at his empty hands—no gift and no flowers. His letter had said he wasn't an extravagant man. He'd neglected to say a miserly man.

He reached into his coat pocket and withdrew a gold band. "Cost me ten dollars."

"It's nice."

"All right then, let's join the others so we can get this over with."

"Mr. Filmore," Fiona hesitated, "have I done something to make you angry?"

"You've cost me unnecessary money."

"I'm afraid I don't understand. I only have the bride's money that was given for travel expenses."

"Because of circumstances, I was only able to build a one room cabin. Now I have to pay for your board at the rooming house until I get a second room added and furnished."

Her hand trembled as she reached out to touch his coat sleeve. "I-it was part of the contract. The lawyer in Philadelphia said so."

Isaiah walked over. He crossed his arms over his barrel chest. "There a problem here, Fiona?"

Her fingers twisted through the folds of her dress. "Mr. Filmore was explaining about his cabin. I can make do with one room, honest."

Isaiah squinted first at her then at the weaselly man who was to be her husband. "Nope, you'll do no such a thing. Mr. Filmore, here, done been told."

"So be it." The log-splitter snarled. He grabbed Fiona's hand. "Ain't no need in keeping the preacher waiting."

Isaiah laid a hand on the man's arm. "Feller, I'd advise you to speak a little more kindly to the lady."

Although his grip tightened on Fiona's hand, Filmore managed a contrite smile. "My apologies, Fiona. It isn't your fault that I neglected to read the fine print on the contract before signing it."

Isaiah corrected him. "Didn't need to read it. Lawyer Daggert spelled it out loud and clear for all you fellers. And as I recall, all you men clambering for a bride agreed hands down to the terms."

The challenge in Isaiah's eyes was evident as he stared at the man. As the tension continued to build, Fiona was relieved when the minister announced he was ready to begin the ceremony.

Filmore said, "If you'll excuse us." Still holding Fiona's hand, he fairly dragged her to stand with the other couples.

Over the course of a half hour she listened to the minister. First he prayed, then he instructed the couples to join hands.

He opened his Bible and read several scriptures then began the exchange of vows.

"Brides and grooms, you are gathered here this sixteenth day of September, 1847, before man and God, to join in holy wedlock. Otto Hackett and Althea Smalley, Arn Johansson and Gerda Olsson, Jacques Medoro and Bird LeBlanc..." He continued down the line, calling each couple by name until reaching the last—"Henry Filmore and Fiona Quinn, do you promise to honor, obey and cherish one another through sickness and sorrow, through good times and poor times, until death do you part?"

A chorus of "I dos," filled the pavilion. Fiona crossed the fingers on her right hand as if by doing so, she was protected by the lie of speaking a vow she didn't wish to honor.

Oh, my dear sweet Mercy. The selfish part of me wishes you were still alive. I think your life with Mr. Filmore would have been like living in hell. At least you've gone to a far better place. He isn't a nice man, Mercy. I fear I will die my own slow death while suffering from his mean spirit.

The minister's voice intruded upon her thoughts. "If any man shows good cause why any one of these couples should not be joined in holy wedlock, let him step forward and state his reason."

Fiona silently beseeched Isaiah to speak on her behalf. When no voice of objection was raised, Reverend Harris continued. "What God has joined together let no man put asunder. By the power vested in me by the holy church and the territory of Oregon, I now pronounce each couple husband and wife."

Over a din of voices, he shouted, "Settle down, folks. Let me finish." He said, "Grooms as soon as you slip the wedding band on the finger of your wife, you may kiss the bride." He smiled as he turned and signaled the band. "Let there be music, merry making and feasting."

Chapter Twenty-Six

"Come along, wife. We will spend our honeymoon night at the cabin."

Fiona didn't like Filmore's tone of voice or possessive attitude. "I thought you were to take me to the boarding house."

"Not much privacy behind thin walls." Henry Filmore laughed. "Man's got a right to enjoy his weddin' night without prying ears."

Searching his face, he reminded her of Blackie Sledge, the brothel owner in Philadelphia. A shudder ran through her, and she had to will her legs to move.

Leaving her to climb into the buckboard unassisted, the timber cutter stepped up to the seat and gathered the reins. "Giddup, horse."

They rode in hard silence. A little moon peaked behind waning clouds by the time he pulled the horse to a halt in front of a square structure with a flat roof. He lifted her valise from the rear of the wagon and handed it to her. "Get yourself ready while I unhitch the horse and stable him. I'll be in directly."

She glanced around at the forested steep banks that surrounded the compact cabin. The sound of rushing water reached her and thought at least she'd have a place to bathe.

Feeling helpless, she wanted to scream. *Oh, dear God, What have I done? I'm wed to a man I already hate.*

Trudging to the house, she lifted the latch to the

door and stepped inside. At least he had banked a fire in the fireplace. Setting her valise next to the door, she surveyed the small room and determined it wasn't much larger than the shanty she'd rented in Philadelphia. A bed, a crudely built stand with a wash basin, a rough-hewn table and two chairs comprised the one room with windows on either side of the only entrance.

Her body quaking with emotion, she sat in the chair nearest the fireplace, her hands gripped together in her lap and stared into the smoldering embers. A short time might have passed—or perhaps an eternity of dread, as measured by the terrified thudding of her heart.

A squeak caused her to look up. Filmore stood in the doorway. He stopped before her—he was shorter than she, and suddenly grabbed her around the neck and jerked her up and kissed her. She reeled back, shaking and darted for the door.

He moved so he stood between her and the way to escape. His eyes glittered. "So you want to play, huh?"

She heard her teeth chatter. She moved a step backward, bumping against the bed's footboard.

Now the moon had moved from behind the clouds and its rays shone through the glass panes illuminating the room.

Filmore gripped her arms. His rough patting reminded her of the two brothers who had kidnapped her. He pressed her breasts together. She struggled. Briefly he was gentle. And just as quickly he reached his hand into the neck of her gown and jerked, ripping the garment all the way down to her waist.

"I asked you nicely to make yourself ready, and now look what you've made me go and do." He laughed at his triumph.

While he lit the lamp, he silently scourged Fiona

with his gloating gaze. He said he had something to tell her for her own good. Was she listening? He said it was all right for her to carry on a bit. But soon she had better cooperate—help along. A husband expected it.

He shed his clothes and tossed them to a corner. Then he grabbed Fiona and threw her on the bed. He straddled her body, touched her shrinking form, and then rolled off.

"Get up," he ordered. "I've got to be flat on my back."

"I don't understand."

"Get on your knees."

She rose, rubbing her arms. She could hardly stand. Her ripped gown exposed her breasts, and as she grabbed for the coverlet to hide her body, Filmore snatched the blanket away.

Then he told her exactly what he wanted her to do. She gulped, shook her head in mute negation. He told her again, his voice growing ugly. It was the only way he could reach full satisfaction, he said. "You'd better do what I say if you don't want me to make you sorry."

Her head shook; her hands begged. She crossed her arms upon her breasts, weeping. "No, I won't. It's indecent."

Filmore grabbed her by her loosened hair and yanked her head down. "Do it—or I'll tear your hair out by the roots."

"I-I can't. I don't know what to do." She sobbed.

"You knew how to nurse at your mama's tit, didn't you? No different." He growled. "Get started or by all that is holy, I'll take my shaving strop to you."

"M-my throat is dry. Let me take a drink of water first," she implored.

"Now why didn't I think of that? I have something better than water. He rolled off the bed. Moonlight played over his stork-like legs. His bony chest was covered with a thick mat of fur that ran from his shoulders to the narrowing apex below his waist.

He grabbed a bottle and two glasses from the fireplace mantle. In his haste to pour, brandy spilled over his hand and into a puddle on the table. He thrust a glass at her. "This should help you relax. Now drink."

She lifted the glass to her lips.

"No more excuses, damn you." He laughed grimly as he grabbed for her. In desperation to loosen his grip she tossed the fiery liquid in his face. The hairs on his chest glistened with moisture.

Her mind working frantically. She used the table as a shield. He snarled at her. "A waste of good brandy. Cost me a day's wage."

His hand rested in the puddle of liquor. He made a game of taunting Fiona. As he zigged one way around the table, she zagged in the opposite directions. Obviously growing impatient with the game, he made a mad grab across the table, knocking over the lamp. There was a crash, the tinkling of breaking glass, a flare, a horrible male scream.

There was a gush of heat from something that resembled only a shrieking pillar of fire as the flame traveled up Filmore's chest. As he batted at the hot glowing mass, the hairs on his arm ignited. In a wild moment, he picked up the bottle and brought it down hard against the edge of the table. The brandy exploded in a ball of orange and blue fire. Fiona watched in horror as the writhing column which seemed like nothing human ran to the door. Unable to open it, he leaped through the closed window and left a bloody char as he entered the woods in a wild shriek that ended in a splash below the cabin.

Fire traveled along the trail of brandy, down the table leg. Flames seemed to come alive as it licked thirstily to where alcohol had splattered on the bed. Moth-eaten blankets quickly ignited. Flames fingered up the walls.

Fiona felt jabs of pain as drops of burning oil touched her feet. In a precious instance, she grabbed her valise and rushed to the door. She clawed at the latch, remembering that earlier she had used her thumb to open the door from the outside.

She leaped through the opening and ran from the flames before falling to her knees. Coughing and retching stopped her breath. Cold penetrated her flesh and seeped to her bones.

She screamed, but the sound was lost among rushing water and the whispering wind through the vast wilderness. Trying to cover herself, she fumbled with the torn bodice of her dress before letting weakness conquer her. As she allowed blackness to take her mind, she wondered if she would ever feel safe again.

****

Fiona awakened in a cheerfully decorated room. For a long time she only wanted to huddle in the security of the blankets. What had happened at Filmore's cabin seemed unbelievable—a nightmare. But, it had all been real—horribly real.

A tear squeezed from the corner of her eye and trickled down her cheek. Her only comfort was in knowing that Filmore's death wasn't her fault, and there was nothing she could have done to save him.

Gradually, she realized that someone was standing over her. "Althea." She tried to smile. "How long have I been here? How did I get here?"

"Whoa. One question at a time." Althea's hand was tender as she placed a fresh damp cloth over Fiona's forehead. "You feelin' up to some broth?"

Fiona nodded.

"Good, after you've eaten and then rested, we'll talk. Right now, I'm just glad your fever's broke."

As the woman rose to leave, Fiona clasped her hand. "Thank you."

Althea winked and left the room only to return with a bowl of steaming chicken broth, a slice of cornbread and a pot of willow bark tea.

Fiona's hand trembled as she lifted the spoon to her mouth, spilling a little on the napkin Althea had draped over the bodice of a new flannel nightgown.

Setting the empty bowl aside, Fiona polished off the cornbread down to the last crumb. "The last time I remember eating was at the—" her voice trailed off.

"At the barbeque." Althea finished the sentence for her. "Close you eyes and rest. We'll talk later."

Fiona shook her head in protest. "Please, now. You have questions. I can see it in your eyes."

Althea reached for Fiona's cup and refilled it with tea, and filling her own, she settled back in the chair. "To answer your first question, you've been here four days. As to how you came, it seems there was a fire. Some timber men went to investigate. They found the cabin burned nearly to the ground and you half out of your mind. You asked to be brought here."

"What about Henry Filmore—did they find him, too?" Fiona shivered at the recollection of the fire.

"They did. He was charred to a crisp, but recognizable."

As her thoughts turned back to that night, Fiona attempted several false starts, each time her voice cracking with strain. Piece-by-piece the tale of her wedding night unfolded. And when she had finished, her shoulders rose and fell with each sob. Suddenly, she felt very old.

Althea's chin trembled as she reached over and embraced Fiona. "The devil take him for what he did, and I'm not ashamed to say that I'm glad the worthless scoundrel got what he deserved."

Brushing away a tear, she added, "As soon as you're up to it, Lawyer Daggert wishes to speak to you."

Fiona's eyes widened. She shrank back against the pillows and pulled the blanket up to her chin. "Am I in trouble?"

"He assures me you are not. What with him being the only law in Glory, he needs all the facts to lay the case to rest."

"What day is it, Althea?"

"Thursday."

"Then if you will go with me, I shall see lawyer Daggert tomorrow."

"It can wait 'til the blisters on your feet heal."

A flash of panic raced through Fiona. She propped against her elbows to glance around the room. "Althea, my valise. All that I own in this world is inside it."

"It's tucked safely under the bed." Althea gave a half-chuckle. "The men who brought you here had to pry it from your hands.

Fiona lay back and groaned. "I wasn't naked was I?"

"The front of your gown was ripped to the waist, but you somehow managed to keep yourself covered. Don't worry. You were shivering so hard one of the men wrapped you in a blanket."

"Althea, I have a terrible confession." Fiona fumbled with her thoughts. "I'm glad Mercy is dead." She watched the struggle of emotions on the woman's face. "Mercy deserved everything good, and Filmore was all evil." She considered her statement. "Do you think I'll go to hell for such thoughts?"

"Likely as not, but you'd have company 'cause I feel the same as you." Althea stood. She lifted the tray from Fiona's lap. "Would you like me to send word to Bannon?"

Fiona's heart thudded in her throat. "No. Not

today, not tomorrow, not ever." Her voice was emphatic. "You must give me your word that you won't send for him. He isn't to know what happened, please."

"Hear me, child. You fulfilled your contract. Now that the sorry lout is dead, you're free to do your own choosing."

Fiona leaned back against the pillows and released a weary sigh. "Too much has happened since leaving Philadelphia. I don't even know my own heart." She didn't know what else to say.

Althea turned toward the door. "You have my word. Bannon won't hear any of this from my lips."

Narrowing her eyes, her mouth pressed tightly. "Nor from anyone else's, Althea."

Although her eyes spoke disapproval, Althea nodded as she left the room.

Chapter Twenty-Seven

In late October, Fiona stood with other passengers waiting to board one of the river sloops that would sail to San Francisco.

The morning chill invaded her new russet colored woolen cloak. She had scarcely noticed the lovely beginning of the new day on her one-mile trek to the shipping docks. She had resisted all offers for a buggy ride from Althea and Henrietta, preferring to say good-bye to her friends in private. After a lengthy silence had passed between them, each woman holding the gaze of the other, hugged once more.

Althea said, "It's been a month, Fiona. You don't have to go. Let me send word to Bannon."

Tears swelled in Fiona's eyes. "We've been through this before, and my answer is still the same."

"You're in love with Cordell Bannon."

"Don't be absurd," Fiona nervously countered. "I'm not. I don't love him."

Althea cut a glance at Henrietta who smiled and nodded. "Oh, but you do, Fiona. It's something we women can see in the eyes of another."

The last vestiges of Fiona's denial crumbled. "All right. I care deeply for him. But it's an affection that isn't returned. You saw how he left the wagon train with some lame excuse about an emergency. A month has passed since we arrived in Glory, and how many times have any of us seen him—none." She drew herself up. "Beside, he isn't the kind who accepts another man's cast-off."

"And that is nonsense," Althea objected. "Very well, have it your stubborn Irish way. But I don't like any of this."

Fiona didn't like it either, anymore than she liked porridge, but there was no changing the past. It was time she looked toward the future.

****

At the end of the hour's ride, Bannon tossed the chestnut gelding's reins over the hitching post in front of Hackett's General Store and waited for Isaiah to light down from the buckboard. "Isaiah, I don't plan on lingering in town any longer than I have to. We'll get what we need then head on back to the ranch."

Isaiah grumbled, "Ah, dagnabit, Cordell, I was plannin' to wet my whistle. Been a blue moon since we were in town."

Bannon laughed at his friend's dog-sad eyes. "Go on. I'll load the supplies and meet you at the saloon. Could use a cold beer myself."

Isaiah stepped up on the boardwalk. "Reckon I'll poke my head in and give a howdy to the new Miz Hackett."

The men had no sooner entered the store than Althea charged around the counter and wrapped Isaiah in a bear hug. She left him and planted a kiss on Bannon's cheek. "Where have you two hoot owls been hidin' yourselves?" She stood back with her hands on her hips, a wide grin on her face.

Otto Hackett appeared through a rear door, his arms laden with bolts of fabric. After depositing his load, he shook hands with the men. "Althea, I bet these two would enjoy a scoop of that fresh blueberry cobbler you just baked."

At Bannon's objection, the store owner said, "Leave your list, Cordell. I'll fill it while you and Isaiah visit with my wife." He cast a grin at Althea and made shooing motions with his hands. "Go...go...enjoy." He called over his shoulder, "Jacob."

A gangly youngster about the age of fourteen came from the stockroom. "Yes, sir?"

"You help me fill this order and load the wagon while these gentlemen enjoy a good visit with Mrs. Hackett." He winked at the boy. "When we are finished, we'll get her to fatten us with a little cobbler."

Althea looped her arms inside Bannon's and Isaiah's. "You heard what my husband said." She led them through a door and into the living quarters at the rear of the store.

Bannon itched to ask about Fiona. He gritted his teeth and decided to let Althea monopolize the conversation.

Althea set bowls of warm blueberry cobbler topped with fresh churned clabber in front of Bannon and Isaiah.

"Where you two been keeping yourselves?" Pouring cups of coffee and setting out cream and sugar, she set the pot in the center of the table. Bannon stood and pulled out a chair to seat her.

"After being gone for most of a year, there was a lot of work that needed my attention at the ranch." Bannon smiled and shoveled a large bite of cobbler into his mouth.

Althea smoothed a wrinkle in the blue and white checkered tablecloth. "Did you hear the news?"

Both men looked up and shook there heads. "The Lone Tree is over an hour's ride from town. We don't get much news." Bannon reached for the coffee pot.

Isaiah polished off his bowl of dessert and drained the coffee from his cup. "Don't mean to be rude, best I ever ate, but I got me an appointment." He winked at Bannon.

Althea laughed. "If beer and cobbler don't set

well on your stomach, I can fix you some blackstrap molasses."

Bannon nearly choked on his coffee at the look of disgust on the old scout's face.

After Isaiah was gone, Bannon grew serious. "What news were you referring to, Miz Hackett?"

"Listen here, Cordell Bannon, we spent six months crossing the prairie, fightin' Injuns, and burying friends. I think it's high time you called me by my given name."

"All right, Althea. What news?"

"Take it that you didn't hear about the fire?"

He scooped up another bite of brown crust and berries and chewed appreciatively. "Fire...nope."

She thrummed her fingers on the table. "I ain't one for making small talk. You gonna ask about Fiona or not?"

He set the spoon aside. "Look Althea, Fiona is another man's wife. She and I both knew we were bound by contracts. I didn't stay for the wedding because there was no need to heap hurt on top of more hurt."

Althea had certainly touched on the more disagreeable aspect of his life. "Figured I'd drop by on my way back to the Lone Tree to see if Filmore finished the cabin." His eyes shifted to look out the window.

She harrumphed. "No need. You'll only find a charred skeleton of the cabin and a grave."

He reached out and gripped Althea's hand, a flurry of turmoil roiled inside him. "Whose...grave?"

She released her hands from his powerful grip. "Filmore's."

"What about Fiona?"

Althea held up her hand. "Just hold your taters. You've waited a month. You can wait a little longer for me to tell it."

Sagging back against the chair in relief, he

didn't miss the sarcasm in her voice. Forcing himself to relax, he toyed with the ear of the coffee mug. "Maybe you'd better start from the beginning."

As she filled him in on the details of Henry Filmore's unfortunate demise, she finished by saying, "The land and the cabin never belonged to Filmore. It sat on Grantham Timber Company's holdings. The sorry coyote could've filed homestead on the parcel, but he never got around to filling out the papers, and he hadn't started any improvements on the land or the cabin, either.

"When she was well enough, Fiona asked me to accompany her to lawyer Daggert's office. That's how we found out about the homestead part." Althea sucked in a relieving breath and exhaled. "All wasn't lost. Though it'd never replace the hurt he did to Fiona, Filmore's stinginess paid off. He left most of his pay vouchers untouched with the timber company's bookkeeper. With Fiona being his legal widow, the money went to her—six hundred dollars."

"Why didn't you send for me?" Bannon flexed his shoulders in a weary gesture. "I would've come."

Althea stirred sugar into a fresh cup of coffee. "Couldn't. She swore me to secrecy. I was honor-bound to keep my word."

Bannon pushed back his chair and stood. He grabbed his Stetson from the hat rack and situated it on his head, pulling the brim down over his forehead, and headed out the door. "Is she at the boarding house?"

"Nope, but if you hurry you might catch her before the riverboat sails on the noon tide."

His brows furrowed in confused agitation. "Which sloop?"

She smiled. "The *Pacific Belle*. Said there was nothing to keep her here so she's striking out for San Francisco."

Bannon growled. "Why the hell is she going to

San Francisco? Doesn't she know it's a dangerous place for a young woman without a chaperone?"

Althea jabbed a finger against the center of his broad chest, her voice terse. "Listen here, Bannon. Philadelphia was a dangerous place, so was the prairie, and so was Henry Filmore. Once the boat docks in San Francisco, Fiona plans to buy passage to Ireland. She has aunts and uncles, cousins, and a grandmother there. She thinks she'll feel safe surrounded by family. She thinks she can forget the past and build a future."

Althea continued poking him as she spoke. "You're in love with Fiona, and she's in love with you. And you're about the two most stubborn blockheads I've ever known. Now, if'n I was you, I'd stop standin' around jawin' and get on down to the docks before that boat sails and takes our Fiona with it."

Her sharply spoken words raced through him like wild-fire. Fiona's face flashed in his mind. His voice was thick and forceful. "Until I draw my last breath, no man will ever hurt Fiona again."

He nearly tripped over a barrel of pickles on his way out of the store. He yanked the reins loose, grabbed hold of the saddle horn and swung into the saddle without using the stirrups. The fractious bald-faced chestnut gelding reared. Bannon cursed as he brought the animal under control. He set spurs to the horse and galloped toward the docks.

Chapter Twenty-Eight

Fiona stood at the railing of the *Pacific Belle.* Her coppery hair blended with the russet hue of the new cape and hood that she drew closer around her face with a gloved hand.

Her new clothing blowing in the wind, she watched the hive of activity as dockworkers loaded timber, bundles of fur pelts, barrels of salted fish, and other merchandise aboard the line of river sloops.

She wondered why she had been so stubborn about contacting Bannon. With one word, she thought, she could insure that she'd never again be threatened or degraded. She would enjoy the respect that comes to a prosperous rancher's wife.

She looked upward past the billowing sails as though seeking help in her decision to return to Ireland. She sighed deeply, thinking of Bannon and wanting to be with him. She could think of nothing more wonderful than becoming his wife. Once he found out that she was now a widow, she hoped he could forgive her for running away.

She frowned darkly. She knew she loved him, but with all the recent and tragic events in her life, she feared he might think her only reason for wanting him was money and security.

Suddenly, tears rushed upon her green eyes, but she lowered her gaze and discreetly brushed away the evidence of her melancholy. It occurred to her that Althea or Henrietta might break her confidence and send word to Bannon.

Feeling perfectly miserable, she paced back and forth wishing the time would pass and the captain would order the gangplank raised.

****

Bannon's insides crawled with apprehension and dread that he'd never see Fiona again. He urged the gelding faster as he raced frantically toward the river sloops where they lay at moorage.

His stomach churned, and he felt sick. He blamed himself. Why hadn't he swallowed his pride and ridden out to check on Fiona. Why hadn't he sought advice from Lawyer Daggert as to ways to break Fiona's contract with Filmore? Had he not let her down, she wouldn't have felt the need to runaway. But mentally and emotionally castigating himself wouldn't solve the problem.

Forcing himself to remain calm, he quickly closed the distance between the township and the docks. He prayed he'd find her sitting on a bench and not yet departed. Yes...God yes, let him find her there.

He slowed the gelding to a walk as he approached a man dressed in the heavy canvas garb of a boatman. "The *Pacific Belle*, where will I find her?"

An old gentleman with a gray beard and wearing a stocking cap pulled a pipe from his lips. He pointed. "She's first in the line."

Bannon urged the gelding to a fast pace weaving in and around passersby until reaching the boat. When he dismounted he was unable to suppress the tremble rocking him from head to toe. He called out, "Here, lad, take care of my horse." He flipped the boy a fifty-cent piece.

A freckle-face boy of about thirteen caught the coin, immediately set it between his teeth and bit down on it. He grinned as he clutched the reins. "Thankee, sir. I'll guard 'im with me life."

A brisk breeze swept over the water. Tugging his hat further down on his head, Bannon arrived as the *Pacific Belle's* captain was shouting orders for the gangplank to be hauled away.

Bannon searched the passengers lined against the railing. A few women, mostly men and a rough-looking crew at that. "Permission to go aboard, Captain," Bannon called.

"Your ticket, sir?"

"I don't have one. I'm looking for someone...a young woman with red hair." Bannon raised his hand to indicated Fiona's height. "She has eyes the color of the ocean."

The captain smirked. "And what is your business with one of my passengers?"

Bannon's brusqueness was meant to diminish his emotions. "To ask for her hand in marriage."

"Aha. Then come aboard, sir. You have three minutes to find your runaway bride." The captain guffawed.

Bannon sprinted up the ramp. His eyes darted back and forth, searching until he spotted a petite woman clothed in a russet cloak. She stood facing the leeward side of the sloop, apparently watching the water. He knew what he hoped to find when he called her name, and yet afraid to consider the alternate possibility.

"Fiona?"

She spun around, her eyes wide, her mouth agape. "Bannon."

He opened his arms and when she flew into them, circled her shoulders and drew her up against her chest. A frown pressed his brow. Questions nagged at him. She was running away—did she want him?

Chapter Twenty-Nine

Fiona stood before the mirror as Althea fussed over her, tucking in a wayward curl, straightening the gossamer veil, and tugging at the bodice of the cream-colored wedding gown.

"You're pretty as a picture, Fiona, in your mother's dress." Althea tucked another pin to secure the delicate headpiece lined with seed-pearls atop Fiona's head.

"Is everyone at the pavilion?" a nervous Fiona asked.

"Here's your bouquet," Henrietta said, enthusiastically tucking it into Fiona's hand. "Everyone who is anyone is waiting for you to make your appearance."

Fiona hugged her friends one last time before the ceremony. A sharp knock echoed the door. Althea opened it to a crack and peeked out.

Isaiah fidgeted in his new black suit. He ran a finger around the stiffly starched collar of his white shirt. Althea opened the door and stood aside.

"I come to collect the bride and walk her down the aisle." His hand tenderly shaped itself around Fiona's.

Bannon wondered how it had gotten so blasted hot on a mid-October day. He stood before the altar that had been erected and looked toward the general store where his Fiona would soon descend. He felt as nervous as a stallion waiting to be broke to the saddle.

When Isaiah escorted her up the steps for the

short walk to the altar, Bannon drank in her beauty. Her emerald eyes gleamed through the diaphanous veil. His eyes held her gentle gaze, and he had to cough down the lump of adoration that rose in his throat. Nodding politely to his best friend, he accepted her hand from a beaming Isaiah Thomas.

Bannon felt her light touch on his arm and looked down at her smiling face. There was relief in her eyes and a silent message meant only for him. A surge of warmth filled his chest.

The minister's smile gave silent approval to him. He began, "Dearly beloved, we are gathered here in the sight of God..."

****

"White linen, candlelight, champagne, I didn't expect all of this Bannon." The flickering flame brought a burnished glow to Fiona's mane of auburn hair.

"This is a very special evening for a very special lady."

Fiona sipped at her champagne, laughing softly. "I feel like this champagne, all sparkly and bubbly."

Closing his eyes, Bannon drew in a deep breath. "I was told brides were the ones who were nervous on their wedding nights. Now I'm not so sure."

Biting her lower lip, Fiona also drew in a long breath.

Bannon stared at the outline of Fiona's body through her gossamer gown. With a seductive smile curling her lips, she lifted her eyes to gaze into his. She raised one hand and lightly traced the steely ripples of flesh over his ribs.

His arms encircled her, crushing her to his chest and taking her breath away. He whispered against her hair, "You promised to cherish, honor, and obey."

"That I did." She turned her head to eagerly accept his kiss.

He sucked in a silent breath to calm his

quickening heartbeat. The smell of her, her silken skin, the feel of her slender frame molded against him was too much for him. He wanted her as he'd never wanted any other woman in his life. Not even his departed wife, Annie. And he felt no guilt.

He would guide Fiona, instruct her, and lead her to a heavenly place she would long remember and desire again. His hands slipped the straps of her gown over her shoulders.

The material floated to the floor to pool at her feet. She broke loose from the searing kiss and placed her hands against his chest.

She looked up into his face. "Bannon...I'm..."

"Hush," he murmured against her lips. "I promised once not to hurt you. I still stand by that promise."

Cupping her face in his hands, he lightly brushed his lips against hers, nipping and teasing, while he fought the urgent cravings of his body.

Fiona eagerly and passionately accepted his kiss as her hunger for Bannon grew hot and demanding. Slipping her arms around him a delicious moan escaped her when his mouth followed the long, slender column of her throat to a shoulder and down to her breasts.

Firelight glimmered in his sun-kissed hair and caressed the strong line of his jaw. A muscle in his cheek flexed as he eased toward her. He removed his jacket, letting it fall to the floor, pulled his shirt from the waistband of his breeches and tossed it aside.

In the soft candlelight, she took in his sensuous mouth, his lean throat, the muscular expanse of his darkly tanned chest, flat belly, snug-fitting breeches that left little to the imagination.

She let her head fall back as he trailed a hot path to a rose-colored peak.

His wide hands caught her around the waist and held her steady as he touched hungry kisses to her parted lips. Her fingers entwined themselves in the mass of his hair as if to guide him and hold him close.

Bannon swept her into his powerful arms, carrying her to the bed where he bent his knee upon the mattress and gently fell with her upon its feathery softness. He rolled her beneath him, his mouth covering hers, and his kisses became savage and fierce, his hand caressing her naked breast.

His breathing quickened and passion ran high. For a brief moment, Bannon left her to shed his breeches. A long sensuous while passed as he hungrily feasted upon her nakedness and the lust burning in her eyes.

Towering over her, he parted her trembling thighs with his knee and slowly lowered himself down, his hands braced on either side of her head, her lips parted, expectant of the kiss.

The flickering light of the candle on the bedside table danced alluringly over Bannon's handsome face, enhancing his bronze complexion and vividly accentuating the gleaming muscles of his shoulders, chest and arms.

The masculine scent of him, his rugged good-looks, and the dark, lustful gleam in his blue eyes turned Fiona's blood to fire.

The manly boldness of him touched the soft flesh of her womanhood, teasing, tempting, throbbing urgently, and Fiona arched her hips. A fiery wave of pain shot through her once his probing staff hit its mark, and she gasped, her body stiffened.

"It will pass," he whispered tenderly, his kisses trailing to her throat as he held her close, and before a protest formed in her mind, a warmth spread deep within her, reigniting the fires of passion and urging her on. Their bodies met in the wild frenzy of love, moving, arching, soaring to new heights as he thrust his manhood deep inside her. His open mouth sought hers, and he responded to her urgent need to be as one.

And when at last spent, his fingers lifted to brush a tear from her cheek. "Did I hurt you?"

"No." She whispered and drew in a quick breath of air. "It's just that..."

When she shyly attempted to cover herself, he took her hands and held them to his chest. "Don't, Fiona. You have nothing to be ashamed of."

He kissed away the tears before they lost themselves in her hairline. "Are you sorry, Fiona?"

She reached up and touched his face. "So much has happened. I never thought to see this day." Her eyes stung with emotion, and her throat was dry. "I wasn't sure you wanted me, and that's why I left."

"You're home, Mrs. Cordell Bannon, and you're safe. No one will ever hurt you again." He surveyed her face solemnly. His arms came around her, solid and strong, and fiercely protective.

Her head fell back to rest against his arm. She shifted allowing herself to be warmed by his gaze, her mouth easily surrendering to his seeking one.

Her arms circled his waist and as the moon rose above the clouds, she was content to rest against him, her head against his shoulder, his rhythmic breathing touching softly against her hairline. Without realizing she'd intended to speak, she whispered, "Bannon's bride."

Waves of fire consumed her as their bodies molded into one. She drank in the sweetness of his breath with every kiss, greedily accepted the probing of his tongue.

The muscles of his back were like tight knots beneath the caresses of her fingers. And when he entered again, she reveled in the fullness of him that felt so natural, the spasms of fulfillment echoed like a beautiful memory within their bodies.

The night was long...their love exquisite.

****

Fiona sighed, gently disengaged herself from her true husband, and laid his hands lightly on his chest. She lowered her mouth to kiss him tenderly, and with love. Easing from the bed, she tiptoed to where she'd left her satchel next to the fireplace. She bit her lower lip as she carefully undid the strap and removed her journal. On the way to the window seat, she lifted a shawl from the chair back and draped it over her shoulders, then nestled against the pillows stacked on the seat. Drawing up her knees, she tucked the nightgown around her bare feet, then opened the book and lifted the pencil nub from the page that marked the spot of her last entry. As the moon cast its light on the blank page, she wrote:

When I was but a wee child, I never understood the secret smile on my mother's face when on certain afternoons she and my father returned from bringing the sheep down from the meadow. In those days before leaving Ireland I was too young to know about the special pleasures shared between a husband and wife in their private hours. Perhaps one day, my own wee daughter or son will wonder the same when they see my secret smile.

Tears filled Fiona's eyes and spilled down her cheeks. She glanced to where moonbeams played across Bannon's face, and then finished the entry— *At last, I am where I belong.*

A word about the author...

Loretta C. Rogers is a fourth generation Floridian. She considers herself an eclectic reader, but is partial to stories about the Old West.

A retired teacher, Loretta and her husband's home overlooks a spring-fed creek where she enjoys watching otters, wood ducks, and an occasional alligator.

When not writing, she and her husband take road trips on their touring bike.

Loretta would love to hear from her readers
and to receive their emails at
loretta@lorettacrogersbooks.com

Visit Loretta at: www.lorettacrogersbooks.com